For teresa,
Nephi's story is
one of faith,
courage and
forgiveness. May
it touch your
life

Bob Moss

I, Nephi...

I, Nephi...

A Novel of the Sons of Lehi

Robert H. Moss

International Standard Book Number
0-88290-245-8

Library of Congress Catalog Card Number
84-80989

Horizon Publishers Catalog and Order Number
1960

Printed and distributed in the
United States of America
by

**Horizon
Publishers &
Distributors, Inc.**

———————
50 South 500 West
P.O. Box 490
Bountiful, Utah 84010

Preface

We all need heroes. During my youth I was fortunate enough to have many heroes: my father, my strong pioneer forebears, many Church leaders, plus the mighty men from the Book of Mormon. These men—Nephi, Ammon, Alma, Alma the younger, Helaman, General Moroni, Mormon and his son, Moroni—all influenced my life. Each one of them had special characteristics to teach me—such things as loyalty, faithfulness, commitment, courage, and humility, to name a few. To read the life stories of the Lord's prophets has strengthened my faith and given me models around which to structure my life.

I have desired to gain a greater understanding into the lives of the characters of the Book of Mormon. What were they really like? What was their family life like? What was involved in just growing up in their day? How did they gain their fervent testimonies? These were questions that intrigued me.

Each of us can identify characteristics which we feel are important in our lives. By observing or reading of the lives of those great people who exemplify that characteristic, it becomes more real to us. Then, by applying the "as if" principle, it can truly become a characteristic of our own.

When Nephi's father Lehi prophesied the destruction of Jerusalem, and had to take his family and flee the Holy City, Nephi was the youngest son. Yet he was the one who took the leadership and who had the greatest faith. He is the one to whom the Lord continued to speak.

This story of Nephi is a work of fiction. I have searched the scriptures and conducted research concerning the time and the culture of the people. I am totally responsible for the material presented herein. In some cases I have gone far beyond what is recorded in the scriptures.

This book has been written for all youth—ages eight to eighty. Know that you are vessels of the Lord—that He does speak to youth and then chooses his leaders from those to whom he has spoken. May this book and those which follow strengthen your testimonies and give you role models to follow as you strive forward in your eternal lives.

I dedicate this book to my mother, Olive Hafen Moss. She has truly been a Sariah to my father—giving full support and encouragement to him most of the time. Yet, like Sariah, she has not hesitated to let him know where she stood.

Contents

Prologue

Joseph, the dreamer, was a prototype of Nephi. He became a leader over his brethren. This was a shadow of things to come.

"Who am I, that I should go unto Pharaoh?" the lonely shepherd, Moses, asked, but God knew his man. Moses was called to lead the people back to Canaan—the land their God had promised them. With God's help he humbled Pharaoh and lead his people, the *Beni-Yisrael*, Children of Israel, through a hostile wilderness to the homeland, *Eretz-Yisrael*, promised them since Abraham's time. Joshua, a mighty conqueror, led the people into the promised land, but the people of the promised land had difficulty remembering who it was that had brought them forth from the slavepits of Egypt. The Children of Israel, living among the surviving Canaanites, adopted many of their gods. Worship (as Jeremiah would later explain) was conducted "on every high hill and under every green tree."

Kings were raised up to govern the promised land. Saul—called by the prophet, Samuel—defeated the Philistines and united the Kingdom. He died as he had lived—with the sounds of battle ringing in his ears. David of Bethlehem, the next king, was an extraordinary man, a hero to his people, the subject of ballad and psalm. Under his leadership, Jerusalem became a capital city—a city of glory. He prepared the way for the building of the temple, further uniting the people.

Solomon, David's heir, inherited many of his father's winning ways and added a wit and wisdom of his own. He built the temple to house the Ark of the Covenant—the symbol of God's covenant with His chosen people.

The Hebrews became strong during the reign of these great kings. Then the nation became divided and weak. Israel was conquered and the Ten Tribes were carried away, while the tribes of Judah and Benjamin, held together by the sacred city of Jerusalem, persisted. The people, beset by idolatry, were easily conquered by the Assyrians, Babylonians, and Egyptians.

Josiah, a young and popular Hebrew king, attempted to return Judah to her former glory by destroying the altars of Baal and by teaching the people of the law of God. As the armies of Egypt moved northward to aid the Assyrians in their battles against the Babylonians, Josiah bravely met the invaders at the city of Megiddo. He was killed and Egypt once again ruled the promised land.

It was to this age that two great prophets were born—Jeremiah and Lehi. Jeremiah, a gentle, sensitive melancholy man who yearned for affection and for a normal life, was instead propelled by the prophetic fire within him to preach doom—to antagonize the very people whom he loved. He prophesied their death and destruction.

Lehi, a wealthy merchant and leader of caravans, was also called to raise his voice in calling the people to repentance. When they failed to heed his message and turned on him, threatening to kill him, the Lord commanded that he take his family and leave Jerusalem—to travel to another "promised land." Nephi, son of Lehi, shared that responsibility. As the youngest of the sons of Lehi, he became another Joseph—a leader of his older brethren. It is of him that this story is written.

Chapter 1

A Young Israelite

The light fell slanting across the garden, gilding the walls and the cistern with rich luster and turning the sand of the path a flaming red. The flowers which Sariah had so carefully planted seemed to glow with extra color and beauty.

Lehi stood in the doorway, breathing in the tableau.

"He is a beautiful boy," exclaimed the midwife, Tamra, as she carefully placed the squalling baby in Sariah's arms. "He is as fair-haired as Laman and Lemuel are dark."

Sariah cuddled her newborn son to her breast. "He looks much like his grandfather," she said looking proudly at her helpless son, whispering little nonsense words to him.

Lehi stood watching, admiring his infant son from a distance. He had watched as Tamra rubbed the newborn baby with salt and wrapped it in swaddling clothes from its toes to its head. He stroked his tawny-red beard. "Another son. Blessed be the name of the Lord," he mumbled inaudibly. He looked with pride at his wife, Sariah. Even so soon after the travail of childbirth she was beautiful. Her oval face looked pale against the damp auburn hair which framed it, but her brown eyes sparkled with a great love of life. Her firm and dimpled chin displayed an austerity which Lehi loved.

His reverie was interrupted as Sariah asked, "Lehi, where are the boys? They should be here to see their new brother."

"I'll find them," he murmured. Laman and Lemuel were playing in the garden and Lehi soon rounded them up. Sam was nowhere to be found. Lehi chewed absent-mindedly on a sapling twig, then snapped it between his fingers. "That boy is always running off," he muttered. After a short but futile search for the missing three-year-old, Lehi placed a large hand on each of the two older boys' shoulders and guided them in to see the baby.

Sariah's eyes lighted at the sight of her eldest sons. "Come and see your baby brother," she motioned to them.

"He is sure ugly, "Laman commented.

"And very wrinkled," Lemuel chimed in, looking at Laman for approval.

Sariah smiled indulgently at her sons. "He looks very much like you did when you were just born," she said. "Come, see his tiny hands and feet."

The boys stood. The flickering lamp played upon the face of the infant, eyes shut tightly, his tiny mouth moving in an instinctive sucking motion.

After the boys had gone back out to play, while Sariah rested, Lehi pulled out his roll of papyrus and wrote: *Our sixth child born this day, a boy. The date is August 6, in the twenty-seventh year of the reign of Josiah, King of the Jews.*

* * *

On the eighth day, the baby was taken to the village rabbi to be circumcised. As the bronze knife cut into his tender skin, he let out a scream of outrage at this mutilation of his body. When the rabbi had finished, Lehi took the tiny bundle in his huge hands, nestling him against his broad shoulder, softly cooing as he rocked back and forth. The child, comforted, settled down to a soft whimpering.

As Lehi rocked him, he looked at the sleeping infant with an expression of great love on his bearded face. He held him out and gave him a name—a name he had long harbored in his heart. It was an Egyptian name—picked up in his travels. "I name you Nephi," he said. "In Egypt it means noble one or prophet. I bless you that you shall be a nobleman among our people. You will be one who speaks with God."

* * *

Nephi loved his big-boned and red-haired father. Though Lehi was away much of the time on his caravans, he was a compassionate and loving patriarch. Nephi sat often on his father's lap, listening as Lehi told him stories of the places he had been and the things he had seen. Laman and Lemuel rode with the caravan on their very own camels. Nephi could hardly wait until he was old enough to go, too.

Sam and Nephi played together in the fields, but when Sam grew old enough to be apprenticed to the caravan, time went by even more slowly for the lonely Nephi. He wandered through the hills and fields of Beith Lehi, often finding himself at his Uncle Ishmael's villa. He played with his nephew, Ishmar, and his cousin, Ishmael's youngest daughter, Miriam. Nephi, Ishmar, and Miriam spent many hours roaming the fields, making clay villages, and pretending to travel to distant lands in their own caravan.

Beith Lehi, Lehi's country estate, was a day's journey southwest of Jerusalem. Lehi's ancestors had been herdsmen and traders. The ancestral home, built by his grandfather out of sun-dried bricks, was old and comfortable. Nephi enjoyed the cool feel of the plastered and white-washed walls. The doors, hanging on leather hinges, creaked with age as he went in and out. All of the brothers shared one bedroom. Their straw pallets were scattered along the wall. But, now that Nephi was alone, he spent most of his time in the large main room of the house or on the roof. The main room served as kitchen and living room. A large table, a small heating brazier, and a brick oven near the garden entrance were its only furnishings.

The home was built around a square garden with every room opening onto it. In the garden were his mother's favorite herbs: coriander to flavor her bread, garlic for the stews, mint, dill, cummin, and many others which Nephi could not name. Sariah loved flowers, and the garden was often a profusion of color with the blooming of the dazzling yellow narcissus, the stark white of the lovely myrtle flowers, and the reds and purples of the hyacinths, tulips, anemones, and irises.

The roof was Nephi's very favorite place. In the evenings the family met there to relax. Stone steps led up from the outside of the house, and another set of stairs from the garden patio. When Nephi couldn't sleep he often took his pallet to the roof and lay there looking at the magnificent heavens. Evenings were cool on the roof and the smell of drying figs and spices was pleasant. Often a slight breeze would bring the sweet smell of the hyacinths and narcissus up from the garden.

Nephi enjoyed taking care of the garden. He loved the feel of warm soil sifted through his fingers. It was a constant wonder to him how a small seed could produce a large bush of beans or a tree heavy with fruit. As seeds were planted and he waited for the first green shoots to spring forth from the ground he learned the meaning of faith. It was a good lesson.

Harvest time was fun for Nephi as he picked the beans or lentils, the cucumbers with their prickly skins, or the smelly leeks. Picking fruit at his Uncle Ishmael's was fun for him, too. He ate more than he put into the goatskin buckets. Sometimes he filled his sleeves with pistachio nuts and almonds and then just sat on the hillside eating nuts and thinking of what life was about. As a six-year-old he decided that he was either going to be a trader like his father, or a farmer like his Uncle Ishmael, his mother's brother.

At age seven, Nephi began his schooling. Most of the other children of Beith Lehi were taught by their fathers or the village rabbi, but Lehi sent Nephi to stay with his oldest sister, Annah, in Jerusalem. Lehi selected the school of Ben Ashmed, the most famous teacher in Jerusalem, for Nephi's education. He could afford the best and that is what he wanted for his son.

Nephi was excited about school. He had watched with interest as Lehi faithfully wrote in his journal, and now he would also be able to write. Lehi brought him a flint stylus from the land of two rivers, and Nephi could hardly wait to use it. School was very formal. The children sat in a semi-circle on the ground around the rabbi. He sat cross-legged in the center of the circle with a large platter of sand in his lap. Using his finger, he traced illustrations of what he was teaching. Then Nephi and the other boys would laboriously copy what he had written on their clay tablets. Erasing was easy. Nephi just balled up the clay and was ready to start again.

Ben Ashmed illustrated each letter with some saying or story from the history of the Jews. Nephi loved the stories of the chosen people. He memorized the words of Isaiah and other prophets, learned the covenant Abraham had made with Jehovah, and studied the Law that God had given to Moses. The deeds of the great kings—David, Saul, and Solomon—inspired him. The story of David killing Goliath was his very favorite. He set a youthful goal to be strong like David.

Jerusalem itself was part of the thrall. Jerusalem, City of David, City of God. For hadn't David fashioned it? Had he not named it? Was it not toward Jerusalem that one turned to pray? Was it not to Jerusalem that every good Jew made his pilgrimage?

Nephi, robust, muscular and a head taller than most of the boys, was a serious student. His favorite friend, Daniel, was a boy of his own age. Their mutual friends were three brothers, Hananiah, Mishael, and Azariah. They often walked together through the streets of Jerusalem, discussing the day's lessons. Because of their deep spiritual faith, they were concerned about the pagan gods of Baal which had taken over the hearts and minds of most of the people.

The boys loved to visit the temple after their classes. It was the true gem of the city. The temple seemed to soar to the heavens in its splendor, stirring profound emotions in Nephi. It gave him a special feeling. It was as if the Lord wanted to talk with him. Often he would leave the other boys, find a quiet corner, and offer a silent prayer.

The boys often stood in the courtyard near the altar of sacrifice, surrounded by the chambers where the temple tithes were stored. They watched as the priests mounted the ten broad steps leading to the two beautiful cypress doors, overlaid with patterns of gold. On the sides of the doors were huge incense burners shaped like pillars, lavishly decorated with chains and pomegranates. Nephi hoped someday to see inside the temple.

As often as he could, Nephi returned to Beith Lehi. He liked to be with Miriam. She was three years younger but almost as tall as he was. He showed off his Hebrew writing as he sat with her and Ishmar. He didn't know why, but he felt it was important that he learn well the art of writing. Ishmar teased him about how serious he was about learning, but Miriam stood up for him. She would toss her head and say, "Nephi is going to be an important person some day. He will need to know how to write."

As a reward for learning Hebrew, Lehi gave Nephi a camel foal for his very own. When it was only a few weeks old the foal was already taller than he. It had a comic face—loony, serene, and disgusted. Its fleece was soft and fine, its cry like the bleat of a lamb. He fed it cucumbers, turnips and greenery from the garden. Usually all he got for his troubles was a nip on his arm or a disdainful look from the camel's liquid eyes.

Nephi named the creamy-white foal Armed. He led it all over with a tether, and soon the beast followed without the sinew. It went everywhere he went, placidly standing around chewing its cud or munching what grass it could find. Armed ate everything; thorns, leaves, dried plants—everything!

Each year Lehi took his family to Jerusalem to celebrate Passover. Passover was celebrated in the springtime when flowers bloomed profusely alongside the roads. It was Nephi's favorite holiday.

Nephi remembered well the Passover celebration when he was nine. For weeks Sariah and her maids worked to prepare food and clothing for the journey, offerings for the temple, and the traditional Sedar meal. On the tenth day of Passover, Lehi selected a yearling kid to offer as a sacrifice.

The family started out on foot for the holy city. The King's Road was jammed with hundreds of other pilgrims walking slowly toward Jerusalem. Nephi had never seen so many people.

Lehi carried the sacrificial kid on his shoulders and Sariah led the loaded donkey. The boys played and chased on the sides of the road. It was after dark when they finally arrived, hot and tired, in Jerusalem. The moon was full and brilliant, lighting the last part of their journey.

At sundown the next day, Lehi gathered his family around him. On an altar of piled-up stones, he killed the yearling kid, making sure not to break any of its bones. After draining the blood into a cup for later use, Lehi skinned the kid and Sariah roasted it over the fire. Nephi was assigned to turn the spit.

That night Lehi and his family stood at the table to eat, symbolic of the Children of Israel prepared for flight. The shank of the kid, seasoned with bitter herbs, was their main course. It was served with unleavened bread, nuts, wine, and a charoseth sauce made of apples.

Lehi presided. He filled and blessed a first cup of wine, giving thanks to God for this holy night. He prayed: *"Blessed thou art, o Lord, who has chosen us above all peoples, and has exalted us above all tongues and has hallowed us with thy commandments. And thou has given us . . . sabbaths for rest, seasons for gladness, holidays and times for rejoicing. This day of the festival of the unleavened bread . . . an assembly day of holiness. . . ."*

At the end of Lehi's prayer, each member of his family dipped a piece of unleavened bread into the charoseth sauce and ate it. Lehi blessed a second cup of wine then it was Nephi's turn. As the youngest son, he asked the traditional question: *"How is this night different from other nights?"*

Lehi responded by telling the story of the escape of the Children of Israel from Egypt. He ended with these hallowed words: *"Therefore, it is the duty to thank Him . . . who brought us forth from slavery to freedom, from sorrow to joy, from mourning to festive day, and from darkness to great light."* The family finished the ritual Passover observance by singing psalms and passing the third and fourth cups of wine. Then Lehi splattered some of the lamb's blood on the door lintels. There was a quiet, sacred feeling throughout the entire evening. Even Laman and Lemuel were silent.

The next day Lehi took his boys to the temple. There was such a crowd that Nephi couldn't see what was going on so Lehi hoisted him onto his shoulders. Nephi was amazed. From his new vantage point all he could see were people. It made him dizzy to look across the swaying sea of white and colored headdresses. Judean soldiers armed with long spears and dressed in tight-fitting shirts, short pleated tunics, and turban-like helmets stood on the fringes of the crowd. To Nephi the temple walls seemed to tower over him, even though they were still some distance away.

After returning to their city home that evening, Nephi could tell that something was troubling his father. He listened as Lehi told his mother of what he had heard in the marketplace: that the Babylonian army, under Prince Nebuchadnezzar, had met and crushed the Egyptian forces.

Lehi said, "It may affect our entire caravan trade. Egypt is our biggest customer. Almost every month we transport salt, potash, wine and olives to Egypt, returning with linen and cotton goods."

Sariah patted her husband on the shoulder. "There is probably no cause to worry."

Nephi was tired and he didn't listen to much more, but he did hear his father mention that the Babylonians were reputed to be just as cruel as the Assyrians. Lehi asked Sariah, "Do you think it wise that we continue to live outside the protection of Jerusalem? Perhaps we should move our family back to the city."

Move back to Jerusalem? Nephi had mixed feelings about that. Jerusalem was an exciting city and he enjoyed living here while he went to school, but . . . to leave his friends and cousins . . . and where would he keep Armed?

Chapter 2

A Caravan Apprenticeship

A hundred ill-natured, kneeling camels, groaning and growling, were being loaded with goods bound for the Phoenician port of Sidon. The bright colors, the pungent odors, and the babble of hundreds of strident voices made Nephi groggy. The blond, freckle-faced ten-year-old Nephi finally had his wish come true: He was going on the caravan! Lehi had assigned him to apprentice with Jacoth, his Egyptian scribe and accountant, but Nephi didn't care what his assignment was. He was just excited to be a part of it.

With camels loaded, the caravan slowly wound out through the gate. Laman and Lemuel waved derisively at Nephi as they rode past. Following them were the pack camels, tied together with goat's-hair ropes and loaded with chests and goatskin bags. Bells on trappings of the camels clonged to the rhythm of their steps. A camel driver led each group of five camels, guiding them down the road. Sam rode by on a big, reddish-brown camel. He waved cheerily and Nephi waved back then turned his attention back to the pack camels, walking dopily along with half-lidded eyes.

The last pack camel finally passed. Lehi and Jacoth were walking and leading their camels. Nephi was supposed to stay close to Jacoth, but for the first few miles he gamboled about the caravan with all the friskiness of a young pup. As the sun rose higher in the heavens, he dropped back and fell into step beside his father. For awhile he kept up, but soon his pace slowed. His feet were sore and his legs ached. By the time they pitched camp Nephi was so tired that Lehi just washed the dust off, gave his son a light supper of fruit and nuts, and put him to bed.

The caravan—strung out for miles like some huge, crawling snake— crossed broad valleys and rocky hills. The warmth of late summer lay on the land like a golden haze. The smell of rich, loamy soil rose from the earth.

Each day was a new experience for Nephi; each night a time of learning and study. Jacoth was a demanding teacher and Nephi was an eager learner. As they traveled, Jacoth taught him the spoken language. In the evening, they pored over the papyrus rolls by the light of the flickering lamps. Carefully Nephi wrote the strange Egyptian characters. He studied hard because he wanted to be like his father. Lehi could write and speak several languages. Because of his learning and wisdom, he had become a wealthy

19

man. Nephi's other motivation to learn this new language was an inner voice which seemed to whisper to him to study hard—to learn the language well. Nephi had learned to recognize that voice, which had finally come in response to the faith which was so much a part of him. He had prayed often and the answer was always there. He just had to learn to recognize the voice.

Being involved in his studies did not prevent Nephi from enjoying the strange new scenery. Now that they were nearing the coast of the great sea, the air was filled with seagulls and terns, their wings aglint with flashes of silvery feathers. The road they were on became broader and harder as they neared the Phoenician city of Sidon; beaten down by the many feet which had journeyed on it and rutted by the wheels of chariots and ox carts.

Topping a hill, Nephi had his first view of the great sea. It was all shades of green and gray with white flecks over its surface. The coast was craggy with many little inlets. The hills were heavily wooded, but on the plains leading to the sea grass waved in green patterns beneath shifting clouds. In the distance, sharp blue mountains looked as if they had been erected as special temples of worship. Blue fingers of the sea and purple ridges of the mountains came together in the distance—seeming to blend into each other. Nephi tried to imprint the various colors and vistas on his memory so he could tell Miriam about it when he got home.

The last night before reaching Sidon, the caravan made camp near the sea. Nephi sneaked away to climb down the rocky cliffs to the white sandy beach. The air was hot and muggy near the water and Nephi took off his robe and carried it on his arm. He looked around. Seeing no one, he stripped off his tunic and waded into the surf. The sand beneath his feet was cool and delightful. Joyously he struck out, diving into the waves, churning the water with his feet, luxuriating in its coolness and cleansing effect after the long, dusty trip. He came out of the water, shaking his mop of hair. The warm wind dried him before he reached his pile of clothing. His first experience of swimming in the great sea had been delightful.

Early the next morning they reached the outskirts of Sidon. Nephi was amazed at the traffic already on the road: processions of heavily laden camels rhythmically lifting their haughty noses with every step; long trains of pack-asses weighted down with clumsy burdens; men, women, children, slaves, carrying bundles and baskets of every size and shape. Smothering dust rose in clouds, almost obscuring the camels ahead of him. Contrasting with the dust of the road were fertile green fields which surrounded the city. Nephi was impressed. Streets leading to the marketplace were filled with ceaseless activity: convoys of pack camels and mules and carts; teams of clerks and government workers taking stock of the merchandise and reckoning taxes; a motley assembly of drovers and military escorts; and warehouses built of wood and brick where trade goods were stored. As their caravan entered the marketplace Nephi heard the angry and wheedling tones of the merchants; he saw women with dark faces and baskets of fruit on their heads; smelled exotic and pungent odors.

The drivers guided their camels to stalls on a side alley near the market-place. Lehi himself supervised storage of their trade goods. While the camels were being unloaded, Sam and Nephi set out to explore. Lehi admonished them to be careful and to be back before dark.

They left the marketplace, working their way to the docks. In the port of Sidon were ships of every sort. The air smelled of fish and pitch. Merchants thronged the area, moving between the dock and the anchored ships. Colorful sails gleamed in the sunlight. To Nephi the ships, with wings of embroidered linen, seemed almost alive—like huge birds.

Leaving the harbor, Sam and Nephi walked back up the street towards the marketplace. In one street Nephi saw rope-makers in three-man teams working on ropes for the large ships. Nephi thought it was such a fascinating operation that he would have stayed to watch but Sam impatiently pulled him along.

They came upon the stall of a metal worker. Nephi watched as the artisan put copper into a clay crucible, then placed charcoal all over the crucible to heat it. An assistant pumped the bellows which blew air through a *tuyere* into the fire, fanning it to a high temperature. Nephi was enchanted by the process. The spirit within him whispered to observe carefully. He stood at the stall a long time, watching the metalworker pour out the metal into a flat mold, then hammer the object into shape. The artisan held up the finished item, an axe blade, for him to see. Nephi nodded with interest before he moved to the next stall.

It was the stall of a weapons-maker. Nephi sucked in his breath in astonishment. He watched as the artisan heated the iron until it was white hot, then hammered it into long, thin strips on an anvil. Next he pressed strips of iron into place on each side of a laminated wood bow. Two pieces of thin wood had been glued together onto a smaller center piece, then the pieces of metal were glued to both sides. Nephi was fascinated by the bow. He wanted it more than anything he had ever seen.

That night, after Lehi had finished compiling his day's transactions, Nephi told him of the bow. Lehi listened, smiling. The next day, after seeing that the goods he had bought were being loaded properly on the camels, Lehi accompanied Nephi to the weapons-maker's stall. He took the bow from the artisan. He drew it clear back, holding the gut string against his cheek, then he handed it to Nephi.

Nephi held the bow out at full length. He pulled on the string as hard as he could pull but he could not budge it. He tried again, but still could not draw the bow. Feeling somewhat foolish, he looked at his father. Lehi was smiling, his look proud. Nephi did not understand. Lehi put a hand on his shoulder. "I will buy the bow for you, my son, but it is up to you to make it a useful weapon." He paused for emphasis. "Promise me you will not put an arrow to your bow until you are able to draw the string to your cheek."

The ten-year-old Nephi looked up solemnly. "I promise, father," he said.

Nephi carried the bow carefully back to his sleeping quarters. He tried drawing it again, and again, but he could not move the bowstring. Laman and Lemuel taunted him, but Nephi didn't care. As he held the bow in his hand, he committed himself to the goal of being able to pull the bow to his cheek by the time he was considered an adult—on his thirteenth birthday.

When the camels were loaded with glasswares, fine metal ornaments, linen from Egypt, imported copper from Cyprus, vessels of bronze, garments made of brightly colored wool, maplewood, boxwood, and ivory, the caravan made its slow way out of the city, heading south to Tyre. Lehi's next stop was to purchase murex purple dye for which Tyre was famous.

The next days were tedious. The deep, rutted highway was crowded with creeping caravans and filthy with dust. Nephi lost patience with his camel which kept insisting on heading off the road to eat little clumps of thistles. He tugged on the rope, pulling the animal back to the road. A camel boy, riding just behind Nephi must have noticed his growing frustration and when Armed wandered off the road again, the young man shouted gently, "Wolloo-wollow-wollow." Armed turned and went back to the road. Nephi looked around at the camel driver. Between his studies of Egyptian and his curiosity about the country he hadn't really become acquainted with anyone other than Jacoth. Now Nephi looked intently at the camel boy who didn't look much older than he was. Tall and so thin his ribs showed on his naked chest. His head was wrapped in a turban. He sat at ease on his camel's back, a small prod-stick in one hand.

When they stopped at midday to rest the camels and to eat lunch, Nephi picked a spot under a tall chestnut tree. As he sat down, he noticed the camel driver watching him. Nephi beckoned for him to come join him. They sat under the tree talking and sharing Nephi's lunch of bread and cheese. He learned that the driver's name was Shemin. He had been born in the desert and knew everything about camels which impressed Nephi. To him, the camels were merely beasts of burden, except for Armed which was still a pet, but Shemin talked of camels with reverence. To him the camel was a member of the family.

"We eat them, ride them, and use them to carry our burdens. We sleep in their shadow, race them, bet on them, drink their milk, and even wash in their urine. We use the hair of our camels for our clothing and tents. Their droppings provide fuel for our fires. If we are choking on the desert, we might even cut them open for water." He shrugged his shoulders eloquently. "We do everything but marry them!"

Nephi looked upon Armed with a new respect, though he still didn't care for the camel's unpleasant disposition.

On the fourth day after leaving Sidon, they camped in a grassy draw, knowing that on the morrow they would be in Tyre. After Nephi's Egyptian lesson was finished that night, Jacoth talked of the fabled Phoenician city.

"Tyre is a pestilential den," he said emphatically, his eyes glinting in the light of the fire. "It constantly stinks of urine and gutters and the unwashed hides of men and camels and goats and asses."

Lehi added, "Yes, Jacoth, it is all you describe and more. If it were possible to get the murex dye any other place, I would do so." He looked at Nephi. "I guess the thing that disturbs me the most is the sensual religion of the Phoenicians. Their worship of Baal, whom they call 'king of heaven and earth' is sickening to one of the true faith."

Nephi was curious to hear more. "What is their worship like?"

Lehi stood and stretched, faking a yawn behind his huge hands. "That is enough discussion tonight. Tomorrow we will be in the city and need to be rested. It is time for bed." With that, he strode towards his tent.

Nephi looked at the other men who were all gazing intently into the fire. Disappointed, he ran after his father.

The next morning the caravan passed through a heavily wooded gorge. From the top of the pass they could see the white and rose-colored walls of Tyre. It looked like a beautiful place between the purple mountains and the blue sea. The caravan passed through plains colorful with orchards, vineyards, palm groves, and villages. Nearer the city, the road was thronged with merchants and farmers on their way into the city.

Like Sidon, there was noise and confusion throughout the city streets. The marketplace on the outskirts of the city was especially uproarious. Nephi watched as Lehi supervised the unloading, then joined his father as he left to bargain for the purple murex dye for which Tyre was famous.

Tyre was an unending maze of narrow, cobbled streets baking under a seemingly unending sun. It was a city of walls built in the oriental manner with secluded gardens and courtyards beyond them. It was winding roads and stinking gutters and blazing white skies and loose dogs and camels and sheep and goats roaming the streets. It was also a city of markets, where the noise level was high-pitched and raucous. Ships of many countries were at anchor in Tyre. The roisterers who roamed the streets were dressed in the garments of a score of nations.

While his father bargained for purple dye, Nephi was again drawn to the stalls of the metalsmiths. Once more he watched as men changed ore into molten metal and then molten metal into something useful. He watched until Lehi had finished his business and was ready to return to the caravan.

The next day Sam and Nephi returned to the marketplace. It was an exciting, bustling city. Nephi was excited by the motley crowds of people. A foot squad of Babylonian soldiers tramped down the street. They looked strange to Nephi in their close-fitting metal helmets and mail vests. Each had a sheathed iron sword at his waist. Beside each archer to carry his long bow was a shield bearer with the soldier's shield of woven wicker covered with leather. Hemmed in by the troop of soldiers was a nobleman dressed in heavy, richly ornamented clothing, with his hair and beard crimped.

In the center of one square was a raised platform. Nephi could not see what was going on, but he could hear much shouting. He and Sam pushed and shoved until they were closer, finally finding themselves against the platform. On the stand was a black woman dressed in a loose-fitting thread-bare robe. Her eyes were wide with fear but she held herself erect, arms wrapped protectively around a tiny baby. A boy of about four clung to one leg. The boy's ribs protruded and there was a hungry lean look on his face. Nephi's concentration was interrupted as a loud voice yelled "What am I bid for these three? Take any one or all . . ."

Nephi had heard his father and Jacoth talking about slave markets. Without intending to, he and Sam had stumbled into one of the vile places. He looked up, right into the large, pleading eyes of the little boy. Finally the bidding was over. Large hands reached up and tore the woman from the stand, pushing back the young boy. He cried out in anguish, reaching out his arms for his screaming mother. She had been sold without him.

Nephi was sickened inside. How could people be so cruel as to separate children from their mothers? The boy was sold for a few coins and the bidding moved on. Sam pulled him and they left the square, but the memory of those pleading eyes lingered.

That night Nephi was pensive, dabbling at his dinner of fish and fresh fruit and goat's milk. After dinner, Lehi took his two youngest sons to the wharf where the ships were docked. They watched as men ran to shift packages and boxes, shouting as they carried box after box onto the galleys. It was an exciting scene under the light of flickering torches as men stooped and heaved and labored to get the ships loaded in time for the evening tide. But Nephi saw little of it. His mind was still in the slave market.

He hung tightly to Lehi. "Father," Nephi began. "Why do people treat other people like mere animals?"

"What do you mean, Nephi?" Lehi responded.

Sam chimed in. "On our way back to our encampment today, we saw the slave market . . ."

Nephi interrupted breathlessly, ". . . and father, there was a woman and her babies being sold, and they sold the mother without her little boy, and . . ."

"Wait a minute, son. Not so fast. What were you doing in the slave market?"

"It was not intentional, father," responded Sam. "But we were curious and . . ."

Lehi again interrupted. "My sons, there are many things in this world which are cruel and unjust. Slavery is one of them. It is not God's will that one man be in bondage to another, but he has given man the freedom to act for himself—even when he does things which are wrong."

Nephi shuddered. "I couldn't stand to be a slave. To not be able to go where I want to go . . ." He left the thought unsaid. It was just too terrible to think about.

Dropping to one knee, Lehi put a large arm around each of his sons. "My boys," he began, "even though a man is branded a slave and manacled with irons, if he says in his soul, 'I am a free spirit, though someone controls my body, no one can control my mind,' then he is not truly a slave. One wise man has said, 'Only man can make himself a slave in his soul.' "

He squeezed his sons and stood up. They continued the walk in silence back to their tent.

Nephi thought of what his father had said. He asked himself, "Then, is freedom truly only within me?" It was too much for him to comprehend. He decided this experience was one he wanted to talk over with Miriam when he got home.

The next morning, Lehi's men, working with the speed and skill of experience, leveled their camp, rolled up the tents, and packed their wares. By sunrise they were on the road to Jerusalem. As they topped a rise near the city, Nephi turned for one last look at the dark purple sea under a purple sky. Ahead, in the east, the sky was lilac and gold.

Nephi walked beside Jacoth, occasionally seeing his father riding up and down the long caravan. He was a striking sight, his great, red beard flowing behind him as he rode, his white cloak and hood standing out in contrast to the blue of the sky. Seeing him made Nephi proud.

It was autumn. The fields on each side of the road were various shades of browns and yellows. Often they passed flocks of sheep with their shepherds in rough robes standing watch nearby. The caravan moved past small villages with houses of pale brick and stucco. The houses were small with children usually hanging out of slitlike windows or playing in yards of hardpacked earth. Walls of yellow stone covered with vines often marked the edges of the roadway.

As the caravan traveled further inland, cypress trees gave way to silvery olive groves heavy with green or dark fruit, then to rows of dark-leaved citron or pomegranate trees bending under yellow globes like burnished copper. Gray boulders and high thistles clustered along the roadside.

They passed Megiddo, and Lehi explained to his sons that here was where the great King Josiah met his death. Nephi gazed across the Carmel mountain range into the plain of Esdraelon. It was a magnificent sight.

Little brooks and rivers shone in the tawny autumn light. The country seemed to shimmer with a light of its own. Fields of barley and wheat— yellow now after harvest—stretched into the distance. He saw farmers toiling along roads toward the town, carrying baskets of fruit and grains. Herds of cattle and flocks of sheep grazed in the stubble-fields. Haystacks dotted the yellow land and stacks of wheat and barley added more texture to the pastoral scene. Several farmers plowed in their fields getting the soil ready for the next planting. Nephi was once again seeing the endless nature of the seasons: plant and sow and reap; plow and plant and sow and reap.

Day after day they made their way homeward. As they neared Jerusalem, the land became more rocky and hilly. Hills were gray and worn to nubs of what must have been their former height. Goats clambered on terraced hillsides and herders waved as the caravan slowly snaked its way down the road.

Laman and Lemuel, seeming bored with the daily monotony of the caravan ride, challenged Nephi to a camel race. He knew he had to accept the challenge or be laughed at for the rest of the journey. Armed was almost four years old and was large and gangly, but the camel was not yet a racer. Laman and Lemuel's camels were older and bigger, standing almost seven feet tall. Nephi looked at their long legs and wondered if his Armed had any chance to beat them. With Shemin's help, he brushed down Armed, and put on his well-padded oak saddle. Shemin took a gaily colored tassel and hung it from Armed's neck. Nephi felt he was ready. He spoke a guttural "GHRRRR," and Armed knelt. Nephi climbed on, and with the command of "KHIKH!" Armed laboriously clambered to his feet.

Laman, already as big as a man, winked at Lemuel. "Let's make this fair for little brother," he said. "Nephi, we'll give you a head start. We'll race to that fig tree on the next hill."

Nephi grimly nodded his agreement, checked his saddle once again, shrugged at Shemin, and with a "HUT" Armed was off. Within moments, Laman and Lemuel were alongside him. They laughed and teased as they rode, knowing that Nephi couldn't keep up with them. He tapped on Armed with his camel stick, but Armed was already at full speed. Laman rode close and, leaning over, gave Nephi a shove.

He was so surprised that he didn't have a chance to grab hold and he fell with a crash to the ground. The breath went out of his lungs in a painful whoosh. He had a difficult time catching his breath. The feeling passed gradually, leaving him giddy. He propped himself on his elbows and saw Armed standing unconcernedly a short distance away. Laman and Lemuel were returning on their camels, laughing and pointing at him. He was bruised, winded, and frustrated, besides being angry at Laman for pushing him. He picked up a stone to hurl at Laman, then put it down. Laman was so much bigger that Nephi knew he would just get beaten up more. He waited until his brothers had passed on their way back to the caravan, then picked up the camel's rope, and walked back to join Shemin. He had been beaten but he was not defeated. He vowed that someday he would race Laman and Lemuel fairly and beat them.

The rest of the journey was uneventful. Within a few days they had almost reached Jerusalem. Now for the past hour the caravan had been plodding up a long hill. At its crest, a very impressive spectacle confronted them. They gazed upon the turrets and domes of Jerusalem, aglow with the smouldering fire of sunset. The city was ablaze with glory. In the intense evening light Nephi could see mighty walls and gates, rooftops and spires and towers, and—above everything else—the soaring spires of the Temple.

The ostlers and porters struck up a song. It was a slow march, but not a sad one. Nephi caught a word here and there. It was a song of thanksgiving, a song of homecoming, a song of Jerusalem.

The caravan wound its way into a valley, then struggled up the last steep, rocky road. Nephi looked across bare hills and saw, rising above them, the stout, high wall—a massive wall built of enormous stones that shone pink and gray and purple in the evening afterglow. From the walls rose towers marking a gate, and beyond it the majestic outlines of the temple, heavy, ornamental and brooding. They were home.

Chapter 3

The Maturing Youth

The years passed quickly for Nephi. Lehi had moved his family to their city home in Jerusalem where they would be safer during the unsettled times. Lehi's caravan business depended upon stable governments, and he was concerned over what was happening. Until Nephi was five, Palestine was controlled by the Assyrians. After King Josiah's defeat at Megiddo, the Egyptians ruled Jerusalem, selecting Jehoiakim, Josiah's son, as king. He was oppressive, cynical, headstrong, and an apostate. Lehi told his sons that Jehoiakim was wicked and that what he did was evil in the sight of the Lord. He paid a heavy tax to the Egyptians, his masters, seeming to take pleasure in exacting tribute from his fellow Jews.

When Nephi was nine, the Egyptians and Assyrians were defeated at Carchemish by Babylonians under the command of Prince Nebuchadnezzar. At age ten King Nabopolassar died, and Nebuchadnezzar, his son, was crowned king of Babylonia. He swept his armies through Judah on his way to Egypt, swallowing it up as if it were not even there.

King Jehoiakim rebelled against Babylon when Nephi was eleven. Nebuchadnezzar sent his armies into Palestine, and for more than two years they ravaged the country. Finally, in December, just before Nephi turned thirteen, Nebuchadnezzar attacked Jerusalem.

Lehi, warned by the spirit, had moved his family back to Beith Lehi. It was just in time. Jehoiakim died, which put his eight-year-old son, Johoiachin, on the throne to face the Babylonian legions. The siege of the capital lasted for three terrible months. On March 15, the city surrendered. Nebuchadnezzar carried off ten thousand hostages, then raided the temple and took its treasures. With the hostages went Nephi's four friends, Daniel, Hananiah, Mishael, and Azariah. Nebuchadnezzar put Zedekiah, a younger brother of Jehoiakim on the throne. He was a weak king, caught in the middle between the scheming elders and the might of Babylon.

With the temporary peace, Lehi received a prompting to move his family back to Jerusalem. Family members once again packed their belongings and moved back to their home on the south wall of the city. Sariah loved this large home with four rooms facing an open court. In the court were trees, shrubs, and flowers. There was a cistern in one corner to catch rain water and to store the limited water supply. Hard-packed earth floors were easy to clean. The roof was cool, made of built-up dirt with pebbles scattered on top.

* * *

The sun was barely peeping above the eastern hills when Nephi awakened. He raised his arms high above his head, stretching and feeling the strength of his youthful body. As he lay there, he was conscious of his maturity—the hair on his body, the rippling strength of the muscles in his arms and legs, the tautness of his belly. He inhaled deeply, enjoying the coolness of early morning air. The scent of roses and herbs drifted to him from the garden below. He rolled off his pallet to his knees. After his prayer he looked over the parapet. His mother was not yet in the garden.

He looked across the valley outside of the city walls, noting that roads were already jammed with people; some walking, some riding camels or donkeys, but all seemed cheerful as they made their way toward Jerusalem. There was excitement and a sense of anticipation in the air. Today was the beginning of Sukkoth, the Feast of the Booths. Now that olives and grapes were gathered and pressed, grain harvested and threshed, and other crops in, the people were ready for merrymaking and for praising God in His Holy Temple.

This was to be an exciting day for Nephi. Today was the day that he would go to the temple with his father to officially become an adult. A thirteen-year-old, under the law of the Torah, was to be considered a man and would be known as a "son of the law." It was his age of accountability.

As an adult, Lehi had told him he must be careful not to touch anything that was unclean such as hogs and dead bodies. He would be able to walk only a certain distance on the Sabbath day and he would now wear the prescribed men's Sabbath dress and join in prayers in the synagogue. It was so exciting to grow up! He took another deep breath—expanding his chest and wondering what he looked like now as a man. He held his breath as long as he could, finally releasing it slowly through his nostrils.

Then he remembered his bow. This was the day to complete the goal he had set three years earlier. Reaching down he picked up the steel bow from beside the pallet. He liked its solid and hefty feel in his hand. Shifting it to his left hand, he flexed his fingers and gently placed them on the taut gutstring. Tensing his muscles several times, he tested its pull. He drew it just an inch, feeling the tightness of the bow and its resistance to his pull. A little smile played on his lips. Each day's pull over the past few weeks had been longer and more steady.

He stiffened his left arm, holding it straight out. The bow was almost as tall as he. He took another deep breath and let it out between clenched teeth. As he applied his strength, the bow curved until his thumb rested solidly against his cheek. He had done it! For a few seconds he held the bow fully drawn. When his hand started trembling he carefully eased the string back. A feeling of accomplishment welled up within him. He could hardly wait to tell his father and Miriam.

Setting the bow down, he looked once more across the valley. Even though it was still pleasantly cool on the roof, this fall day promised to be very warm. Across the Valley of Kidron morning sunlight danced on leaves of the myrtle and sycamore trees. Olive groves on the Mount of Olives were a shining, shimmering silver in the light. Beyond the city to the south, fields of grain stubble were golden with patches of green where clumps of weeds still grew. Nephi could see orbs of yellow fruit on the citron trees. Young grapevines marched in straight rows across the fields, their leaves still green and bright. Nephi knew that even though most of the grapes were harvested, there would still be succulent bunches hidden high in vines beneath the leaves. He thought of the many times he had sat in the shade of the large vines eating his fill of grapes from above his head. His mouth watered.

He slipped on his sandals and walked down the stone stairs. Standing in the garden, he smelled the sweet and urgent fragrance of grass and trees and flowers. He splashed water on his face from the cistern and ran his fingers through his long, thick hair. It crackled as he chased away the snarls. He rubbed his face, wondering when his beard would begin to grow. His older brothers now had beards and he felt he should have one, too. Each day he looked in the polished metal mirror to see what progress his beard was making. There was no beard, only whorls of gold down growing on his ruddy cheeks.

A thrill went through him as, once again, he thought of the significance of this day. He walked absently through the garden, feeling more than thinking, his feet finding the narrow path. Dampness from the dew wet his sandals and felt good on his bare feet. He climbed back to the roof, and gazed once again over familiar rooftops. His eyes were drawn to the spires of the temple. Winding streets and dirty, crowded alleys were forgotten as he looked at his beloved city. It was glorious in the dawn, showing golden walls and towers in the tawny light of morning. In that light the streets of Jerusalem quivered and sparkled with new life.

Nephi loved the temple. With his friends he had spent hours in its courtyard. He was fascinated by its spires, its many courts, its gardens and walls. He loved to run his hands over the rough bark of cypresses in the outer courtyard and imagine to himself all that happened inside that holy place.

He pictured the seventy-thousand men Solomon had employed to build it; great donkey and camel caravans traveling from Tyre and Sidon with loads of cedar beams, gold, silver, and precious stones. He looked with awe at the great, multi-colored stones in the walls, huge cedar columns, palms, fountains. Lehi, with tears in his eyes, had talked of the glory and splendor of the temple, how it was the pride and the lifeblood of the people, their very heart and soul. Lately he had spoken of desecrations against the temple and of the need of the people to return to the worship of the God of their fathers.

Now, here he was, today. . . . His reverie was interrupted by his mother's call. "Nephi, it is time to eat." He left the roof, washed in the basin at the door, and went inside. His father and Sam were already seated at the table. His mother, Sariah, bustled around, putting food on the table. She would eat by herself after the men had finished.

Nephi noted the absence of Laman and Lemuel but he said nothing. He didn't want to add to the sadness of his parents over the behavior of his older brothers. They just didn't seem to want to participate with the family in anything—even their meals. Again Nephi silently vowed that he would never do anything that would make his parents sorrowful or ashamed of him.

He ate some bread and cheese and took a long drink of goat's milk, but he was too excited to eat much. He was anxious to be off, but he knew that his father would not be hurried.

Finally Lehi smiled and spoke. "Come, Sam and Nephi, let's go to the temple."

Sam shook his head and grunted. Sariah wagged her head sorrowfully in a silent signal to her husband. Walking up behind Sam, she put her hands on his shoulders in a protective gesture.

"Why don't you and Nephi go by yourselves today," she said, as she squeezed her son. "Sam can help me in the garden. We will pick cucumbers and lentils for our supper."

Lehi nodded and shrugged. "All right. Nephi, let us be off."

Nephi quickly followed his father secretly glad to have him all to himself. They were immediately swept up in a mass of humanity surging through narrow streets toward the temple. Sukkoth, The Feast of Booths, was the most popular of the annual festivals and many people had traveled great distances in order to celebrate in Jerusalem.

Nephi turned to Lehi. "Father," he began.

"What is it, son?"

"Do you remember buying me the steel bow in Sidon?"

Lehi smiled. "How could I forget! I didn't think I would be able to leave the city unless I did."

"You made me promise never to put an arrow to the bow until I could draw it clear to my cheek."

"Yes, I remember," Lehi said.

Nephi walked silently for a few minutes. "Father, I made a full draw today." He looked up expectantly.

Lehi stopped in midstride seeming to know how important this accomplishment was to his son.

"My son, I'm proud of you. That is a man's bow. There are few men in this city who could draw it fully." He squeezed Nephi's hand, noting the color rising in his son's cheeks. "I recommend that you start to practice shooting. Drawing a bow is of no use unless you can hit what you shoot at."

Nephi beamed.

They turned, walking arm in arm toward the temple. Lehi felt a swelling of pride for his stalwart son. For his part, Nephi sensed anew the love and support from his father.

Men, arms filled with myrtle, palm, and willow boughs streamed through the gates into the city. With these branches, along with corner poles and hemp cord, they were building small huts everywhere. They lined the narrow streets, filled squares and courtyards, and even appeared on roofs.

Lehi, watching his son as he tried to see everything, asked, "Son, tell me about the huts of Succoth."

Nephi was pleased to show his knowledge. "The huts represent crude shelters the Children of Israel lived in on their journey from Egypt to the promised land. The people interlace roof branches in such a way that a man sleeping in the hut can awaken in the middle of the night and see the stars." He continued, "Part of the Sukkoth celebration is that people live in the huts for seven days and eight nights. This is symbolic of the lonely years on the desert when the Hebrews came to know Yahweh as their God. So now, each year, all men of Judah take to their booths in memory of that experience."

Lehi nodded approvingly. "You have learned well."

Nephi stood a little taller. Receiving a compliment from his father was the greatest of rewards.

As they hurried along, Nephi was startled to hear the loud blast of trumpets close by.

"Hurry," Lehi said, "or we will miss the procession."

They pressed forward, joining the procession moving slowly toward the temple. Many people carried barley, fruit, vegetables, wine, and other things to be used as offerings. Led by the priests, they marched to the sound of pipes and cymbals, singing psalms of thanksgiving. Lehi and Nephi joined in the song, "Give thanks unto the Lord, for he is good . . ."

When they arrived in the temple courtyard the procession of priests was just leaving on their way to the Pool of Siloam. Lehi and Nephi waited, engrossed in watching the people around them. There were small, dark, poorly dressed Jews from Ethiopia, fair-haired Jews from Tarsus, richly dressed Jews from Alexandria.

The procession of priests soon returned, a pitcher of water from the Pool of Siloam held high above their heads. Nephi, standing on tiptoe, could see over the heads of the crowd. He watched as priests ceremoniously carried the pitcher of water to the front of the temple and solemnly poured the water over the altar. Nephi looked up at his father, a question in his eyes.

Lehi whispered, "The ceremony symbolizes our need for winter rains to begin the cycle of crops for next year. The pitcher of water is a 'Symbolic rain' which is poured on the altar as the beginning of autumn rains."

As the ceremony continued, heat became oppressive. The sky was almost white with heat and the sun's rays reflected off walls and streets with an eye-searing glare. Thousands of stamping feet sent myriads of yellow dust particles into the air. With no breeze, the dust settled right back down upon the crowds. Cypresses in the streets were covered with dust. Nephi's mouth was gritty, his lips and throat dry.

The crowd moved slowly toward the temple, following the priests. Lehi guided Nephi through the great doors. He was inside the temple! He looked around seeing the beautiful cypress floor, walls and beams of cedar and sandalwood. Everything was ornamented with palms, and chains, and cherubim with wide-spread wings. Nephi saw the small cedarwood altar overlaid with gold, a golden table for shewbread, the seven-branch gold candlestick. Beams and doors and posts were patterned with gold. It was more beautiful than he had imagined. Everything seemed to pulse and glow. He could see steps leading to the temple veil, and the veil itself of blue, crimson, and purple hanging across the doorway. He knew that only the high priest entered there, for this was the sacred room known as the Holy of Holies.

The priest blessed Nephi and each of the other thirteen-year-olds, performing the age-old rites that granted them the responsibilities of adulthood. He then handed each of the boys a lulab—a switch made from branches of myrtle, palm and willow trees. Nephi saw that many of the men were also carrying lulabs.

As priests circled the altar, worshippers, including the novice adults, waved their lulabs in the air and joined in chants and singing. Everyone acted happy and carefree, and Nephi joined in the spirit of the occasion.

Suddenly the dancing and chanting stopped. A man, thin, gray-haired and narrow-faced, with deep-black searching eyes, wearing a long, plain robe with yellow fringes, stood with arms outstretched, stopping the happy ceremony.

"Thus says the Lord of hosts, the God of Israel," he shouted in a voice that thundered across the courtyard. "Amend your ways and your doings and I will let you dwell in this place."

Nephi stepped closer to his father, not sure what was happening.

"What is it?" he whispered.

Lehi put his arm around Nephi's shoulders. "It is Jeremiah, one of the Lord's prophets."

A chill went up Nephi's spine. Jeremiah, the prophet! He had heard his father speak of him. Lehi said he had heard him preach many times as he warned the people that Jerusalem would be destroyed unless they repented. Now Nephi strained to catch what the man was saying.

"You stand here pretending to worship the God of your fathers," Jeremiah shouted. "The God of Abraham, Isaac, and Jacob, but you leave this place and what do you do?" He paused. "Behold, ye trust in lying words that cannot profit. Will you steal, murder, and commit adultery, and swear falsely, and burn incense unto Baal, and walk after other gods whom ye know not; and come and stand before me in this house, which is called by my name, and say, 'We are delivered!' . . . and then you go right back out and continue doing all those abominations. Is this house become a den of robbers in your eyes?" [1]

Several temple officials, looking angry, pushed through the crowd toward Jeremiah. A priest stood on a porch and shouted indignantly, "How dare you interrupt this sacred procession?"

"I am Jeremiah," he defiantly answered. "God has called me to call you to repent or this city will be destroyed."

The priest shouted, "Seize that man. You have heard how he has prophesied against this city. He deserves to die!"

Jeremiah, his arms pinned to his sides by those who had seized him, stood calmly. Nephi marveled at the prophet's courage as he shouted, "The Lord has sent me to prophesy against this house and this city the words you have heard. Now, therefore, amend your ways and your doings . . . and the Lord will repent of the evil which he has pronounced against you. Kill me and you will bring innocent blood upon yourselves and upon this city and its inhabitants."

The men holding the fiery-eyed prophet stepped back seeming to fear God's wrath. Pashur, one of the chief priests, seized a lash from a camel driver. Turning, he struck the prophet, slashing him across his face and back, driving him to his knees. Jeremiah knelt there, hands covering his face, as he tried to dodge the blows.

Nephi, indignant at this cruel treatment of a man of God, tried to push through the crowd to give aid to the stricken Jeremiah. Lehi laid a restraining hand on his shoulder, holding him.

Jeremiah stood, cut and bruised from the flogging, but still with an air of dignity. The crowd was hushed, anticipating an angry outburst from the riled prophet but Jeremiah looked at Pashur with quiet contempt. "You, Pashur, shall go into captivity; to Babylon you shall go; and there you shall die, and there you shall be buried." [2]

Pashur blanched at the prophetic statement, then sneered, "Take him away. Lock him in the stocks at the Benjamin gate. We will see what a night in the stocks will do for his spirit." He spat in the dust at Jeremiah's feet, turned on his heel, and stalked back to the temple. Two guards, girdled with bright yellow sashes from which hung short, curved swords, grabbed Jeremiah by the arms and propelled him through the crowd and away from the temple grounds.

Priests attempted to revive the ceremony, but the people had lost their zeal. They finally dispersed, the ceremony spoiled. As he and his father trudged slowly home, Nephi hoped that his father would explain what had happened, but Lehi was strangely silent. Nephi could tell he was deep in thought. His brow was wrinkled and drops of sweat stood out on his forehead.

* * *

Nephi didn't know it, but his father was seeing again that dreadful scene, with the emaciated Jeremiah crying, "Has this house become a den of robbers in your eyes?" The words kept flowing through his mind. Had it? Had he been so blind as to not see what was happening to his beloved Jerusalem? He knew that good men must stand up for their beliefs, especially when they saw things they knew were wrong. If they were unwilling to take such a stand, evil would eventually take over and they would lose everything. Have I been derelict in my duty? he asked himself. Have I waited too long to do something? He thought of his beautiful land; of how the idol worshippers had desecrated every grove of trees with their profane worship. He shook his head sadly as they walked. Nephi had never seen his father so glum.

Even Lehi's beloved Sariah could get no response from him when she wiped bread dough from her strong hands and ran to her husband.

"What is it?" she asked.

Lehi shrugged, averting his eyes. He squeezed Nephi's shoulder, but Nephi was too excited about what he had seen to get the message.

"Mother," he said. "We saw Jeremiah. He called the people to repentance, and then he was beaten by a priest and . . ."

"Nephi," his father said sharply, "that is enough. Let's not be troubling your mother over the happenings of this man."

Nephi, not understanding why he was chastized, bit his lip. What had he said wrong?

At dusk, Lehi, Sam, and Nephi worked their way through the streets of the old city. They carried a small sack of provisions and a large gourd of water. It was almost dark when they finally arrived at the Benjamin gate in the northern wall of the city. Jeremiah was a sorry sight. His clothing was torn and ragged, his face bruised and bloody from the flogging, his hair straggly and hanging in his face. Only his hands and head protruded from the stock that held him. He was forced to stand in a stooped-over position, his feet spread wide to give him support. Nephi felt very sorry for him. He could see that Jeremiah would have a very uncomfortable night. A group of unruly children stood in front of him, throwing sand and pebbles at his face and laughing at his discomfiture. Jeremiah bore their taunting with a stolid indifference.

Nephi and Sam chased the children away while Lehi sponged off Jeremiah's bloody face with cool water. Then he took the gourd and held it to the prophet's parched lips. Jeremiah looked grateful, but he did not speak. When he had drunk his fill he shook his head, letting it sag once again in weariness and discouragement. Nephi and Sam stood back, in awe of the prophet, while Lehi talked to him. He and Jeremiah whispered hoarsely together for a few moments, words Nephi could not pick up. He watched Jeremiah curiously, then met his eyes, deep and piercing. Nephi felt as if his whole soul was exposed to the view of those eyes.

The time came when Lehi felt he should return to Sariah so she wouldn't worry, but he didn't want to leave Jeremiah at the mercy of street hoodlums. It was a difficult decision, but finally he called Sam and Nephi.

"My sons," he said, "stay here tonight and see that no harm comes to this man. I believe his words. I feel it is important that we protect him. I will return to your mother and come for you in the morning." He paused. "Are you willing to do this?" They both nodded, looking proud because their father entrusted them with such a responsibility. "Will you be all right?" Again the boys nodded.

Lehi gave each of them a hug and a final admonition. "Be careful . . . and keep your torches lighted." Saying a last goodbye to Jeremiah, he stalked off, wondering if he were doing the right thing, sure of Sariah's displeasure when he arrived home without the boys.

Nephi was impressed with this man of God. This was the closest he had ever come to one who called himself a prophet. He watched him carefully, observing his patience, his willingness to suffer adversity in order to spread his message. Several times he glanced up to see Jeremiah looking intently at him. He thought, It's as if the old prophet knows something about me that I do not know about myself.

It was a cool night so Nephi put a long shawl over Jeremiah's back, making him as comfortable as possible. Sam was soon dozing against a nearby wall, but Nephi couldn't sleep.

He sat deep in thought, arms around his knees. Suddenly Jeremiah spoke. Nephi jumped. It had been so quiet that the voice sounded almost like thunder. Yet the prophet's voice was quiet and kind, not at all like Nephi remembered it from the temple courtyard.

"Come here, my son," he said. Nephi moved closer to the prophet who looked at him from beneath white, shaggy brows. "My son," he said, "your name is Nephi. The Lord has whispered to me that He has a mission for you." Nephi's eyes opened wide. He was shocked that God should speak to this man about him. Jeremiah continued, in an almost reminiscent tone. "I was about your age when the Lord first spoke to me, calling me to

prophecy to His people, and commanding me to call them to repentance."
He lapsed into a thoughtful silence, remembering all he had seen in his life-
time. A sad look crossed his face as he contemplated his efforts to save the
Chosen People, and his lack of success.

"Yours will be a sacred and holy calling," he said. "I admonish you—
train yourself to listen to the voice of the Lord in your heart. He will only
speak to you if you are worthy to receive His voice. God will direct you if
you will just listen to that still small voice. It is important for you to follow
the words of Solomon, 'Trust in the Lord with all thine heart, and lean not
unto thine own understanding. In all thy ways acknowledge him, and he
shall direct thy paths.' " [3]

Nephi was puzzled. All his life he had felt nudges of some unknown
power within him. Could it be that the Lord really had a mission for him to
perform? Was this prophet speaking the truth? Nephi knelt to look directly
into Jeremiah's eyes. "But I am yet a youth. Why would the Lord call me?
I have not even learned the Book of the Law."

Jeremiah smiled wryly. "I know not why the Lord does what he does,"
he responded, "but I do know His voice. He asks that you prepare yourself
fully because you will be called for a special task. Trust Him. He will tell
you of your mission in His own time." With those words he lapsed back
into silence.

"Please tell me more about my mission and how to listen to the inner
voice," Nephi asked. The prophet was silent. Apparently he had said all he
was going to say.

Nephi sat awake long into the night, wondering what it all meant. Near
morning he finally fell into a restless sleep, with the voice of the prophet
jumping out at him in his dreams, calling, "You have a special mission to
serve . . . prepare yourself."

He woke suddenly, stiff and cold, unsure where he was. Then he remembered what had taken place. A pink light was brightening the east. He
glanced at Jeremiah. The prophet seemed to be sleeping, his head hanging
low in the stocks, long hair obscuring his face.

Guards came early and released him, prodding him with their staffs
toward the gate. Jeremiah's body was obviously stiff from long confine-
ment in the stocks and he fell several times under the staffs of the guards.
Nephi ran to help but he was held back. Jeremiah turned for one last, mean-
ingful look at Nephi, and then he was gone so fast that Nephi had not even
said goodbye.

The boys started for home, tired but excited by their adventure. Sam
seemed not to notice that Nephi was more quiet than usual.

Sariah was thankful to see them as they entered their home, but Lehi
was gone and she told her sons that she was almost beside herself with

worry. "It's not like your father to go somewhere and not tell me," she said, wringing her hands.

Attempting to console her, Nephi said, "If you want, Sam and I will look for him, won't we, Sam?" Sam nodded.

As if she had not heard what Nephi had said, Sariah continued. "He left before light this morning without explanation, heading out of the city. I just know something terrible has happened to him."

* * *

Lehi was distraught over the experience with Jeremiah. He lay awake, pondering what the prophet had said. Finally, to avoid disturbing Sariah by his tossing, he went to the roof. As soon as it was light enough he left the house to find a secluded spot where he could offer up his prayers in secret. Far into the Kidron Valley he walked. In a quiet place he knelt. He needed an assurance that Jeremiah was right. Had the nation of the Jews slipped so far that it no longer had respect for individuals, but only for the masses? If so, its day was done.

All day Lehi prayed. Then, as he was ready to give up his vigil and return home to his family, a blinding flame burst forth from the rocks near him, rising straight up to the heavens. He fell backwards in astonishment. While he lay there a vision opened before his eyes. He saw the destruction of the city of Jerusalem. He saw the temple destroyed and desecrated. Not one stone stood upon another where the Temple of Solomon had stood so proudly through the centuries. He saw the people slain by barbaric soldiers and he cried out in anguish as he saw the rest of the population carried away into slavery. A voice came into his consciousness saying, "The words of Jeremiah are true. These things must shortly come to pass. The people will not heed the voices of my prophets. Therefore, they will be destroyed."

Lehi trembled in anguish. What he had just seen and heard had been terrible. What could he do? What would happen to his family? He moaned to himself as he contemplated the awfulness of what must shortly come to pass. He sat up, but he was too weak to stand. He looked around. The pillar of fire and the voice were gone. Everything was just as it had been before. Could he have just dreamed it?

He made his way across the now dark valley to his house. Sariah was relieved to see him but, in her distraught state, all she could do was scold him.

"Where have you been? Don't you know we have worried about you? Why don't you tell me where you are going so I don't get so frantic? I've had the boys looking for you. Why don't you answer me?"

He wearily dismissed her prattle—not answering—and went straight to his cubiculum where he cast himself on the bed. Lehi was exhausted. His mind was racing but he couldn't make any sense out of what he had seen.

He lay thinking, and soon fell into a troubled sleep. Immediately he was carried away in a vision. The heavens opened before his eyes. It was a glorious place. Streets of gold were filled with people dressed in white. Buildings were beautiful and spacious. One stood out above the rest. As Lehi approached the building in his vision, he was made aware that this was the place where God dwelt. The building seemed to open up before him, and he saw God Himself sitting upon His throne. The building was filled with numberless angels, standing and singing praises to the Lord.

The scene of his vision changed. Once again he stood upon the earth looking into the heavens. From this vantage point he saw One who had a special radiance and luster descending from heaven to earth. This lustrous and great Being was followed by twelve of lesser luster. Whereas the first had a brightness greater than the sun at noonday, these had a brightness more like the radiance of the stars on a dark night. The special One came forward until Lehi was engulfed in His radiance. The One handed him a book with a golden cover, and said to him, "Read."

Lehi read, and as he read he was filled with the Spirit of the Lord, telling him that this glorious being standing before him was the Son of God. In the book he read about Jerusalem, how it would be destroyed along with all of its inhabitants. Many of the people would perish by the sword, but some would be carried as slaves to Babylon. He shook his head in wonderment, saying, "Wo, wo, unto Jerusalem, for I have seen thine abominations."

After reading through the book, seeing awesome and marvelous things recorded there, Lehi turned once again to that great Being who stood before him. Setting the book down, he knelt before the Son of God, praising Him, and saying, "Great and marvelous are thy works, O Lord God Almighty! Thy throne is high in the heavens, and thy power, and goodness, and mercy are over all the inhabitants of the earth; and because thou are merciful, thou wilt not suffer those who come unto thee that they shall perish!" [4]

He was shown other great visions, becoming so distraught that he cried out in his agony. Sariah ran to the bedroom. Lehi was writhing on the bed. Sweat stood out on his forehead. His clothes were tangled and twisted. Sariah sat beside him, gently stroking his face, talking to him in a soothing voice. Finally, he opened his eyes—eyes reddened by tears and strain.

He sat up, recalling clearly what he had seen. He rocked forward, resting his head on Sariah's bosom. "Oh, Sariah, it is so painful to me. Our city, Jerusalem, is to be destroyed because of the wickedness of her people. Jeremiah is right. No wonder he always has such a sad and pained look. Now I understand more fully his prophecies and his mission." He moaned, "Oh, that the people could but repent so that the city could be spared." Sariah tried to comfort him, but Lehi would not be comforted. It was almost more than he could bear. He truly loved this city of Zion—this Holy City.

By the next morning he had made his decision. He realized the significance of that decision. He knew that the road would not be easy. But he
knew the decision was right.

He called his family to him and told them what he had seen. He noted
the skepticism of his older sons, but he kept on with his story. Then he
paused and looked at each of these family members he loved so much,
knowing the impact his decision would have. He sighed, letting his shoulders
sag in weariness. "Dear Sariah and my precious sons. I have made a decision.
I cannot stand by and see the city destroyed. The Lord has given me visions
and I have now resolved that I must join Jeremiah in prophecying to the
people. I must warn them of what is going to happen. I must call them to
repentance and hope that, through their repentance, Jerusalem can be
saved."

His words were received in shocked silence. Finally Laman shook his
head. "I can't believe it. My own father going to make a spectacle of himself on the streets." He stalked from the room with Lemuel at his heels.

Nephi could tell that Sam had been moved by his father's words. He
had stepped forward and placed a hand on Lehi's shoulder. Nephi knew
Sam would have spoken if he could. With compassion, Nephi—speaking
for both of them—looked into his father's eyes. "Father, it is wonderful to
know that the God of our fathers has spoken to you. Sam and I are proud
to have a prophet for a father."

Chapter 4

Flight from Jerusalem

Nephi glanced over his shoulder to make sure the street was empty before darting around the corner and into the dim alley. He didn't want anyone to see him. He looked down at his disheveled clothing and torn tunic. What would his mother say? She was always scolding him for being careless with his clothes. He touched his bruised cheek, wincing. He thought, Well, it isn't the first time Ive had a black eye.

He limped to the end of the alley and pulled himself up and over the mud wall. He walked the short distance along the arched wall to a low, flat roof. Nephi jumped to the roof with an agility which belied his size, and made his way home, keeping to alleys and rooftops. As he went he mused aloud, "What will I say to father?" He jumped a narrow archway and thought back over the last few hours.

His mother, Sariah, had sent him to the maktesh—the Jerusalem marketplace—to buy fresh produce. He couldn't resist buying a piece of honey-candy. Savoring its sweetness, he had started for home. Without warning he was surrounded by a gang of shouting youths.

"Josephite!" "Arab lover!" "Pig of Sidon!" He was taken by surprise. He had heard Lehi say that Jerusalem was a city divided: that dissension between the pro-Egyptians and the pro-Babylonians had almost ripped apart the unhappy city and that passions ran high.

As a man of affairs, Lehi had gone throughout Jerusalem telling his friends and anyone who would listen that unless there was repentance there would be a terrible destruction of both city and people. For his efforts, he had almost lost his life. All this rushed through Nephi's mind as he warily backed up, watching as the street urchins and toughs formed a tight cordon around him. They circled, chanting and mocking, poking him with their sticks. Nephi turned, too. His assailants began another chant. "His father is a prophet! His father is a prophet! His father is a prophet!" in derisive and mocking tones. They punctuated each chorus of the chant with a flailing of sticks.

Red-faced with anger, Nephi jumped at one of the boys which acted as a signal for the others to pummel him with fists and sticks. He dropped the produce and raised an arm to shield his face. He was tackled in the back of his knees and knocked face-forward to the hard-packed dirt street. He grabbed one of the boys in a tight grip as he fell. They rolled on the street, first one on top, then the other, while those on the sidelines whacked Nephi with their sticks.

He could see it was going to be a losing battle. The odds were too great. Suddenly, with a shout, the gang faded away. Surprised, he stood up and looked around. Up the street a squad of Jewish soldiers in full armor had rounded the corner. Nephi tried to pick up some of the produce, but it was no use. Nothing could be salvaged. He dragged himself into the alley and started for home.

Now here he was, almost home and still no plausible story to tell. He smiled good-naturedly and shrugged his broad shoulders. What could he tell but the truth? He could already hear the snickers and snide remarks of his two eldest brothers. Though he was only going-on-fourteen, Nephi was as big as Laman and a head taller than Lemuel. They were always picking on him and treating him like a servant. "Do this!" and "Do that!" He was glad that his brother Sam was more agreeable. In fact, he wished Sam *could* say something.

As he approached the door of their city house, he straightened up the best he could, ran his fingers through his hair in an attempt to comb out some of the tangles, slipped off his sandals and stepped inside. Laman spotted him immediately. "Ho, little brother. Now what has happened to you? Lemuel, come here and see your ragamuffin brother." The two of them chided him all the way to the kitchen.

Sariah was standing over the small brazier, stirring a thick broth, when she saw Nephi. She straightened up in surprise. "Son, what has happened to you? And where are my groceries?"

Nephi looked sheepishly at the floor. Laman and Lemuel stood in the archway enjoying his discomfiture. Lehi, hearing the commotion, came in from the reading room. He looked at Nephi and asked, "Tell me what happened, son."

"I was on my way home from the *maktesh* when a gang of toughs cornered me." He calmly attempted to explain what had happened.

Lehi was sympathetic, but Laman and Lemuel turned angrily to their father.

"See what you have caused!" Laman's breath came fast and his eyes gleamed with rage. "We cannot even walk down the streets of our city because of you and your cursed preaching."

Lemuel chimed in, looking at Laman for approval. "Father, give up this madness before we lose all of our friends." Then he added, "The Jews are right. You are a troublemaker."

Sariah stepped between them. "Boys, stop it! You will not talk to your father that way. He is only doing what he feels has to be done."

"But why does he have to preach in this city?" Laman asked bitterly. "Our friends have deserted us. We are made fun of in the marketplace. Our house is a target for rotten eggs, and still our father continues to tell the people they are wicked and need to repent." He angrily turned from the room. Lemuel was close behind.

Nephi said, "I'm sorry, Father. I didn't mean to start an argument." He turned to his mother. "And, Mother, I'm sorry I spilled the groceries."

Lehi put his arm around Nephi. "Son, you didn't start this. Laman and Lemuel have been festering for some time. They will not accept that God has spoken to me, telling me to call the people to repentance."

Nephi looked up at his father in admiration. Lehi was now over forty-five years of age. The once dark-red beard which flowed broadly over his chest now had streaks of white. Nephi had always respected the quiet dignity of his father. He knew that, in a pinch, his father would be a mighty fighter.

* * *

Afternoon sun beat down upon the roof with brilliant intensity. Lehi, sitting cross-legged on his rug, did not seem to notice. Once again the Lord had spoken to him. Since receiving his first vision, which warned him about the destruction of Jerusalem, he had spent his time telling the people to repent in order to save the city. He had been rejected by the people, who had called him a dreamer. His own relatives felt he had been deluded. His children had been ridiculed and beaten. His home had become an object of desecration by roving street mobs. He and Sariah could no longer appear on the streets of the city without a protective escort.

Lehi had spent much time on his knees imploring the Lord to lift this awesome burden from him. Now the Lord had spoken to him again. The voice had said, "Blessed art thou, Lehi, because of the things which thou hast done; and because thou hast been faithful and declared unto this people the things which I commanded thee, behold, they seek to take away thy life." [5] The Lord had then commanded him to take his family and leave Jerusalem. Now he rocked back and forth on the rug, contemplating once again this latest command of the Lord. Leave the city of his birth? Leave his friends and relatives? Leave his business? His gold and silver? Just pack what he could and disappear into the desert? He didn't for a moment think of disobeying the Lord, but he was grieved.

He took a deep breath and straightened his broad shoulders. Sariah and the boys must be told. He stood up, brushed the dust from his robe, and went down the steps to the garden. In the kitchen Sariah was busily making honey cakes for their supper. She was wearing a slim, ankle-length tunic caught in at the waist with a broad sash. Her long, black hair was braided in two thick braids and coiled around her head. One wisp of hair had escaped the braid and was hanging damply on her forehead. She looked so lovely. How was he to break the news?

Laman and Lemuel were gone somewhere. Sam? Faithful Sam was by the door grinding wheat, his arms rhythmically moving back and forth, his lips whistling a tuneless song. Sadly, Lehi's mind flashed back to Sam's return from his last caravan journey. It had almost been two years now. The caravan had been plundered by a band of Assyrians who had taken Sam and several of the younger men as hostages. The grieving family had lost all hope of ever seeing Sam again.

Yet he had returned. The day of Sam's return was imprinted on Lehi's memory. Thin, clothes ragged and dirty, he staggered into the house and into his father's arms. Lehi cried out a welcome, throwing his arms around this son returned as if from the dead since few captured by the Assyrians ever returned. Yet here was his son. Lehi held him tightly, tears running down his cheeks, his hands digging into Sam's back.

He pushed him away to get a closer look at him, but Sam ducked his head, not looking at his father. Something was wrong! Had something terrible happened to his son? "Sam," he said, alarm in his voice. "What is it?"

Sam glanced up, then again dropped his bloodshot eyes. He had walked and crawled over two hundred miles from the Assyrian camp. His only desire had been to get home—to get back to the family that loved him. He had been a slave to the cruel Assyrians but now he was home. He felt weak. He started to sag, then he straightened and looked at his father.

Sam shook his head and uttered a low croak then, with a pleading look in his eye, he opened his mouth and groaned audibly.

Lehi gasped and sat down. His head dropped to his chest and he rocked back and forth in agony as tears ran down his cheeks. They had mutilated his son! They had cut out his tongue and relegated him to a mute life. Lehi drew his son to him, cradling his head on his chest. Sam—barely seventeen.

A slight cough brought Lehi back to the present. Nephi was standing behind him. A smell of charcoal smoke clung to him, and Lehi knew that he had been to the street of the metal workers again. Nephi had spent much time there this past year, befriended by the Philistine metal worker, Sharaz.

Sharaz, noting Nephi's intense interest, had taken him in as an apprentice. Nephi pumped the bellows, stoked the charcoal, and poured molten metal into moulds. Lately, he had even been able to do some pounding and shaping of the pliant metal.

Lehi looked now at his fourteen-year-old son. Nephi was a handsome youth, large for his age, with a barrel chest and broad shoulders. Years of loading camels, of consistency in drawing his steel bow, and hard work at the metal forge showed in muscles that rippled beneath his skin.

Sariah looked at Lehi, a question in her eyes. Lehi thought, How do you tell your family that you are going to leave everything you have worked for and just walk into the inhospitable desert? He cleared his throat, breathed deeply, and asked, "Where are Laman and Lemuel?"

Nephi shrugged. Sam continued grinding corn. "They left this morning to check with the caravan overseer," Sariah replied.

Sweat beaded on Lehi's forehead. He tried several times to tell about his vision, but each time his voice failed him. Finally, frustrated and alone in his knowledge, he pushed aside the door and walked into the night. Sariah looked after him, her brow wrinkled with worry.

That night Lehi lay quietly on his back, staring into the blackness. His hands were clasped behind his head and he tried to breath normally so as not to disturb Sariah. She was not fooled. She rolled over and laid an arm across his chest. "What is it, my husband? What is troubling you so?"

Lehi smiled in the dark. After more than twenty years of marriage Sariah knew his every mood. He rolled on his side, drawing her to him. While running his fingers through her long hair, he groped for the right words. They lay there for a few moments, cheek to cheek, drawing strength from each other.

Finally he said, "The Lord has spoken to me again." He breathed out in a long sigh. "He has commanded me to take my family and leave Jerusalem. He told me that if I don't my enemies would take my life." He paused. "We are to depart as soon as possible, and to leave most of our possessions behind." He paused again, hoping for a response from his wife. Hearing none, he ended lamely, "The Lord told me he will lead us to a promised land—far from Jerusalem and our enemies."

Sariah's composure melted like snow on a hot summer day. Tears rolled down her cheeks onto her pillow. She loved Jerusalem! She loved her fine home! Her family was here—why should she have to leave them? She held tightly to Lehi, needing his strength.

When her tears subsided she whispered in his ear. "I'll go wherever you want me to go, my husband. I will stand by your side regardless of what may come."

Lehi squeezed her tightly, his own eyes filled with tears. His joy was full. What more could a man want in life than a wife who gave him her total love and support! Someone to stand by him, regardless of his decisions. He slept peacefully for the first time since receiving his latest vision.

But sleep had departed from Sariah. It was she who now stared into the blackness. What a challenge this was going to be. She was forty years old! Was she up to leaving her home and possessions to travel in the desert toward some nebulous promised land?

At the breakfast table, with the entire family assembled, Lehi broke the news.

"My family," he said, "I have something very important to talk over with you." The boys stopped eating and looked at their father. Groping for words, he began. "The Lord has spoken to me again." Laman frowned and shook his head at Lemuel. "He listed the abominations of the people of Jerusalem:

'They worship stumps of wood and idols of stone;
they have created heathen gods for every town and city;
they have persecuted and killed My prophets;
they have shed innocent blood;
they offer up human sacrifices to Moloch;
they practice gross immorality, wife swapping, adultery;
harlots are in My holy temple;
the judges are corrupt;
they won't listen to the true prophets.'

"All of these things and more the Lord rehearsed with me. Then He told me that if we stayed here, the people would take my life." He sighed. "So the Lord has told us to depart Jerusalem into the desert. He will then lead us to a promised land, reserved for us and our posterity."

It was a long speech. For a moment the boys sat motionless, then Laman jumped up. The veins stood out in his throat. His hands balled into fists.

"You mean to take us away from the city of our birth? The land of our inheritance? Where all of our friends and relatives live? Take us out to some forsaken desert where we will die by ourselves? I won't go!"

Lemuel chimed in. "Nor will I." The two eldest sons pushed their chairs back from the table and stomped out.

Nephi sat there, stuned. Leave Jerusalem? The city he loved so much? God's holy temple? Sam mutely looked from one to another. Sariah sat still, tears running down her cheeks. Finally Nephi spoke. "Father, it will be hard to leave this city, but if the Lord has commanded, we must obey."

* * *

The next day was Friday. The Sabbath began in the evening, when all work ceased at sundown. At the sound of the ram's horn, which echoed through the city, Sariah lighted the Sabbath candles with the traditional prayer, "Come let us welcome the Sabbath. May its radiance shine forth in our hearts. The Lord is my light and my salvation. . . ." She spoke the prayer this day without enthusiasm. A pall had hung over the hearts of the family since Lehi had announced that this would be their last Sabbath in Jerusalem.

Sariah served a big meal, setting out trays loaded with figs, melons, apples, oranges and roasted locusts along with a cooling pomegranate drink. Lehi blessed their dinner and they ate silently, each with his own thoughts.

Lehi, on his stool at the head of the table, enjoyed the moment, watching his family. He knew of the anxiety they were feeling. Sariah poured the pomegranate drink then sat beside him. Lehi didn't look at her. He just put his broad hand on her knee. They sat in companionable silence.

Sariah gazed around the room that had become part of her very being. Walls were glazed with a patina from thousands of smoky fires in the brazier. Strong timber beams were hung with pots and baskets filled with herbs and household articles. She looked at her sons. They were fine boys and handsome men. She knew that soon they would marry and have children of their own. What kind of a life would the children be born to? Would they be wanderers over the deserts like the Bedouins? Her shoulders slumped.

Lehi's attention was drawn by her small movement. He squeezed her leg. "Tired?"

"A little. Thinking of what is going to happen to us makes me tired."

He smiled at her gently. "Under the Lord's leadership, the future will be very rosy." Lehi was seeing beyond their home, visualizing their future in that land which the Lord had promised him for his posterity.

* * *

The Sabbath passed slowly for Nephi. Now that the decision was made to leave Jerusalem, he wanted to get on with it. He listened to Lehi's deep voice during scripture reading, but his thoughts were not on what was being read. He could see that Laman and Lemuel were also nervous. Nephi knew they wanted to be out with their friends and that they thought the Sabbath laws were stupid.

Saturday evening finally came, and with it the packing of the camels. Laman and Lemuel, still complaining, had gone to the caravan encampment and had picked out twelve camels for the journey. Eight of the camels were for riding and four for baggage. Nephi's camel, Armed—now fully grown—was one of the riding camels.

All night they worked, loading the camels. Lehi strapped tents across the backs of three camels, forming saddles upon which the women would ride. Panniers, hung on the sides of pack camels, contained the few possessions they would take with them: dried foods, cooking vessels, clothing, tools, and huge sacks of grain and seeds. Water bags were hung on the panniers, and Lehi reminded Laman to stop at the well to fill them before they started out.

* * *

The eastern sky finally brightened with morning. The outlines of their home became more distinct. They no longer needed the torch that burned beside the door. Lehi felt the dearness and love of their home—its permanence and safety. It had been built with love and now they must leave it. He put an arm around Sariah's shoulders and for a moment they stood gazing at it. Then, trying to cheer her, he said, "Don't worry, my dear, we will have many homes." She cried silently in his arms.

The sky was gray now. After comforting his wife the best he could, Lehi went, for the last time, to the caravan encampment. Jacoth and the overseer greeted him warmly, kissing him on both cheeks. Lehi looked from one to another of these old friends. Together they had traveled many miles, had overcome many hardships, had shared many campfires. For their faithful service to him through the years, he presented them with documents making them legal owners of the caravan. They had just become rich men. From the caravan, Lehi hired three camel drivers, one of whom was Nephi's friend, Shemin.

Following the tearful goodbye, Lehi returned to his home, bare now, devoid of the family which had filled it with love. Sariah was in the garden, picking the last of her precious herbs. She packed them carefully in one of the panniers, and they were ready.

As the family caravan started out, Sariah turned for one last look at her home. Then she resolutely turned forward, looking to her future—and the future of her family.

Chapter 5

Journey in the Wilderness

It was autumn, and hot. The air was still, with even the restless palms unstirring. Leaves of cypress and karob trees hung listlessly as the small caravan passed. The sky, a hard and brilliant turquoise laced with wispy wind-driven clouds, contrasted with distant, scarlet mountains. The valley deepened, showing a panorama of bronze fields ready for harvest.

Sariah half-reclined on the back of her camel between the panniers which carried cooking utensils, a stone for grinding meal, dried fruits, meal, herbs and other staples, a few pottery jars, several lamps, floor pads, skins and water bags, a bucket with goats-hair rope and a few special female ornaments.

The center area between boxes was softly padded and lined so Sariah could either sit or recline. Over the top was stretched a green awning to shade her from the glaring sun. She tried to be comfortable but she was unutterably weary. Her worries about the future of her family made her even more tired. The rocking motion of the camel often lulled her to sleep, but she would suddenly awaken, with the startling realization of what was happening to her family.

Lehi marveled at her. She had ridden all day without complaint, either of the early morning cold, dry east wind which lashed grit in their faces and made them cringe in their cloaks, or at the fierce contrast of the daily *khamsin*, blowing its hot, stifling breath from the desert.

The camels interested Sariah. She had never been on caravan with Lehi, and this was her first view of a camel fully loaded for desert travel. Not even love could make the haughty and disdainful beasts beautiful, but she did think they were poetic animals. She observed their motion, their long and elastic step, their sure and soundless tread, the broad careen as they walked, and the long, graceful neck of swan-like curvature. She could tell that the drivers took pride in their camels. The scarlet-fringed bridles covering the foreheads and the throats were garnished with chains, each ending with a tinkling silver bell.

They had left Jerusalem in the early morning light, before their enemies were awake. Sariah would always remember the harsh, grating, melancholy sound as grim-faced soldiers swung open the gates to let them out of the city. They had taken the south caravan route from Jerusalem, through

Bethlehem and Tekoa. They ate lunch at the Spring of Philip, resting during the hottest part of the day. By evening, they arrived at their country estate in Beith Lehi.

Squealing and grunting, Sariah's camel dropped to its knees. Wearily she stepped off and entered her home. Moray, Lehi's elderly caretaker, and his wife, Edna, greeted her warmly. Sariah hugged them and then left them to greet Lehi while she wandered through the cool rooms, remembering events that had taken place there. Her simple furnishings were intact—beds, chairs, and rugs. She looked at her garden area, now grown over with tall weeds, then she looked across fields she had loved as a young bride. She sighed. Now she would have to leave this home also. Father, she prayed silently, it is sometimes difficult to follow my man. Help me to understand. She paused in her prayer. And Father, she pleaded, please let us stay right here. We're out of Jerusalem. We're out of danger from those who would take Lehi's life. Let us stay here and live our lives.

The men unloaded the camels in the front yard. Lehi, knowing Sariah's misgivings, stopped in the doorway. He could see the lines around her eyes and he knew of her tiredness. He turned to his sons.

"Bring in the bags from the camels. We will stay here for a few days." He walked into the room and drew Sariah to him. Now he almost wished he had taken a different route and bypassed their country home. It had too many memories for Sariah. They stood for a long time, not saying anything. Sariah drew comfort from his nearness.

Finally shaking off her lethargy, she pushed away. "Well, my husband, it is time that I helped Edna fix our dinner." She bustled off into the kitchen, rattling pans she found, giving directions to Moray and Edna. Lehi smiled. Sariah would be fine.

* * *

As soon as the camels were unloaded, Nephi slipped off to visit Miriam. Approaching Ishmael's home, he called to Miriam as he had done so many times in the past. The door opened and she ran out to meet him, her youthful figure illuminated by lamplight from the door. She was even lovelier than Nephi remembered. Her maturity was obvious and he suddenly felt embarrassed and tongue-tied. She stopped before she reached him, and they looked at each other timidly across that short distance. It had been over six months since he had seen her. She had been a girl, almost a little sister. Now she was a woman.

"Hello, Miriam," he blurted. "Can we go for a walk?"

She nodded and moved ahead of him, her robes catching in the oleander bushes. In the garden area behind the villa he caught up with her. They walked hand in hand between bushes, finally sitting on a large rock, silently, listening to the chirp of insects in grasses and trees. Somewhere a pariah dog was yelping—a wild and eerie sound. A swish above their heads signalled the darting of a bat as it dipped and turned under the starry skies.

Miriam arched her back, leaning against the rock. Her face was a white oval in the light from the stars, her hair a dark mist. Nephi had an urge to take her into his arms. He hadn't realized how much he cared for his cousin.

He cleared his throat. "Miriam?"

She sat up, leaning closer to him. "What, Nephi?"

"Miriam," he started again. "We are leaving the Land of Jerusalem and going into the desert. Perhaps I will never see you again." There was melancholy in his voice. Then he added impulsively, "Miriam, come with us. We could become betrothed."

She jumped like a frightened deer, moving quickly away. Throwing a look at him over her shoulder, she ran for the villa. He stood up, shaken and baffled, regretting what he had said. He wanted to cry out for her to stop, but he watched mutely as she reached the doorway and slipped inside.

Dejected he walked through the garden, scuffing his sandals in the dirt. As he passed the villa, he gave it one look then took off for his own house. He carried no torch and the familiar path was strange in the darkness. He reeled through the bushes and careened through small draws. When he arrived at his father's villa he was scratched and unkempt.

In his cubiculum he knelt and prayed. "Why, Lord? What did I do wrong? Is it wrong to desire Miriam for my wife?" He prayed for a long time but no answer came. It was as if the heavens were shut to him. He lay on his pallet wondering what he had said to upset Miriam. He finally fell asleep, dreaming of running after Miriam, but never catching her.

* * *

Morning gave Sariah a chance to wash clothes before their journey into the wilderness. Keeping busy helped her to keep her mind off her thoughts of losing her homes. She had the men fill a large wooden tub with water from the cistern where the hot sun had warmed it. Then she carried linens into the yard and started them soaking. She pounded and flailed and wrung the clothes with a passion. She loved to wash. It helped to work out her frustrations. She shook the clothes and spread them to dry on walls and nearby bushes. Nephi called from the house. Sariah wiped her hands on her tucked-up skirt and hurried inside.

He sat at the large table, his head in his hands. "Mother," he said, looking up, "How old were you when you and Father were married?"

Sariah looked at him, smiling. "I was fourteen and your father was twenty. Why?"

Nephi mumbled a response and stepped outside. It had begun to rain. A few large drops spattered cooly on his face, but he knew the late-summer shower would not last long. He stood listening to the drumming of rain, leaning against the white-washed wall where he had stood so often as a child. In a few minutes the only reminder of the shower was the sweet smell of earth and a soft, rhythmic dripping from the beams. For once the peaceful scene had no effect on him.

At supper that night Nephi was very quiet. Sariah and Edna had prepared bowls of lentil soup, a large plate of lamb mixed with parched grain and chickpeas, and cheese and fruit for dessert. None of it tasted good to him. He was too miserable. Lehi tried to converse with him, but Nephi didn't feel like talking. Laman and Lemuel didn't help. They had spent all day at Ishmael's villa and now sat across the table laughing and joking over the fun they had with Miriam's older sisters. Nephi tried to ignore them.

The next day was their final day in Beith Lehi and Lehi invited Ishmael's family to join them for dinner: Ishmael and his wife, Elizabeth; Esther, Lehi's oldest daughter and her husband, Shazer, and their children, Ishmar, Vivian, and Zippah. Ishmael's five unwed daughters—Cleopha, Marni, Leah, Miriam, Eva—were all there. The only family members not present were Lehi's daughter Annah, her husband Arneth, and their children Tamna and Rebecca. Against Lehi's advice, they had remained in Jerusalem where Arneth was a guard in Zedekiah's court.

It was an enjoyable gathering and, Sariah thought, probably our last one. She held her grandchildren to her, loving each of them.

Lehi and Ishmael secluded themselves in a corner, deep in conversation. Nephi overheard the words "dream," "but why?" "the Lord commanded," "wilderness," "join with us," "too old."

Nephi visited with his friend and cousin, Ishmar, and tried to catch Miriam's eye, but she wouldn't look his way.

* * *

In early morning light, the drivers rounded up the camels and repacked them. Lehi added seed from his granary as well as gold and silver coins from his treasury. Lehi left the other treasures there, including silver goblets and plates, gold necklaces and jewelry, their fine linens and other valuables. Before they left, Lehi drew up a deed giving the villa to Moray and Edna. As he read it to them, tears of joy coursed down their cheeks.

The air was warm and the sky was blue as they left Beith Lehi. White clouds gathered over mountains to the east, but Nephi paid them little attention. He turned again and looked toward Ishmael's villa. There was nothing to see except vineyards and orchards. Resolutely, he turned forward, thinking, I will never see Miriam again.

The caravan strung out as it moved through fields and onto the caravan road that stretched toward Hebron. In front of the camels walked the small herd of black and speckled goats. Lehi said they would need the kids for sacrificing and the nannys for milk, butter, and cheese. They could also use goats' hair to repair their tents.

As they passed through Hebron, Lehi pointed out the Oak of Mamre where Abraham had worshipped, and the tomb of the Patriarchs. Almond trees dotted hillsides covered with dazzling yellow desert roses. Tall date palms lined the caravan route, clusters of fruit hanging below their coronet of leaves. From Hebron, Lehi led them south through Adoraim, where he told his family Noah had been buried, then through Ziph and Maon. They ended their first day of travel just north of the ancient town of Beersheba. They had covered almost thirty miles.

They pitched their brown and black tents or *ohels* beside a spring hardly more than a trickle from the rocks. Pitching the tents was normally the women's responsibility, but Lehi directed the drivers and his sons to help. They laid a tent out in the sand, stuck in three seven-foot center poles, and hoisted them upright. While Lemuel, Sam, and Nephi held the poles, Laman helped the women put in rows of parallel outside poles. Then he and Lehi, using rings of leather sewn into the tent, staked it to the ground.

The tents that would be their homes were woven in three-foot strips of goats' hair sewn together and reinforced with cross-strips. Lehi's large tent was divided into two apartments by a fabric curtain. The front room was reserved for the men, the rear one used as the women's quarters and kitchen. The floor was covered with mats of straw and coarse camel hair. Along the sides, bed rolls and pallets were piled in tiers. Scattered over the floor were camel saddles which would serve as seats.

While the tents were being erected, Nephi gathered branches from tamarisks and acacia bushes and built a fire while Sariah, using the last rays of the sun for light, began baking. She scattered several handfuls of grain on her oblong millstone and ground them with a second, slightly rougher stone, dampening the rough flour from time to time with water from the spring. After she leavened the flour with starter from the previous day, Sariah kneaded it into the thumb-sized cakes. By this time the fire had burned down to a heap of white ash. She laid the raw cakes on a flat stone, heaped a pile of hot ashes on them, and left them to bake. Nephi watched her with pride knowing that even though his mother was the wife of a rich man she took pride in her household skills.

Beersheba, the gateway to the Negev desert, was just a grouping of water wells—a wayside station for caravans. Lehi, knowing what was ahead, had their leather water bags and allowed the camels and goats to drink their fill. After Beersheba, the rolling green hills abruptly gave way to treeless plains and barren desert.

Nephi turned to his father. "What a land of contrasts!"

Lehi smiled. "Yes, and yet this is the land through which Moses wandered in search of the promised land."

"But why here?"

"Palestine is the crossroads of the world—the bridge between darkness and light. God didn't intend His people to be a weak and helpless people. He gave us a strong, untamed land to make of us a strong people."

Nephi nodded. Ahead he could see that the land was bare and lifeless, the yellow earth rocky and crumbling. The day glowed with heat as if the doors of a furnace had suddenly opened over the endless slate fields and deep gorges and canyons. The landscape was somber, ravished by erosion, the sky glassy and pale.

Thorny shrubs, some as tall as a man, grew rampant alongside the roadway. Lehi showed his family the sabra, a cactus with fruit which was hard on the outside, but tender and sweet inside. He told them that without a knowledge of the desert they would not survive the desert.

Lehi guided his small band southward over the caravan trail. It was a route his caravans had traveled many times as they transported spices and incense from the land of the Sabaeans to Jerusalem and Egypt. Waterless stretches of sun-scorched rock and sand dominated the area. Occasionally they passed a hummock of clay and cemented sand, but most of the time it was just sand, sometimes as smooth as the wave-leveled beach, sometimes heaped in rolling ridges, or just rippled like a lake in a windstorm. The sand was so crusted on the surface that it shattered into rattling flakes at every step of the camels. Dissecting the desert were numerous *nabals*, or wadis. The caravan trail followed an undulating pattern as it dipped and rose.

The second night of their journey they camped at Ein Avdat—a glorious oasis with springs, beautiful pools, green fields and stately date palms. Nephi and Sam took advantage of the pools and went swimming, washing off grimy dust of the caravan trail. Sariah, under Lehi's direction, restocked supplies, because there was nothing to hunt or to gather for food in the *midbar* or wilderness through which they would be passing. Game was plentiful around the oasis, and Nephi increased his skill catching partridge and quail.

After Ein Avdat was another desert. Every day was the same—sky a brassy blue, landscape stretching monotonously for miles without sign of vegetation except for a few tamarisk, acacia or terebinth trees. Early caravaners had dug cisterns a day's journey apart, so each night they camped near water. Rope marks, worn deep into the chalk-white limestone edges of the cisterns, told of the centuries they had been used.

The caravan trudged onward, the people suffering in silence except for Laman and Lemuel. They had complained so much that not even their mother listened to them. From the Sinai they entered the wilderness of Zin, a wild and lonely place with rocky canyons, scorched by burning sun and wind—empty of everything except sand and stone.

As they descended through barren hills to the oasis at Kadesh-Barnea, the weary travelers were greeted by the welcome sight of date palms lining a sparkling stream. They set up their tents next to tall myrtle bushes. Sariah picked some of the purplish-black berries, called *mursins*, by the Hebrews. She would dry them and use them for poultices.

They stayed several days at the oasis, to rest their livestock and refresh themselves. From Kadesh-Barnea the small caravan followed a trail called The Way to the Hill Country of the Amorites, which led across the chalk and limestone plateau marking the Wilderness of Paran. It was not an easy trail, but Lehi said it was smoother than many others, avoiding as it did both mountains to the northeast and deep ravines and heavily eroded valleys to the southwest. Ahead of them the terrain climbed steeply. As they topped the mountain pass leading into the Arabah, all they could see were saw-toothed peaks, eroded slopes, and desolate valleys. Sariah shuddered and whispered, "Is this where we are to die?"

They dropped eastward through the desert, finally intersecting another trail which Lehi identified as the Way to the Red Sea. A wild and desolate region, it was a land of hot winds, waterless stream beds, and undulating hills of burning sand and flint. On their right, to the south, steep cliffs dropped abruptly to the valley floor and forbidding canyons cut into the cliff face.

It had been two weeks since they had left Beith Lehi, and day followed monotonous day. Nephi attempted to alleviate the monotony by hunting, but there was little game. Crows and ravens and an occasional eagle soaring effortlessly high in the sky were the only wildlife.

The Arabah was a wide sandy plain with occasional salt flats. Black seams snaked across the barren ridges and reached down to the desert like unearthly fingers. Millions of stones, worn smooth by winter's flash floods, littered the mile-wide wadi. It was a wilderness of rock. As they continued south the tilt of the land changed with drainage toward the Red Sea.

There was little feed. Hundreds of caravans passing through kept the grass cropped short. Nephi was thankful for Lehi's knowledge of an occasional oasis. These were lush, palm-fringed stopping places where springs came from porous limestone rocks which had trapped the little rainwater beneath their surfaces. Wildlife was abundant near the oases and Nephi became an expert with his bow. He shot Barbary sheep with their long curving and pointed horns, but most of their meat came from the hartebeest. Sometimes Nephi was lucky enough to get a shot at the fast gazelle.

Turtle doves were abundant in the rocky crags near the springs. In the evenings the valley seemed to reverberate with their soft-plaintive cooing. Nephi and Sam snared them in nets made of woven goats' hair in wooden frames. The hillsides were covered with star thistle and buckthorn and many times Nephi returned to camp scratched and bleeding, but he usually had meat for the caravan.

Nephi enjoyed sitting at the edge of the canyons watching the forked-tail swifts as they darted from their little mud huts plastered on the canyon walls. They were superb aerialists, twisting and turning, soaring and diving as they pursued insects on the wing. He loved to be by himself especially at night when the desert was as still as the sky. Often he left the camp to feel the quiet of the night and to communicate with his God. He would lie on his back, staring at the night sky as the light of the sun faded in the west. He often thought of Miriam, wondering what she might be doing, wondering if he would ever see her again. It was natural for him during these alone times to talk to the Lord. He also learned to listen to the still, small voice in reply to his questions.

On the caravan's last night in the Arabah, Nephi was again off by himself. As the blackness of night fell around him he picked out the constellations: Orion the hunter with the lion's skin in his hand; The Herdsman with its bright star Arcturus; Taurus the Bull, with the six stars of Pleiades in his shoulder. Looking back at the camp, the only movement Nephi saw was the tall, moving shadow of his father pacing inside his goat-hair tent. Beyond the silent tents, strands of thick hemp curled around four terebinth trees, forming a square corral where the camels huddled together.

A cool breeze blew across the valley. Nephi shivered, then snuggled into the sand, letting its warmth permeate his body. He thought about their journey. Lehi had told them that on the morrow they would pass Solomon's ancient seaport city of Ezion-Geber. He looked forward to seeing this great ship-building city. As he lay there a voice spoke within him: "Watch carefully the shipbuilders in Ezion-Geber. You will need the knowledge."

The next morning their small caravan passed through Timna where Solomon had mined his copper. They looked in awe at large smelting ovens located in such a way that prevailing winds blowing through the canyon entered the smelting ovens and fanned their flames to process the metal. From a rise in the rift they spotted the reddish water of the Red Sea and houses of the port city of Ezion-Geber.

When they reached the city, Lehi led his family to an area where they could camp for the night. While Lehi and Sariah went to the marketplace for additional supplies and provisions, Nephi and Sam went to the docks. The harbor was not as busy as harbors he had seen in Sidon and Tyre, but there were many ships being built in the quays along a narrow inlet from the sea. Nephi resisted Sam's urgings to go down to the white sandy beach. Instead he stood where he could watch the shipbuilders at work.

He asked himself, Was I imagining that the Lord told me to observe the building of ships? When would I ever have the opportunity to build such a vessel? But he was obedient to the promptings of the Spirit, and he observed, carefully, construction techniques employed by the shipbuilders. Finally, as the sun was setting over the sea he followed Sam back to the caravan.

Lehi and his caravan followed the sandy beach for almost a full day, only turning away from the Red Sea when their way was blocked by steep cliffs. As the small caravan crossed the invisible border between Palestine and the no-man's-land of the Arabian Desert, Nephi felt a sudden loss. The land had been a promised land for his people. It was the land of Abraham, Isaac, and Jacob: the land where Saul, David, and Solomon had ruled; the land of the Lord's Holy Temple. Now what would happen to his family?

Leaving the beach they turned up a wadi which went east up through the mountain range. Storms had long ago filled in rough places with sand and gravel, making traveling easy. About halfway to the top they found an area dotted with the blackened fire pits of hundreds of travelers. Lehi signalled that here they would camp. By the time the morning sun peeped over the range of mountains, they were well on their way. At the summit, the trail branched, one fork going eastward across the desert. Lehi turned the caravan into another wadi which headed south. It sloped all the way back to the seashore in leisurely, sweeping curves.

On the third day, the wadi broadened into a wide valley with a winter stream running down its center. An oasis with date palms and terebinth trees greeted them. Lehi halted his camel, turned and swept his arm around, indicating the broad expanse of the valley.

"This is the place we will stop," he said. "The Lord has told me that here we are out of danger from our enemies. This valley has fertile soil which we can till to grow our crops. Here we will stay."

When the tents were set up, Lehi called a family council. "The Lord has directed us here," he said. "We will make this valley our home until He directs us further." He motioned to his sons. "Bring me stones for an altar." As stones were brought, he piled them one on top of another. While his family waited, he went to the goat herd and picked out an unblemished yearling kid. Holding it gently on top of the crude altar, while praying mightily to the Lord, he offered it as a sacrifice for the successful completion of this part of their journey.

He stood, only to face his two oldest sons. They accosted him, anger written in their faces and bodies. Laman spoke.

"Father, I cannot believe that you would lead us to this forsaken place. We left our homes, our gold and silver, our fertile farms, our friends, to come to this?" He flung his arms wide, kicking his foot in the sand in his anger. "If we stay here, we will perish. I don't intend to perish. I am going back to Jerusalem."

Laman and Lemuel turned away. Lehi called after them, attempting to control his indignation. "Jerusalem will be destroyed."

Laman turned. "I don't believe that. It is a great city and will never be destroyed. You are nothing but a visionary man, deluded by your own vain ideas. I don't blame the Jews at Jerusalem for attempting to kill you!"

Nephi was shocked and angry. He started toward his brothers, but stopped at a gesture from Lehi. Lehi spoke again, with a commanding voice.

"Laman and Lemuel, you will obey me. You will remain here with the family as the Lord has commanded. Cease contending with me and your brothers. This is the valley the Lord has led us to and all of us will remain here—including both of you."

Laman, who had turned to walk away, turned back. Nephi saw that he was pale and shaking. Truly his father had spoken with the spirit of the Lord!

Lehi looked far down the river, where it emptied into the sea, and continued speaking to Laman.

"My eldest son, Laman. It sorrows me that you would mock your father. Nevertheless, you are my eldest. I name this river for you. It shall be called the River Laman." He paused and shook his head in sorrow as he looked at where the river poured into the Red Sea. "Oh, that you could be like this river, continually running into the fountain of all righteousness!" Then he turned to Lemuel.

"This valley will be known as the Valley of Lemuel." He shook his head sorrowfully, "Oh, Lemuel. I wish that you could be like this valley, firm and steadfast, and immovable in keeping the commandments of the Lord!"

Nephi returned to his tent. He wondered what would happen next with his rebellious brothers.

Chapter 6

Return for the Plates

His mouth was dry and his throat was sore, but still Nephi prayed. For a day and a night he had pled constantly with the Lord.

He had left the Valley of Lemuel two days before, telling his family he was going hunting. For weeks, since crops were planted near the River Laman, he had felt a need to get away to talk to the Lord. There was a restless feeling inside him—a need for reassurance of what was going to happen to him and his family. Was his father right in bringing them into the wilderness? Where would they go from here? Would they spend the rest of their lives in the desert? Would he be able to have a wife and family of his own? He even wondered if Miriam would someday be a part of his life again.

On he prayed. At last a feeling of peace came upon him. A voice whispered in his consciousness: *"Peace be unto you, Nephi. You have done right to ask me concerning your family. Have patience, my son, and I will lead you and your family to a promised land, a land choice above all other lands."* The voice continued. *"Blessed art thou, Nephi, because of thy faith, for thou hast sought me diligently, with lowliness of heart. And inasmuch as you shall keep my commandments, you shall prosper, and shall be led to a land of promise; yea, even a land which I have prepared for you; yea, a land which is choice above all other lands."*

Nephi found his voice. "But what will become of my brothers?"

The response came. *". . . inasmuch as thy brethren shall rebel against thee, they shall be cut off from the presence of the Lord. And inasmuch as thou shalt keep my commandments, thou shalt be made a ruler and a teacher over thy brethren."*

"I don't think they will listen to me," Nephi said. "They complain daily against my father. If they won't listen to him, will they listen to me, their younger brother? They seem to rebel against all authority." He paused, then added, "Even Your word."

The voice spoke with firmness. *". . . in that day that they rebel against me, I will curse them with a sore curse, and they shall have no power over thy seed except they shall rebel against me also. And if it so be that they rebel against me, they shall be a scourge unto thy seed. . . ."* [6]

Nephi was physically exhausted but his heart was full. Before returning to his father's camp, he pulled a piece of parchment from his pack and recorded the vision. He retrieved his bow and arrows and retraced his steps to the Valley of Lemuel. His hunt had produced no food, but he felt that his prayers had produced a foundation of strong faith that would sustain him through adversity.

He met Sam on the outskirts of camp and excitedly told him of the marvelous vision he had received. He told of the Lord's words to him, especially those which commanded him to do whatever his father told them to do because his father was doing the Lord's will. Sam's eyes shone with excitement. He vigorously nodded his affirmation.

Lehi rejoiced to see his youngest son. Nephi could see that his father was excited. He took a cold drink from a goats' skin bag, then sat on the rug and waited for his father to speak. Sam stood at the flap of the tent, an expectant look on his face. Laman and Lemuel were not in sight.

Lehi began, "My son, I have dreamed another dream." He looked intently at Nephi. "In my dream the Lord commanded that you and your brothers must return to Jerusalem."

Nephi's eyes opened wide in surprise. "But why? I thought Jerusalem was to be destroyed and that the Jews would kill us."

"Apparently the time of destruction is not yet, and the Jews have never sought to kill you or your brothers. They were only angry at me because I condemned their wickedness."

"But why are we to go back?"

"Laban, an officer in Zedekiah's army, is my relative. He has the records and genealogies which have been kept concerning our ancestors. The Lord told me that these records, engraved upon plates of brass, are important for our family's spiritual well-being."

"But . . ."

Lehi ignored the interruption. "You and your brothers are to return to Jerusalem and get the plates." He paused, looking sadly at the floor. "I told Laman and Lemuel of my dream, and they became angry, calling me an old dreamer." He shook his head sadly. "They said it was just too hard a task." He looked at Sam gratefully. "Only Sam was willing."

Nephi stood. "I am willing, too, Father. I will do anything you ask me to do. I know that the Lord won't ask us to do anything without helping us."

Lehi embraced his son, then Nephi told his father of what the Lord had said to him. His eyes brimming with tears, Lehi again pulled Nephi close.

Several days of preparation were required. Before they left, Lehi drew a map of the fastest route. They would not return the way they had come, but would travel straight up the full length of the Arabah to the Salt Sea, then skirt the sea to the west until they came to the Way to Jerusalem. It was a more difficult route, but a much shorter one.

Sariah had been brave and uncomplaining in coming into the wilderness, accepting all that her husband had done and said, but Nephi knew it must be difficult for her to see her sons ride off into the desert. As she waved goodbye, her eyes were filled with tears.

The brothers, young and healthy, required few rests. Their riding camels averaged almost thirty miles every day. They passed through Ezion-Geber and turned up the Arabah, following the trail Lehi had mapped out. Often they traveled far into the night, relying on their sure-footed camels to pick the trail. It was afternoon when they topped a rise and saw the brilliant blue waters of the Salt Sea. A blue-colored mist hovered over the sea close to the white-striped shore.

They traveled past Masada, King David's fortress, and camped that night at the oasis of Engedi. Engedi, the Spring of the Goat, lay along the desolate western edge of the Salt Sea. The lushness of the oasis presented a sharp contrast to the sparse vegetation through which they had traveled since leaving the Valley of Lemuel.

Nephi was awed by the beauty of Engedi. Spring water, instead of coming out of the ground, cascaded down sheer cliffs for several hundred feet. He didn't think he had ever seen such a beautiful place. He bathed his face and dusty hands. His brothers followed suit, and they all enjoyed a cool, refreshing drink. Nephi threw off his cloak, revealing his gray linen tunic, and soon the four brothers were splashing in the cool, fresh water of the pool, washing off the sweat and grime of travel.

After they had bathed, Laman took bread and cheese from a bag on his camel. They enjoyed their meal in the shade of palm trees. Sounds of water cascading over the rocks—joyous music in these hot surroundings—came to them through the lush foilage. It was such a pleasant place that, for the first time in several months, the brothers relaxed and enjoyed each other. Laman in an uncharacteristically playful mood, challenged Nephi to an arm wrestle. Sam chuckled gleefully as Laman and Nephi, flat on the sand, faced each other. On the signal their arms knotted. Grunting and sweating, each tried to put the other down. They were both large men, well-developed and muscular. Laman, being older, was more cunning, but Nephi was stronger. As he strained, the bulging cap of muscles atop his powerful right shoulder knotted, cords stood out on his thick neck. Sweat beaded on his brow and ran into his eyes. Nephi hunkered down even more, applying a crushing pressure to Laman's arm, slowly pushing it down. He had won.

They stood and brushed off the sand. Laman gave him a good-natured slap on the arm then both of them jumped in the pond to cool off and wash off the sand. This was the closest Nephi had felt to his older brothers in years. He wished it could continue.

That night they didn't pitch their tent, but slept in one of the caves which surrounded the spring. The sound of falling water had a soothing effect and they slept late the next morning. By the time they were loaded and on their way the sun was a cauldron of yellow light and heat beat through their clothing like heated rods. Half a day north of Engedi, they started their climb upward through the deeply eroded hills on the well-traveled track to Jerusalem. Even the camels seemed to sense that they were getting close to the Holy City. They picked up their pace and swung forward in a steady trot. The sun sank below the western hills and still they journeyed. A thin moon came up to light their way through the chilly night, and at last they saw the twinkling lights of the city across the valley.

It had taken them twelve days to travel from the Valley of Lemuel. They and their camels were tired, and they were still unsure of what kind of reception they would have in the city. They camped outside the walls near the stream of Kidron. Nephi hadn't realized how much he had missed the Holy City until he looked up again at the huge walls.

That night they huddled around their small campfire trying to stay warm while discussing how to get the plates. From Jerusalem, across the Kidron Valley, came the smell of smoke, incense, and burning flesh from the temple, mixed with the turpentine smell of terebinth trees surrounding their camp.

Laman proposed a plan. "I think that one of us should simply go to Laban and ask him for the plates. After all," he said, "they contain our genealogy. They are rightfully ours."

They all agreed and cast lots to see who would go. The lot fell to Laman. He grumbled, but couldn't very well back out since it was his idea.

Early the next morning Laman reluctantly climbed the path and entered the city. Waiting was always difficult for Nephi, but he tried to be patient. About noon Sam grunted and pointed. Running toward them was Laman, his hair flying behind him. He stopped at the campfire, his chest heaving from the exertion. When he got his breath, he told them what had happened.

He had threaded his way through the narrow streets, his pace slowing as he came to Laban's street. Arriving in front of Laban's home, he fearfully rapped on the door. A servant answered his knock. Laman stated his business and was led to the study. He sat there fidgeting until a large man finally entered, looked at him, then reclined on the couch. It was Laban. A servant placed a plate of fresh fruit at his elbow and Laban picked up a plum and thoughtfully devoured it, never taking his eyes off Laman who was very nervous. Laban was a man about Laman's size, about forty years of age, with graying hair which had once been dark.

Finally he spoke. "What is it that you want?"

Laman straightened his shoulders, hoping his fear wasn't showing. "My father has told me that you have the brass plates with the record of Joseph."

Laban raised his eyebrows, then drooped his head between his shoulders. That, plus his distinctly crooked nose, gave him the menacing look of a bird of prey.

Attempting to make conversation, Laman asked, "Where did you get them?" No answer. "Who has kept them up to date?" No answer. "How long have you had them?" Still no answer from Laban. Sweat beaded on Laman's forehead and he could feel drops trickling down his back and armpits.

Laban tented his fingers, and closed his eyes as if in deep thought. Finally he responded. "The plates you speak of have been in my family since Joseph's time. I pay a scribe to keep them up to date, including the prattlings of mad men like Jeremiah." He paused again, looking keenly at Laman out of the tops of his eyes. "Why do you ask? What is your purpose in coming here?"

"Since we also are of the tribe of Joseph, my father has asked me to ask you if we can have the records."

Laban sat upright on the couch. "Take my records?" he bellowed. "You have the audacity to sit in my house and ask me for the records of my forefathers?" His face got red, the veins standing out on his forehead. Laman stood, backing toward the door. Laban jumped to his feet. "Zoram," he yelled. "Bring me my sword!" He turned back to Laman. "You are a robber, and I am going to kill you!"

Laman jumped through the door, bumping into a servant carrying a large, gold-handled sword. He ran through the atrium, and out the front door, still hearing the bellowing of Laban behind him. Laman hadn't stopped running until he was outside the city gate.

Now he mumbled as he looked at his brothers. "My father is a fool to have sent us on such a foolish errand. It is impossible to get the plates. I say let's go back to the wilderness before we all get killed."

Lemuel nodded. "The plates aren't worth our lives."

Sam looked from one to another, then shrugged.

Nephi disagreed. He said, "Are we going to quit just because we failed in our first attempt? We must persist until we accomplish our task. We have been commanded by the Lord to get the plates. If we are faithful He will help us to get them. We will not go down unto our father in the wilderness until we have obtained the plates!"

Angrily, Laman sneered at him. "What do you propose, little brother? You don't seem to understand how angry Laban was because I even asked for the plates!"

"I have an idea," Nephi said thoughtfully. "Laban is a greedy man. We left all of our gold and silver and riches at Beith Lehi. Let's go there, gather up our riches, and return with them to buy the plates from Laban."

"But why are the plates so important?" whined Lemuel.

"The Lord has told us to get them. That should be enough. It is wisdom in the Lord that we should obtain these records that we may preserve unto our children the language of our fathers. Besides, the records contain the words spoken by all of the prophets. We must have the plates." This last was spoken with such conviction that the brothers agreed to try one more time, and they started down to the land of their inheritance.

Ishmael said he was glad to see his nephews. He and Elizabeth questioned them at length as to what was happening with Lehi and his family. Nephi found Miriam, took her hand, and quietly apologized to her for speaking so bluntly the last time they had talked. She smiled shyly at him. His heart leaped. Miriam still liked him!

The next day they packed all of the gold and silver and precious things onto the pack camel and started back for Jerusalem. When they arrived at Laban's home, Laman hid outside with the camels. The other brothers carried their treasure to the door. Nephi noticed how Laban's eyes slitted greedily as he saw their treasure.

The fifteen-year-old Nephi acted as spokesman. "Sir, it is our desire to obtain the plates of brass which contain a record of our genealogy. We are willing to trade all of our possessions: our gold and silver, our precious cloths, everything we have for them."

Laban sank onto a bench, closed his eyes, and pursed his lips. From time to time he nodded to himself. Nephi watched him, not interrupting. Laban fished an artichoke from the bowl at his elbow. He slowly chewed and swallowed. He licked his fingers, ignoring the finger bowl with its floating rose leaves, and wiped his hands on his shirt. At last he looked up. He stood and spat between his teeth, then motioned to the door. "Take your gold and silver and get out of my house. The plates are not for sale."

Naphi was disappointed. He had so hoped that Laban would be willing to deal. Gathering up their things, the brothers quickly left.

As they were loading the treasure the spirit whispered to Nephi that Laban had sent his guards to kill them and take the treasures. He called a warning to his brothers and just then they saw the guards. Mounting their camels they raced away, leaving the treasure behind. Laban could have it! They raced through the back streets, outdistancing their pursuers. Outside the city walls there was confusion as they wondered where to go.

"To Beith Lehi," Nephi called. "There we will be safe."

They rode silently all day, not sure whether they were still being followed. It was dark when they arrived at Beith Lehi. Then they faced another dilemma. Where to stay? It wouldn't be fair to endanger the lives of old Moray and Edna, or Ishmael and his family. Nephi remembered a small cave he had played in as a child. He led them to it on a hillside behind Ishmael's orchards. The cave was narrow, but big enough for them to hide in. It had a hidden entrance and was right next to a spring. Nephi took the camels and rode to Ishmael's villa. Ishmael, white-haired and dignified, greeted him.

"My young nephew," he said. "Why are you back here so soon?"

Nephi explained what had happened, and he told Ishmael that Laban's guards were searching for him and his brothers to kill them.

The old man listened, then nodded toward his field. "Put the camels in with my herd. No one will be able to identify them. How about provisions? Do you have enough?"

"We have dried fruits and cheese. Perhaps enough for a few days," Nephi lamely replied.

Ishmael smiled, his white teeth showing. "Each evening I will have Miriam bring you your dinner."

Nephi flashed Ishmael a smile of appreciation. "Thank you, Uncle Ishmael. Our family will appreciate your generosity."

For ten days Nephi and his brothers lived in the cave, not daring to come out during daylight hours. Nephi was nervous. To while away the time he started carving with his knife on the soft, limestone walls. He drew pictures of the ships he had seen in Ezion-Geber. Then in large bold letters, he wrote across one wall, "I AM YAHWEH THY GOD. I SHALL ACCEPT THE CITIES OF JUDAH AND WILL REDEEM JERUSALEM." [7]

"Redeem Jerusalem?" Laman derisively remarked. "Father's silly dreams say God is going to destroy it." He laughed at the apparent inconsistency. Nephi ignored him and continued writing. Next to the first inscription he wrote, "ABSOLVE US O MERCIFUL GOD! ABSOLVE US O YAHWEH!" He stepped back to admire his graffiti. Then on the side wall he scratched, "DELIVER US O LORD." [8]

Each day Miriam faithfully brought dinner. Nephi stepped outside each time to visit with her. He felt so close to his young cousin, but he didn't dare approach her again about betrothal.

Days in the cave became more unbearable. The close quarters seemed even smaller, and each day Laman and Lemuel became more irascible—complaining bitterly about having to spend time in a cave when there was so much they could be doing.

One morning Nephi returned to the cave after filling a goatskin with water from the spring. As he entered he felt the tenseness in the air. Laman stood just inside the entrance, hands on hips, a camel prod in his hand. He angrily shouted, "It is your fault! We have to stay in this stinking little cave because you insisted on going back for the plates." He raised his prod. "I'll teach you to listen to your elders." He whacked Nephi over the head. Again and again he hit him. "You, too, you sniveling idiot," he said as he whacked Sam across the shoulders. Sam fell to the floor and covered his head. Nephi shielded his face the best he could with his hands, but the blows were starting to tell. Lemuel stood to one side, a pleased smirk on his face.

Laman continued to strike Nephi, when suddenly the poorly illuminated cave became as bright as noonday. Laman and Lemuel fell backward, shielding their eyes. A being, dressed in white and radiant as the sun, stood before them in the air. *"Why do ye smite your younger brother with a rod? Know ye not that the Lord hath chosen him to be a ruler over you, and this because of your iniquities?"*

Laman and Lemuel were speechless.

The angel turned to Nephi. *"Go up to Jerusalem again, and the Lord will deliver Laban into your hands."* [9]

With these words, the angel departed and the cave again became dark. Laman and Lemuel sat sullenly in one corner.

Laman asked, "How is it possible that the Lord will deliver Laban into our hands? He is a mighty man in Jerusalem. He can command fifty men to do his bidding."

Lemuel added, "He can even slay fifty! Why not us?"

"I have had enough of Laban to do me a lifetime!" Laman said. Lemuel nodded.

Nephi looked at them in disgust. "You just heard an angel tell you that the Lord would help us get the plates and still you doubt! The Lord is mightier than all the earth. Surely he is mightier than Laban with his fifty, or even his tens of thousands. Let us do what the angel has commanded us and go up to Jerusalem."

"I'm going to stay right here," Laman murmured.

"Me too," Lemuel echoed.

Nephi argued, "Is getting the plates as big a task as leading all of the Children of Israel out of Egypt? The Lord helped Moses do that. They crossed the Red Sea on dry ground, and when Pharoah's armies followed them they were drowned. If the Lord can do that, surely He can provide us a way to get the plates from Laban so our family will have the records."

Laman and Lemuel were silent.

"Why do you still doubt?" Nephi cried in exasperation. "If an angel can't convince you, then surely no one can. Well, I am not waiting for you. I'm going to Jerusalem, with or without you. The Lord is able to deliver us, even as our fathers, and to destroy Laban, even as he destroyed the Egyptians." [10]

With that, Nephi motioned to Sam and they went to get the camels. When they returned, Laman and Lemuel were still sitting on their pallets, complaining to each other about what a foolish situation they were in, risking their lives for some silly brass plates. Nephi shrugged, and began loading Armed for the journey to Jerusalem. Laman and Lemuel reluctantly joined them. By noon they were ready to go.

It was dark when they arrived back in the Kidron Valley. In the starlight they could once again look up and see the imposing city walls.

"Stay here and wait for me," Nephi said. "I don't know what I'll do yet, but the Lord will guide me." He started toward the city, then turned to call, "If I am not back by morning, find a good hiding place and wait for me." With that he disappeared into the blackness of the night.

Nephi was thankful that he had spent so much time in the streets of Jerusalem as a child. It was late and there were few lights. Bare, windowless walls of extremely narrow streets gave him an eerie feeling. The only sound was the muted slap of his sandals echoing on the walls as he walked by. His neck prickled as he remembered stories he had heard of how the streets at night became home of the hoodlums. People who had to go anywhere usually went through with lamp bearers and armed guards. To go without them was to invite assault, yet here he was—alone and unarmed.

As he approached Laban's house he was surprised to see a torch burning at the door to indicate that Laban was not yet home. Where could he be? Cautiously Nephi approached. Just at the edge of the circle of light, he almost stumbled over the prostrate form of a man. He thought the man was dead—assaulted by night thieves. But as he bent over the form Nephi smelled the sour smell of palm wine and heard the man's labored breathing. It was Laban. He was drunk!

Nephi nudged Laban with his toe. No response. He was unconscious! Nephi had an idea. Laban was about his size, and he was dressed in Judean armor—a coat of leather covered by bronze mail, a thick leather collar, and best of all a close-fitting metal helmet which could cover his face. He could put on Laban's clothes and impersonate him long enough to get the plates. This must be what the angel meant. The Lord had delivered Laban into his hands!

Nephi started stripping off Laban's clothes. He unbuckled the sword, admiring the superlative quality of the meteoric steel blade and the beautifully carved gold handle. He carefully took off the leathern belt, armor, the helmet, and finally even the tunic. Except for his loincloth, Laban lay naked before him. He was about to put on Laban's clothing when a whispering came from the spirit, *"Slay him."*

Nephi looked around, then shook his head. "No," he said aloud. "I have never shed the blood of a man. I cannot do it."

Again the voice came to his mind. *"Behold, the Lord hath delivered him into thy hands. Slay him."*

Nephi thought of how Laban had sent his guards to slay them, and of how he had taken their property. He knew he was justified in taking Laban's life, but still he hesitated.

Once more the voice came to him. *"Nephi, slay him, for the Lord hath delivered him into thy hands. Behold the Lord slayeth the wicked to bring forth his righteous purposes. It is better that one man should perish than that a nation should dwindle and perish in unbelief."* [11]

Conflicting thoughts raced through Nephi's mind. On the one hand what the voice said was true. His people needed the plates. However, couldn't he get them just as well by impersonating Laban? Without killing him? It sickened him to think of killing an unarmed man. One who couldn't fight back. Then he remembered the words the Lord had spoken to him near the Valley of Lemuel: *"Inasmuch as thy seed shall keep my commandments, they shall prosper in the land of promise."* How could they keep the commandments if they didn't have them? They were written on the plates of brass. The Lord had delivered Laban into his hands and had commanded that he kill him.

Reluctantly he pulled Laban's sword from its scabbard, feeling its delicate balance. He hefted it, raised it into the air, then set it down. He was breathing hard and sweat stood out on his forehead. His stomach was churning and he felt lightheaded. Once more he pled with the Spirit, and once more the voice penetrated his consciousness, *"Slay him!"*

Nephi reached down, grabbed Laban by his hair, raised the sword, closed his eyes, and with all his strength, chopped down with the sword. Laban's lifeless head hung in his hand. He flung it from him, and was immediately sick. He vomited until there was nothing left inside him. He sat for some time against a wall, weak, sick, and completely spent, his skin pallid and damp. But he had to act. The torch at the door was now flickering and would soon die out. He stood up, carefully putting on Laban's necklace and tunic. He laced up his sandals then put on the helmet and armor. He put the leather belt around his waist, wiped off the sword on his own robe and slid it into the scabbard.

Grabbing Laban's body by the legs, he dragged it into a side alley. Resolutely he brushed himself off. He still felt queasy but he was once again in control. He practiced Laban's stride as he stepped to the door. It was unlatched. So far so good.

As he walked towards the treasury, Laban's servant, the keeper of the treasury keys, stepped from a lighted room into the dim hallway. Nephi recognized the servant, Zoram, from his previous visit. He spoke loudly, with a slurred and drunken tone.

"Zoram, come with me to the treasury." Zoram reached for a torch and obediently led the way, opening the treasury wide and stepping aside to let Nephi pass. Apparently it was not unusual for Laban to go to his treasury at night.

Nephi glanced around at Laban's treasures. He smiled. Almost half of what Laban had was what he had stolen from him and his brothers. Zoram's voice startled him. "Master, did you have a good session with the *sarim* tonight?" Nephi remembered his father talking about the *sarim*, the council of elders which governed the city under the rule of Zedekiah.

"They are all a bunch of weak old ladies," responded Nephi trying to imitate the voice and mannerisms of Laban. "Come," he said, "we must carry these brass plates to my elder brethren, who are outside the walls."

Zoram obediently picked up the plates, supposing that his master was referring to the elders of the church. Together they walked from Laban's house. With Zoram's torch lighting the way, they strode quickly through the city.

Outside the walls, the brothers dozed. The crackle and hiss of burning pitch were the only sounds. The conversation around the fire had lagged and halted long before. Laman was awakened by Sam's grunt. Coming toward them from the gate of the city was someone with a lighted torch. Laman could make out the forms of two men. As they drew closer, he saw that one of them was dressed in armor. It must be Laban! He awakened Lemuel. "Quickly. It's Laban. He must have killed Nephi and now he's after us. Run!" The three brothers scattered from the campfire like frightened gazelles.

Nephi called, "Laman. Lemuel. Sam. Wait. It is I, Nephi!"

The brothers halted in mid-stride. They sheepishly walked back to the campfire.

Zoram, apparently realizing that he had been tricked, turned to flee. Before he could take a step, he was held in a vise-like grip.

"Don't be afraid, Zoram," Nephi said. "We're not going to hurt you. I am sorry I had to trick you, but these plates belong to my people." Zoram ceased struggling as he listened to this big stranger. "You have been a slave to Laban. Laban is dead. You can come with us and be part of our people. If you will take the oath of *hai Elohim* you can come down into the wilderness with us and be a free man." He continued speaking in a calm voice as Zoram relaxed. "The Lord commanded us to obtain the plates. Come with us and you will be a free man in the tent of my father."

"With the oath of *hai Elohim* I promise that I will go with you and become a free man with your people," Zoram said. Nephi released his hold, turned Zoram, and clasped arms. He was pleased that Zoram had promised to come with them. Now no one could alert the Jews of their flight into the wilderness. The Jews would suspect that Laban had been killed by ruffians or thieves. The Lord had again fulfilled his promises!

They quickly loaded the camels, putting Zoram on the pack camel with their tent and provisions. In the dark they retraced their path back toward the Salt Sea. On the way, Nephi told his brothers what had happened and how the Lord had helped him obtain the plates. Laman, when he heard how his youngest brother had actually killed Laban, looked at him with new respect.

All night the camels plodded on, their riders dozing as they rocked to and fro. By morning they could see the Salt Sea before them. Morning sun shone down like flaming copper on the turquoise blue of the Sea, burnishing the white crystals that speckled its surface. Across the sea, sun blazed on the mountain peaks and slowly dispelled deep blue mists of the valleys.

* * *

In the Valley of Lemuel, Sariah knelt before the beehive-shaped oven. The bread she had put on the coals to bake smelled hot and delicious. The heat from the oven felt good on her thighs. She sniveled. She was in mourning and Lehi didn't understand. No matter how much he tried to comfort her, she was convinced that all of her sons were dead. They had been gone for six weeks. She carried the hot bread in her apron to the table and called Lehi. Knowing the melancholy mood she was in he had stayed in the field as long as he could. Mealtimes had become times of shouting or of forced silence. He came to the table, washed his hands, splashed cool water on his face, and sat on a stump. Sariah averted her reddened eyes. She loved this man, but he had caused her much grief. Lehi kept his eyes on his plate, not caring to incur more harsh words.

But Sariah was not to be denied. "Lehi, look at me," she scolded. "For half a year we have been gone from our fine home in Jerusalem. We have been hot and thirsty, tired and hungry because of your so-called visions. Laman is right. You are a visionary man. You have led us forth from the land of our inheritance, and now my sons are dead." Her body shook with her sobs.

Lehi stood and put his arm around his quaking wife. He was very frustrated but he didn't say anything. What was there to say? Sariah caught her breath. "Oh, why couldn't you leave well enough alone? Why couldn't we have lived our lives and let others live theirs? You provided well for our family. Now we have nothing—not even our sons." Again she sobbed.

Trying once more to comfort her, Lehi said, "My dear Sariah. I realize it's hard for you to understand. I know I have tried your patience, but you must trust me. Even more important, you must trust the Lord. Yes, I am a visionary man. But if the Lord hadn't shown me what would happen, we would have stayed in Jerusalem and perished with its destruction."

Sariah shook her head, refusing to believe.

"My dear wife, *we have obtained a land of promise, in the which things I do rejoice; yea, and I know that the Lord will deliver my sons out of the hands of Laban, and bring them down again unto us in the wilderness.*" [12] He pulled her close. "My dear, give them time. They will come back. You'll see."

It was dusk, a few days later, when the western skies again showed a sunset of gold and crimson and mauve. It was a fantastic, undisciplined display of reflected color. Lehi stood in awe, his hoe in hand. He never tired of God's artistry. With a start he noticed riders coming from the north. Could they be raiders? A man of the desert, he was ever suspicious.

He started for the tent to warn Sariah, then stopped. That big white camel in the lead—could it be? There was only one long-legged camel like that. He had raised it from a foal! Armed! It was the boys! They were home! He dropped his hoe and shouted for Sariah. "They're home! They're home! Sariah, come quickly!"

They stood in front of the tent, Sariah twisting her apron in her hands. It was just too good to be true. Her sons, whom she had given up for dead, were alive! The five camels kicked up much dust as they approached the dry stream bed where the river had flowed when they had left less than two months before. The camels groaned as they came to a stop and knelt down before Lehi's tent. Sam was the first off, running to throw his arms around Sariah.

Nephi cried, *"Abba"* as he embraced his father. *"Ema, "* and he embraced his weeping mother. Even Laman and Lemuel seemed pleased to be "home." Zoram stayed back with the camels, not knowing what kind of welcome he would receive.

Lehi looked at him and called, "Shalom. Welcome to my humble dwelling. Whatever I have is yours." Nephi was embarrassed that he had forgotten to introduce this new friend.

"Father, this is Zoram," he said. "He was Laban's servant." Then in response to Lehi's unasked question, "We have the plates."

Lehi sighed with relief.

While the weary travelers unloaded their dusty camels, Lehi selected a yearling from the goat herd. Once more he offered sacrifice to the Lord. His boys were home! They dined that night on succulent young kid, vegetables boiled in goat's milk, and melons from Lehi's garden. It was good to be home.

In their tent that night, Sariah knelt before Lehi, her head in his lap. As he stroked her long, shiny hair, she said, "Please forgive me for doubting, my dear husband. Now I surely know that the Lord did command you to flee into this wilderness." She looked up at him. "I also know of a surety that the Lord has protected my sons, and delivered them out of the hands of Laban so they could obtain the plates and return safely to us." Softly she said, "I will doubt no more. I will take comfort in the knowledge that the Lord is guiding us."

Chapter 7

Return for Ishmael's Family

By evening the day's heat had dissipated. Undulating under shimmering heat waves, the desert floor sparkled like thrown rubies. Sariah and her maids rolled up the sides of the tent, letting in a slight breeze blowing up from the Red Sea. Nephi lounged on a cushion, listening intently as Lehi read from the brass plates. Since they had returned from Jerusalem, Lehi had read the history of the chosen people from the creation down to the reign of King Zedekiah. The plates traced his own genealogy back to Joseph who had been sold into Egypt.

Now Lehi was reading some of the prophecies. He set the plates down, a dreamy, faraway look in his eyes.

"Nephi," he said, "the Lord is speaking to me. Write these words."

Chills raced up Nephi's spine as he wrote. *"These plates of brass shall go forth unto all nations, kindreds, tongues and people who are of thy seed. They shall never perish, and even though the earth becomes old in time, these plates will never dim."*

It was Lehi's voice, but the words were not his father's words. It was the Lord Himself speaking. *"It is not meet for you, Lehi, to take your family into the wilderness alone. Your sons shall take daughters to wife, that they might raise up seed unto Me in the land of promise."*

Startled, Nephi stopped writing. He had thought of having a wife ever since he had talked to Miriam. But who would he marry out here in the desert? Lehi's voice continued. *"Send Nephi and his brethren back to the land of Jerusalem. Have them bring Ishmael and his family into the wilderness. I will touch their hearts so that they will accept what Nephi will tell them."*

Lehi's voice rumbled on, prophesying many other things which would take place with his family, but Nephi's mind was elsewhere. Ishmael and his family! Miriam here! Take daughters to wife! He could hardly wait to tell his brothers. Getting back to his duty, he wrote as Lehi talked.

When he was through prophesying, Lehi stretched forth his arms. "Come here, my son," he said. "My heart is full. I have something to say to you."

Nephi obediently moved over on the mat next to his father. As he knelt Lehi put his arm around him. "Nephi," he began, "you have kept the Lord's commandments and I am proud of you." He paused, seemingly deep in thought, then continued. "The Lord has great things in store for you. He has singled you out as a leader of the people. You are a man the Lord feels he can trust." Nephi was squirming under this unexpected praise. Lehi looked at him and added, "Do you know when you became a man in my eyes?"

Nephi shook his head.

Lehi continued, "The day you came into my tent and told me that you would go wherever I would send you. A man is one ,who takes responsibility for his actions and who trusts in the Lord to give him guidance. You have been able to do both."

Nephi looked down, a little embarrassed. Then he looked into Lehi's eyes, squared his shoulders, and said, "Thank you, Father. I hope that I will always be able to carry my responsibility in whatever assignments the Lord may give to me."

Lehi patted his shoulder. "As you have just heard, the Lord has already given you an assignment . . ." his eyes twinkled, ". . . and I don't think you will mind it a bit."

* * *

The brothers were more enthusiastic about this trip to Jerusalem. Lehi assigned Shemin and the other camel drivers to help manage the camels of Ishmael and his family. Zoram would stay in the Valley of Lemuel with Lehi, Sariah, and Sariah's maids. The camels were loaded and the seven men were on their way.

Sariah thought of the great difference between this trip and the last. Now that she had put her total faith in her husband and the Lord, she no longer worried about the return of her sons. She knew that the Lord would protect them. What a relief it is, she thought, to leave worrying to the Lord!

Nephi was amazed at how quickly the miles passed. It seemed they had barely started when they arrived at Beith Lehi. Ishmael greeted them, then ushered them inside his villa while Shemin and the camel drivers took the camels to the enclosure.

"Welcome once again to my humble home," the gray-haired Ishmael remarked. "I have been expecting you." Laman and Lemuel glanced at him, bewildered. He smiled. "The Spirit whispered to me a fortnight ago that you would come and that we would accompany you to the wilderness. We have been preparing ourselves for the journey." He sighed, his bony shoulders drooping. "I told Lehi that I was too old to make the journey, but I cannot argue with the Lord."

"But how"—Laman started to say, then fell silent.

Ishmael, not hearing the interruption, continued. "Elizabeth and I and our family are almost ready. However, we don't have enough camels or tents. It is important, also, that we bring Annah and Nahom and their children from Jerusalem. The Spirit whispered that our whole family should accompany us."

Nephi mentally counted the people in Ishmael's family. There were Ishmael and Elizabeth; his sister Annah, who had married Ishmael's son, Nahom, and their two children Tamna and Rebecca; Esther, his oldest sister who had married Ishmael's son, Shazer, his nephew, Ishmar, and the two nieces, Vivian and Zippah; and Ishmael's five unmarried daughters, Eva, Cleopha, Marni, Leah, and Miriam. That was sixteen in Ishmael's family, plus the seven of them, and he was quite sure that Elizabeth would take a few of her maids with her. It would be a large caravan.

"How many camels do you have?" he asked Ishmael.

"Seven. But Nahom has two and Shazer four. That's thirteen. We will need four for pack animals, and at least three more to ride. I have made arrangements to sell my villa and my orchards. From the sale I will be able to purchase more camels and tents."

Nephi left Ishmael to discuss the details with his brothers and went in search of Miriam. He stepped from the door and saw her in the olive orchard. Silver leaves were shimmering as a slight breeze played through them. She stood tall and straight, her back to him, her black hair cascading free to the middle of her back. His heart leaped at the sight of her.

He called, "Miriam."

She turned quickly and came to him. She was beautiful and slender. Her dress of coarse white linen was bound with a blue ribbon below young breasts. She was barefoot and moved with a litheness and grace that made his heart beat faster. A few feet from him she stopped, gazing intently at him. Her neck was bare and he could see her pulse beat in her pale throat.

Miriam looked at this man from the desert. Winds and dusts of the desert had reduced his body to a leanness of hard rope. Never had he looked so handsome. There was a peacefulness in his countenance, and a fire in his eyes. His resolute chin was sharp in contour, his nose thin and large. He was tanned and seasoned, and yet she felt the gentleness within him.

They stared at each other, shy, embarrassed, both eager to reach out to the other. Nephi had never had much to do with girls. His only desire had been for Miriam. Now the nearness of her both captivated and terrified him.

She smiled, seeming to sense his desire, and her mouth was like a new poppy. Reaching for his hand, she pulled him along the path until they came once again to the large rock in the garden. She sat down, pulled Nephi down beside her, then spoke for the first time.

"Nephi," she said softly. "Long ago we sat together on this rock and you asked me if I would betroth myself to you and journey into the wilderness." Nephi remembered only too well. Miriam continued, "I was afraid, and I ran. Many times I have regretted that." She paused, a pink blush darkening her pale skin. "I am almost thirteen now. Nephi, if you still want to be bethrothed . . ." Her voice broke and she turned her head to hide her tears.

Nephi was astounded. "Still want to!" He reached out and folded her into his arms, holding her tightly to him, his face pressed against her hair. He pushed her to arms length and looked at her. Miriam's eyes were huge and black, her soft cheeks wet with tears. Nephi put one gentle hand under her chin and tipped her face up toward him.

"I'm sorry," she said. "Please forgive me."

"Oh, my dear Miriam," he said, again pulling her close. "You don't know how many lonely nights I have spent thinking of you and wanting to hold you." He held her small, warm body firm but soft against his, feeling the beat of her heart mingling with his own. A shiver went through him, and once again he asked, as he had on that night long ago, "Miriam, will you betroth yourself to me and go into the wilderness with me?"

"Oh, yes, Nephi. I will!" she cried. She reached for his hand, kissed it, and held it against her cheek. He vowed that he would always remember her radiant look: her half-opened red mouth, the gleam of her white teeth, and the shine of her large, dark eyes. They rose together and turned toward the house. "We must tell your father."

They walked hand in hand toward the house.

Ishmael gladly gave his permission for the betrothal and, as he prepared the family to move, Nephi whistled and hummed. The next days sped by as the family finished preparations to leave Beith Lehi, but Nephi was concerned about Ishmael and Elizabeth. Elizabeth, a gaunt and forbidding woman, was stooped and gray. Hard work and raising seven children had taken their toll. Ishmael, though in good health, was already an old man. Nephi wondered how they would hold up in the harshness of the desert. The girls were excited to be going. He understood why when he saw how they looked at Laman, Lemuel, and Sam.

Shemin and the camel drivers went to Jerusalem with Laman and Ishmael to get the camels and Nahom's family. When they returned, all was in readiness. By nightfall the caravan was on its way. Lehi had advised them to bring the caravan on the easier route through Hebron and Beersheba, but after traveling the route beside the Salt Sea as many times as they had, Laman recommended that they go that way. Nephi agreed, mainly because he wanted Miriam to see the beauties of Engedi. By midnight, the moon was huge in the sky. Stars were out in glorious profusion. Balminess of the air was delightful as the camels, with silent tread, picked their way down the rocky trail toward the Salt Sea.

As dawn approached, cheeping birds signalled the new day. The sky awoke with morning, sun coloring the hills. As they topped a final rise to look down upon the sea, Miriam gasped at the panorama spread out before her. Across the sea, the brown hills of Moab were a stark contrast to glittering blue waters.

As they traveled, they dined on a breakfast of bread and cheese and dried dates. By midmorning they reached the oasis at Engedi. Nephi was not disappointed in Miriam's reaction. Engedi still took his breath away, and he had visited the oasis several times. In the morning light the wall of rock stood against ardent blueness. Miriam looked up at the steep and jutting formations, tall and tawny, where from an upper crevice a narrow cataract of green water burst forth, cascading to the ground with a soft though thunderous sound. At the foot of the rocks, now golden in color with the midmorning sun, was a vast pool into which the cataract tumbled. Trees of many kinds grew wild around the pool. Beautiful locust trees, garlanded with large clusters of tiny, pea-shaped blossoms, reared over fifty feet into the air. Masses of wild flowers—morning glories, poppies, lilies of the field—covered the ground with brilliant blue and red and purple blossoms.

Gourd vines stretched their tentacles up the rocky faces of the cliffs, their heart-shaped leaves forming a layer of emerald green. Gourds, green with yellow and orange stripes hung like jewels from the vines. It was a breathtaking sight.

After the camels were unloaded and hobbled, Nephi led the people into a long cave where it was cool and dark. Here they could sleep until evening. Miriam, tired as she was, refused to rest yet. She just wanted to inhale this beauty, to remember it forever. She stood on the edge of a clear pool, seeing all the way to the bottom. While riding through the night she had braided her hair, and now she flung the braid over her shoulder. Nephi watched her, delighting in her every move. Miriam took off her sandals and stepped into the pool near the edge. She scooped the cold but refreshing water in her hand, and drank it. She bathed her face then stepped out beside Nephi.

"I have never seen such beauty," she whispered reverently.

"The only thing more beautiful is you," he said, smiling.

She cupped her hands and threw water on him. Nephi picked her up and dumped her in the pool. She came up sputtering and laughing. He waded in and pulled her to the warm sand. They lay back, the smell of flowers pungent and heady, and soon they were asleep.

Nephi was awakened by a jab in his ribs. He looked up, surprised. He was surrounded by people. He tried to pull his arm out from around Miriam's neck without waking her, but she, too, looked up surprised.

Laman stood there, a scowl on his swarthy face. "Get up," he growled. "It is time you learned who the leader is." He turned to Cleopha, Ishmael's oldest unmarried daughter. She nodded encouragement. He motioned to those around him. "We have decided that we aren't going to be bossed around any more by our youngest brother." He looked around again for support. "We aren't going into the desert to live. We are returning to Jerusalem where we can live like human beings with the comforts of life." The others nodded in agreement.

Nephi looked at those surrounding him: Ishmael's two oldest sons and their wives; Laman and Lemuel and two of Ishmael's daughters; Cleopha and Marni. Standing back from the rebellious ones, Nephi could see Ishmael, Elizabeth, Sam and Leah. Their heads were bowed. Miriam slipped out of the circle and went to them.

"Laman and Lemuel," Nephi said, "you are my older brothers and I respect that. You should be the leaders of this family, helping all of us to be obedient to the words of the Lord. Why is it that you are so blind in your minds that I, your younger brother, need to speak to you and set an example?"

"A fine example you are," Lemuel retorted from behind him. "You should be ashamed, lying out here with Miriam as if you were already married."

Nephi angrily turned on him. Lemuel, smirking, stepped backward. Getting himself under control, Nephi continued. "How is it that you have not hearkened to the word of the Lord?" He looked at Laman. "Have you forgotten so soon that you saw an angel of the Lord, and that he spoke to you?" He looked directly at Laman. "You have even forgotten how the Lord delivered us out of othe hands of Laban and helped us to obtain the sacred record."

His two older sisters looked down, seeming to be unsure of themselves. Laman, Lemuel, Nahom, and Shazer looked defiantly at him.

Nephi continued. "How is it that you have forgotten so soon that the Lord will help us in all things if we are but faithful to him. With faith, we will obtain the land of promise. I know that Jerusalem is to be destroyed, and the Lord will inform us when that happens. Are you willing to take the chance of having your families destroyed, your wives and children killed? You know how wicked the people are. They even tried to kill our father." His voice softened. "The choice is yours. No one is forcing you to journey with your families to the land of promise. But I promise you that if you return to Jerusalem you and your families will perish."

Nephi could see that his words had an effect on the women, but the men were still angry. Laman's face was livid with rage. He turned to Shazer and nodded. Before Nephi could move, the men grabbed him, throwing him face down in the sand. His arms were jerked roughly behind him and Shazer tied them tightly with a leather camel rope. His feet were bent up behind him and trussed with his arms. He lay there helplessly while they argued over what to do with him.

"I heard a lion roaring last night!" Lemuel said. "Let's just leave him tied up and let the wild beasts devour him."

While his fate was being argued, Nephi silently prayed. "Oh, Lord, according to my faith, deliver me from the hands of my brethren. Please give me strength that I may burst these bands."

The ropes didn't break—they just fell from his arms and legs as if they had never been tied. Nephi jumped to his feet to confront his astonished brothers once more.

"You have desired to take my life," he said. "I can understand how you feel. I might feel the same way if my younger brother were attempting to lead me. However, nothing would please me more than to have you become faithful so you can receive the words of the Lord in leading this family. I beseech you to listen to my words and return with me to the tent of our father where we can dwell in unity."

Laman and Lemuel were still angry and were ready to grab him again, but Miriam ran to stand before Nephi. He was so proud of her. She seemed so small as she stood there defiantly facing those who would do harm to the one she loved.

"I am ashamed of you," she said to Laman. "If you don't want to go with us where the Lord has directed, then go back to Jerusalem. But leave Nephi alone." She turned to her brothers, a fiery gleam in her eyes. "And you, Nahom and Shazer, should be ashamed of yourselves!" She burst into tears, and Nephi turned her to him.

Miriam's courage seemed to inspire the others. Elizabeth stepped forward, a determined look on her narrow face. "Cease this contention immediately," she said sharply. "Our families will stay together and not have quarrels. Nahom and Shazer come load the camels. Cleopha and Marni, come with me."

Those who had been unified in their rebellion a few moments before now stood as if they were unsure of themselves. Laman looked at Cleopha but she turned and walked away with her mother.

Nahom stepped forward and put his hand on Laman's shoulder. "Laman, perhaps we acted hastily. If Nephi is right about Jerusalem being destroyed, it is best that we continue our journey."

They turned and walked away, leaving Nephi and Miriam standing alone. Miriam's small frame still shook with subdued sobs as she realized how close she had come to losing this man she loved.

As they stood there, those who had been about to kill him returned. Nephi looked at them, not knowing what to expect. Miriam clung to his hand. Laman and Lemuel looked at the ground. Finally Laman looked up. "We are sorry, Nephi, for what we did. Please forgive us. We desire to go together to the tent of our father."

Nephi's heart was full as he looked at his contrite brothers. He knew how hard it had been for proud Laman to ask forgiveness. "I forgive you," he said as he stepped forward and took their hands in his. "Let us all kneel and pray to the Lord for his forgiveness and understanding, that we may once again be unified as a family."

They knelt in the sand. While those who had been rebellious prayed for forgiveness, Nephi offered a prayer of thanksgiving to the Lord for His constant, protecting care.

In late afternoon, as the air began to cool, they started on their way once again. For four days they traveled, around the Salt Sea and down the broad expanse of the Arabah. Travel was no strain for the younger people of the caravan, but even though they hadn't complained, Nephi could see how drawn and tired Ishmael and Elizabeth were becoming. About halfway between the Salt Sea and Ezion-Geber, he called a halt. A narrow canyon led from the dry riverbed into a small oasis. Towering canyon walls gave shade and protection, and here they made their camp. Ancient cisterns were cut deep into the rock. The camel drivers lowered their buckets and watered the camels.

Nephi caught some young birds and found eggs for their dinner—a welcome change from bread and cheese and dried fruit they had lived on since leaving Beith Lehi. The camels ate mucilage-filled locust pods which the camel drivers had gathered at Engedi. With the people and the camels taken care of, Nephi took Miriam's hand and led her up the canyon.

An enormous, jagged rock several hundred feet high rose to a peak before them. For almost an hour they silently climbed toward the summit. At last they were there, breathless and perspiring, but dazzled by the view below them. Nephi watched Miriam as she stood silhouetted against the blue sky. How very lovely she is, he thought. He sat with his back against a rock, looking out into the vastness of the desert. Miriam sat beside him, leaning against his shoulder. His huge hands gently stroked her hair.

"It is so quiet and peaceful here," Miriam whispered.

"Yes," Nephi agreed, "but we are surrounded by those who dwelt here before. This was the land of Esau. Here Jethro, Moses' father-in-law, tended his flocks." He lapsed into silence, thinking of his heritage. Wherever they had traveled, there was history: remnants of the tribes of Abraham, Isaac and Jacob; Moses and the Children of Israel seeking their promised land.

Miriam interrupted his reverie. "It's almost dark. We must be getting back to camp."

Reluctantly agreeing, Nephi took her hand and started back.

After several days of rest they continued their journey to the Valley of Lemuel with no further problems. When they arrived at the tent of Lehi there was great rejoicing. There they tarried awaiting the Lord's further direction.

Chapter 8

Visions of the Tree of Life

There were times in the next few weeks when Nephi felt that the Valley of Lemuel was the promised land. Now that Ishmael's family had joined them there, even Laman and Lemuel complained less. It was the time of harvest and everyone worked in the fields. Bags of seeds and grain were gleaned from the fields and stored. The first year crop of fruit was picked and dried and the seeds saved for future plantings. People worked together in unity and harmony. With Ishmael's family there, the pairing off that was occurring was natural. In addition to Miriam's betrothal to Nephi, Eva was betrothed to Zoram, and Laman and Lemuel seemed sure of winning the hands of Cleopha and Marni.

The Valley had become a veritable tent city: tents for Ishmael and Elizabeth, their daughters, and their married sons with their families were erected. With such a large camp and with more animals grazing, water was a problem. Only a small stream trickled down the ravine where once the River of Laman raged.

Following the harvest season, the tent city entered into a restful state when fuzzy hours slid by with the stateliness of a camel's silent tread. Relationships were strengthened, romances developed.

On a lazy afternoon, Lehi napped. As dusk approached and the sky darkened, a slight breeze rustled palm leaves. They chuffed together in a resonant dance. Lehi's sleep, fitful at first, entered a new plateau. Then suddenly he awakened—and yet it wasn't like awakening. He felt as if he were floating above the camp, a disembodied person, free of gravity and bodily sensations. It was as if he were viewing the camp as a bird from on high, looking down on the barren hills and the colorful tents. Then he seemed to enter clouds and when they parted, he beheld a dark and dreary wilderness.

A white-robed personage suddenly appeared and asked that Lehi follow him through the dark wasteland. After an interminable time of wandering through the darkness, Lehi fervently prayed for release. Almost immediately he stepped out of the dark waste into a large and spacious field. In the center of the field was a beautiful tree, green of leaf and heavy with white-colored fruit.

After walking through the meadow, Lehi stopped at the tree, picked some of the fruit, and ate it. It was the sweetest he had ever tasted. He desired to share the good fruit with his family. He looked around. Sariah, Nephi and Sam were standing near the river which flowed past the meadow. They looked as if they were lost.

* * *

It was after dawn when Lehi called his sons to his tent. He stood at the flap, his hair and beard so interspersed with grey that it looked more pink than red. His eyes gazed intently on each man as he entered. When they were seated he began to speak.

"Behold, I have dreamed a dream. I have seen a vision." He looked around the tent at his sons. Nephi and Sam were listening with rapt attention. Laman and Lemuel's demeanor seemed to say, So what?

Lehi continued. "Because of the things I have seen, I have reason to rejoice in the Lord because of Nephi and Sam. I have reason to believe that they and many of their seed will be saved." He went on to tell his sons his vision. Nephi listened intently. Each time his father stopped, he encouraged him to go on.

Lehi told them of the tree of life, of its fruit, of the filthy river and the rod of iron which led to the tree. He told them of the straight and narrow path which was by the rod of iron. As he told of the mist of darkness that rose from the earth, he looked searchingly at Laman and Lemuel who squirmed under his gaze.

"Where were we all this time?" interrupted Lemuel.

"That saddened me the most," Lehi answered. "You never came forward to eat the fruit. You joined those who were scoffing. My sons! I fear lest you shall be cut off from the Lord's presence." He stepped to them, leaned over and put a hand on each son's shoulder. "Laman and Lemuel, as your father I exhort you to hearken to the Lord's commandments and to pray that He will be merciful to you."

Laman shook off his father's hand. "I'm not paying any attention to your silly dream. May we leave now?"

"Stay, my son," Lehi replied sadly. "There is more I must tell you.

He told of again seeing Jerusalem destroyed and the Jews taken to Babylon. His voice broke as he worked to control his emotion. Then his eyes lighted as he told them that he had seen the Jews returning and rebuilding the city. "The most exciting thing I saw was the Messiah, such as the prophets have spoken of." He told of seeing a prophet who would precede the Messiah: one who would baptize the Messiah in the River Jordan. His voice dropped as he told of how most of the Jews did not believe in Him, and of how they eventually killed Him.

He continued. "I saw the Messiah rise from the dead."

"How could that happen?" Laman asked, skepticism in his voice.

"I don't know. But I saw it!" As Lehi continued, Nephi saw that each of his brothers was listening intently. "My sons, in my vision I was shown an analogy. I saw that the House of Israel is like an olive tree whose branches are broken off and scattered upon all the face of the earth. The Lord told me that we were one of those branches, and that we would be led to a land of promise where we can live His gospel. Then, through our lineage, the Gentiles will receive the gospel and will come to a true knowledge of the Messiah. That is why it is so important that we reach the land of promise and become a covenant people of the Lord."

It was a long speech. Laman stood up and stretched, followed by Lemuel. "Well, I don't have any belief in your dreams," he said. The two of them left the tent.

Lehi, tears in his eyes, turned to Sam and Nephi. "My sons, thank you for believing. I am worried about your brothers."

That evening Nephi slipped away from the camp. He had many questions and he needed to have some time alone to get answers. He was really curious about the meaning of his father's dream. He worked his way through the brush and rocks until he reached his favorite place of solitude.

He fell on his knees in the soft sand. "Oh, Father," he prayed, "please manifest to me the vision of my father." For several hours he prayed and pondered in his heart the things his father had said.

When he had almost given up receiving an answer, a vision opened before him. It was as if he were carried away to a tall mountain—one he had never before seen. Before him stood the Spirit of the Lord, looking like a man. He spoke to Nephi as a man would speak. "What desirest thou?"

"I desire to see what my father saw in vision."

"Do you believe your father saw the tree of which he spoke?"

"Yes. I believe all the words my father spoke."

"Blessed art thou, Nephi," the Spirit said. "Because you do believe you shall see the things which you have desired. You shall see the tree which bore the white fruit which your father tasted. Then you shall see a man descending out of heaven, and you shall bear witness that He is the Son of God."

The vision quickly passed before Nephi's eyes. He saw the tree and the whiteness of the fruit. But he was not satisfied. He spoke to the Spirit. "I see the tree which is precious, but . . ."

"What desirest thou?" the Spirit asked.

"I want to know the meaning of the tree."

"Look," the Spirit cried and then vanished.

A vision of Jerusalem and the other cities of the Land of the Jews opened before Nephi. He saw the little town of Nazareth through which he had once traveled with his father's caravan on the way to Tyre. In Nazareth he saw a beautiful young woman. As he watched, the heavens opened and an angel suddenly stood before him.

He spoke. "Nephi, what do you see?"

"A virgin, most beautiful and fair above all other virgins."

The angel asked, "Knowest thou the condescension of God?"

Nephi answered, "I know that the Lord loves all of His children, but I don't know the meaning of this thing."

"The virgin whom you see is the mother of God in the flesh." While the angel spoke, Nephi saw the virgin carried away in the spirit and when she returned she was holding a baby.

"Behold the Son of God," the angel said. "Now do you know the meaning of the tree which your father saw?"

"It must be the love of God," Nephi answered. "That is the most desirable of all things."

"Yea, and the most joyous to the soul," the angel added. "Look!" he said again.

Nephi now saw the baby grown to maturity. He watched the Son of God going forth and teaching the people. Then Nephi understood what the rod of iron was. It was the *Word of God*, providing guidance for man to get to the tree which represented the love of God.

The vision continued. Nephi saw the same things his father had seen: the prophet who preceded the Son of God and who baptized him; the Son of God teaching the people and healing them; the Twelve called to follow Him. Then he saw the Son of God taken by the people, judged by them, then cruelly murdered. It was almost more than Nephi could bear. He turned away from the awful sight and saw the building filled with people that his father had seen.

The angel said, "Behold the world and the wisdom thereof; yea, behold the House of Israel hath gathered together to fight against the twelve apostles of the Lamb."

Amazed, Nephi watched the large building fall, carrying all of the people to their deaths. The angel said, "Thus shall be the destruction of all nations and people that shall fight against the twelve apostles of the Lamb."

The pink light of dawn in the east signalled the new day by the time the vision finished. Nephi was exhausted, but he was anxious to share what he had seen. He made his way back to the camp. As he approached, his gaze traveled across the camp to the small breakfast fire where he could see Laman and Lemuel. They seemed to be having an argument. Laman's voice did not reach Nephi, but the anger of his expressions and gestures did. They were apparently disputing over what Lehi had told them.

Nephi grieved. They were his brothers, but through his vision he now knew their fate. Oh, why couldn't they listen! Why couldn't they see that they could inquire of the Lord and find out what the future held for them?

As he hurried toward them, he stumbled and fell, lying motionless on the sand. For some time he lay there, unobserved by those in camp.

Gathering his strength, he struggled to his feet. He walked to the fire.

"I heard you arguing." He raised his eyebrows in an unspoken question.

Laman spoke. "As long as you're here, we are trying to understand what Father meant when he spoke of the natural branches of the olive tree, and what did he mean when he spoke of the Gentiles, and . . ."

Nephi interrupted him. "Have you inquired of the Lord?"

Lemuel sneered, "What makes you think God will listen to us?"

He asked them, "Don't you remember what the Lord has promised—if you will just ask in faith, believing that you will receive, your prayers will be answered."

Laman shrugged his shoulders in wordless acknowledgment.

Nephi thought for a moment about Laman's questions. "The Lord compared the House of Israel to an olive tree. We are a branch of the House of Israel, but we are now broken off. What Father meant when he spoke of the grafting in of natural branches through the Gentiles is that in the latter days, when our descendants will have fallen away in unbelief, it will be the Gentiles who will bring back the gospel of the Messiah to our descendants."

Laman shook his head. "How do we know that our descendants will fall away in unbelief?"

Nephi was patient. "Father, in his dream, saw that our children's children would fall away into unbelief. They will lose the knowledge which we have of the Redeemer. Someday they will regain that knowledge from the Gentiles. That's what Father meant when he said they would once again be part of the House of Israel—being grafted as a natural branch back onto the olive tree."

"When will these Gentiles come?" Lemuel asked, his tone suspicious.

"Father said it would be many generations after the coming of the Messiah in the flesh. The fullness of the gospel shall come to the Gentiles, and through them back to our people. That will fulfill the covenant which the Lord made with Abraham that all nations would be blessed through his seed."

Nephi went on to explain other things to his brothers, including the restoration of the Jews to their promised land in the latter days. He shared with them some of the teachings of Isaiah which he had learned in his schooling: that after the Jews were restored again to the promised land they would never be scattered again. Laman and Lemuel listened intently, for the first time seeming really to want to understand what he was saying.

Laman asked, "What is the meaning of the tree father saw?"

"It's the tree of life."

"What about the rod of iron?" Lemuel asked.

"It is the word of God. If we will hearken to the word of God we will never perish. It will be like a rod of iron leading to the tree of life." Tears filled his eyes as he said, "My brothers, for your own sakes and the sake of our father, please give heed to the word of the Lord and diligently keep his commandments."

Laman had more questions. "Father talked of a river of water. What was the meaning of that?"

"It was filthiness. Those who let go of the rod of iron get immersed in the things of the world and become filthy before God. The river also represents the awful gulf which keeps the wicked people away from the tree of life."

Nephi's brothers stood silently, appearing thoughtful. He added one more point. "My brothers, the filthy river also represents that awful hell which is prepared for the wicked."

Lemuel asked, "Does the hell you speak of come while we are here on the earth or does it come after death?"

"Both," Nephi answered. "The day will come that everyone must be judged by the life he has lived. The kingdom of God is not a filthy place and no unclean thing can enter. The wicked are separated from the righteous, and from the tree of life.

Laman and Lemuel seemed humbled by what Nephi had told them. Laman put his hand on Nephi's shoulder.

"Little brother, tell us how you have come to know these things."

Nephi told them of how he had gone to pray. He told them what he had seen and heard; of seeing their seed in the land of promise, and of the battles and wars and slaughters.

Humbly, he told them of seeing many generations pass away and of the awful mist of darkness and earthquakes and lightnings and thunderings; of cities burned or buried in the earth; of multitudes of people destroyed. Then he told them of seeing the mist of darkness disappear and of the coming of the Messiah—the Lamb of God—as he descended from heaven. Nephi's mouth tightened and his countenance fell as he told them of the total destruction of the people just four generations after the coming of the Messiah.

He sat down by the small campfire, his head in his hands as in his mind he again saw the destruction of his descendants. Laman and Lemuel waited for him to resume his story. He looked up. Then he told them of seeing the land peopled by the Gentiles. He told them of the book which would come forth as the record of the Jews. He added, with excitement in his voice, that a book would come forth which would contain the gospel's fullness.

He said, "That book will go to the remnants of your seed."

Laman looked at him. "You have declared unto us hard things," he said. "More than we are able to bear. We must have some time to think about what you have said."

Nephi spoke boldly. "I know that I have said some hard things against the wicked. But I have also said that the righteous will be lifted up at the last day. And now, my brethren, if you were righteous and willing to hearken to the truth, and give heed unto it, that you might walk uprightly before God, then you would not murmur because of the truth and say: 'Thou speakest hard things against us.' " [13]

He placed a hand on each man's shoulder. "My brethren," he said gently, "let this be a turning point in your lives. You say that what you have heard from Father and me has been hard. Sometimes it takes something hard to wake us up."

Again the impact of the great wars he had seen pressed deeply on his mind. "I plead with you. Keep the commandments of God so that your children and my children can live together in peace in the promised land."

Chapter 9

On the Shores of the Red Sea

The enchanting colors of the late afternoon painted the earth like a fairyland. The hill behind the valley was radiant in golden hues. Nephi, working in the vegetable garden, gazed in awe. He thought, I am like a seed planted in this valley, bursting with life and anxious to grow. Like a seed I know what shape I will take and what fruit I will bear because the Lord has told me. He flexed his muscles, and stretched. It is good to be alive; good to be strong. I am like David of old. I will make a success of my life. Then he added aloud, "Dear Lord, let it begin now. I am ready."

He smiled. Perhaps the reason he felt so alive and excited was that today was his wedding day. For months the women had been sewing tents together from the goats' hair they had collected. They had separated their pans and buckets so that each new family would be self-sufficient. Now the time had come. Tonight was the night, and Nephi could hardly wait. He had loved Miriam since they were children, and now she would be his very own.

The women had been making preparations for days. Freshly picked vegetables were simmering in goat's milk; several kids were roasting on cooking fires; bowls of fresh fruits adorned the heavily laden dinner tables. This was to be a real wedding feast. In addition to Lehi's and Ishmael's families and their maids and camel drivers, Lehi had invited the local nomads to the festivities. After all, how often do families have five weddings all at once?

Lehi, acting on behalf of his four sons and Zoram, had formally negotiated the marriages with Ishmael. Zoram was to marry Eva, Ishmael's oldest daughter. Nephi delighted in that couple. Eva seemed to have become resigned to never being married. Now she and Zoram were a happy couple. Laman was to wed Cleopha, and Lemuel, Marni.

The marriage of Sam to the beautiful Leah was especially exciting to Nephi. Sam might not be able to say words with his tongue, but he and Leah talked "heart talk." They seemed so happy together. And then there was his marriage to Miriam. His heart swelled in anticipation.

As he walked past the table, he noticed the bouquets of wild flowers Sariah had gathered. Their heady smell added special excitement to the preparations. The weddings would not be the formal ones of the Jews, with dowrys, much fanfare, and a week-long feast. Provisions in the desert were scarce and the family would have to settle for a one-night banquet.

As pale evening light turned to darkness, torches were lighted in front of Lehi's tent. The five brides, beautiful in full-length robes, were brought forward by their mother. The grooms, dressed in light tunics, came forward to claim their betrothed. Lehi stepped out of his tent, clothed in his robe of many colors, carrying the precious brass plates. As patriarch of the tribe he would perform the wedding ceremonies.

He read: "And the Lord God said, It is not good that the man should be alone: I will make a helpmeet for him. . . . And the Lord God . . . made he a woman, and brought her unto the man. Therefore shall a man leave his father and his mother, and shall cleave unto his wife: and they shall be one flesh."

He gave counsel to each of the couples, then ended with, "Dear ones, you enter this marriage of your own free choice. Love must be the basis of your union. Marriage represents a total partnership. Treat each other in a manner that will cause your love to grow. For your love to ripen, there must be confidence and understanding, frequent and sincere expressions of appreciation for each other; and most importantly a forgetting of self. Dear sons and daughters, each of you take your mate by the right hand in token of the covenant you now enter into, to become companions and to love, honor and cherish your mate as long as you shall live. I now pronounce you husband and wife, wedded for the period of your mortal lives, with the promise that through your faithfulness God will give you the opportunity to have your marriages sealed for the eternities."

The couples kissed. Nephi and Miriam clung unashamedly to each other, then accepted the well-wishes of everyone before being escorted to their newly dedicated tent. There they were served their wedding dinner.

Outside the tent was feasting, dancing, and merry-making far into the night. Lehi, much relieved, sat beside Sariah. He had now fulfilled all of the Lord's commandments. He had forsaken his home, had launched into the wilderness with his family, had obtained the necessary records to preserve the knowledge of God and all the prophecies of the holy prophets, had his company strengthened by the addition of Ishmael and his family, and now had the gratification of seeing all of his sons united in marriage. The Lord had truly blessed him. He reach over and squeezed Sariah's hand. She smiled at him. His heart was now at peace. He was ready for whatever the Lord had planned for him.

* * *

Nephi and Miriam, alone now, nervously talked as they tried to eat. Nephi's eyes glowed with adoration for his new wife. He leaned over and kissed her. "My darling, it seems unreal that we are finally one."

She looked at him, a tender smile on her smooth face. She held out her arms and murmured, "Oh, my dear one."

Nephi's arms went around her. He kissed her tenderly.

Even in the happiness of his wedding night, sleep didn't come to Nephi. His mind returned to his vision and the eventual destruction of his people. Why have children when you know your descendants will someday be destroyed? He quickly discarded that thought. In his vision he had also seen that many positive and powerful things would happen through his seed.

He opened his eyes.

Miriam lay awake, propped on one elbow, looking at him in the dim, flickering light of the lamp.

"Why aren't you asleep?" he asked.

"I'm still too excited about our marriage to sleep."

He kissed her and whispered, "I love you."

"Oh, Nephi!" she whispered huskily, coming into his arms. Nephi could feel the rapid beating of her heart.

"You are very beautiful," he said.

She put her arms around his neck and pulled him down on the pallet beside her.

They lay there, staring at the colorful tent above them, exulting in their new and wonderful love. Miriam rolled on her side. "Nephi?"

"Yes."

"I want to have ten children, and I want all of them to look like you."

"You silly thing. Why would you want the girls to look like me?"

"Do you think we will have girls?"

"Don't children come in two kinds?" he asked playfully, reaching over and giving her a kiss on her nose.

* * *

Things once again settled into the harmony of life in the desert. That tranquillity was interrupted a few days later when Lehi shouted, "Nephi. Everyone. Come quickly!"

There was a great commotion outside Lehi's tent. Lehi stood with arms extended, holding a bright, shiny ball. As soon as Nephi arrived, he held up a hand for silence.

"My family," he began, "we have dwelt in the Valley of Lemuel for several years. We have learned to patiently endure and submit to privations and hardship. We have planted and harvested our crops. We have learned the things that will help us survive in the desert." He paused for emphasis. "The Lord visited me last night and commanded me that today we would take our journey into the wilderness. This morning, upon leaving my tent, I found this ball at the door." He held it up for all to see. "In the days of Moses," Lehi continued, "the Lord led the children of Israel with a pillar of cloud by day and of fire by night. This ball has been given us by the Lord for the same purpose: it will direct our paths as we cross the desert. Now return to your tents. Pack your belongings. We will take our tents, our seeds, our supplies and our provisions and renew our journey to the promised land."

Nephi was exultant. At last they were on their way. Their campsite in the Valley of Lemuel was soiled now by their beasts. The fleas had multiplied until they were almost intolerable, and there was little pasturage left for the camels and goats. It was time to leave. He noted that Laman and Lemuel and their wives did not look happy while Ishmael and Elizabeth seemed to accept the announcement with the stoicism of age.

Lehi handed the ball to Nephi to examine. It was about three inches in diameter, made of finely crafted brass. Designs on the ball were of curious workmanship, but even more strange were the two spindles inside the ball. No matter which way Nephi turned the ball, one of the needles always kept its direction. The Lord had given them a compass to point the way of their journey!

Almost the entire day was spent packing and loading provisions, including seeds and grains. By late afternoon the camels were loaded and the people were ready. Lehi called them together on the banks of the River Laman. They knelt on the ground where his tent had stood, and where Lehi had received his revelations. There he prayed for guidance as they commenced their journey to the promised land.

Following his prayer, Lehi picked up a handful of dirt and threw it in the air as a goodbye to the campsite where they had spent almost three years. It was part of the ancient Bedouin proverb: Greet your campsite when you arrive and bid it goodbye when you leave, for every spot on the face of the earth has its own guardian angel.

Mounting their camels, they followed the River Laman down to the shores of the Red Sea. Lehi walked ahead with the ball as they traveled south-southeast along the shores of the sea, following the frankincense trail. It was a trail Lehi knew: he had traveled it with his caravans.

On the evening of the fourth day they arrived at a tree-lined oasis, bounded on the west by the Red Sea and on the east by gently rising mountains. Several Bedouin tents were set up near a small stream which ran through its center. Lehi halted his caravan and gathered everyone around him.

Calling the sons of Ishmael forward, he said, "We will stop here and rest for a season. We will call this place *Shazer*." Shazer, Ishmael's oldest son, looked pleased. Lehi continued, "There is much game in the mountains east of here. We will have meat for our continued journey."

After camp was set up, Nephi, his brothers, and Shazer left for the mountains to hunt game. Nephi split off from the rest of the hunters as soon as they had climbed into the foothills. He had always enjoyed hunting alone. As he picked his way up the hillside, he looked for tracks among the sparse bushes. Overhead the sky was hard and blue, like a shimmering tent spread over the flowing browns and golds of the hills—hills that spoke of ancient patterns and rhythms, hills that gave Nephi a feeling of time standing still. When he was high on the ridge, he turned, seeing the green of the oasis far below him. The tents were mere pinpoints of contrasting color among the green. He wondered what Miriam was doing. Beyond the oasis, extending as far as he could see to the horizon, were the glistening waters of the Red Sea.

There were few animal tracks. Those Nephi did see were old. Vegetation was sparse and stunted although some grass grew under clumps of brush.

Soon it was dusk and little time remained for him to hike. Far below, campfires winked at him from the oasis. Slopes below him took on the texture of brushed velvet in the softened light. Nothing was moving, not even a buzzard in the cloudless sky. He gazed at the shimmering northern sky, seeing in his mind's eye the land of Jerusalem some five hundred miles beyond the horizon of crumbling hills and desert. A twinge of loneliness went through him, then he turned to continue upward, picking his way through rocks and brush until it was too dark to see. He found a sandy level place behind straggly brush and made his bed. He would continue in the morning.

Before lying down to sleep, Nephi knelt in the sand. "Dear Father," he prayed, "please bless that when morning comes I may find game." He offered his thanks to the Lord for his blessings, and prayed for those he loved. After his prayer, he lay looking into the heavens. The earth was dark and silent, lit only by the huge and wandering light of the stars. Not a breath of air challenged the stillness. He felt chilly and wrapped himself in the cloak of stiff, unyielding goats' hair which Miriam had woven for him. A breeze started blowing in from the sea. It was an arid wind, smelling of rock and desolation. Nephi's eyes closed and he slept.

Dawn came swiftly. At one moment the earth was blank and dark, hills invisible, and at the next the whole eastern sky was a blazing, amber conflagration. Nephi was already climbing after eating dried fruit for breakfast washed down with water from his gourd.

As he topped a rise, his eyes picked up a movement on the opposite slope. He froze. Several brown Nubian ibexes grazed on the far hillside. One stood aside from the others, motionless, with great, curving horns. The ibexes were out of range, even of his steel bow. Nephi stood, silently planning his strategy. There was no wind which meant he must approach the animals from above. Dropping to a crawl, he moved across the hillside. For over an hour he stalked the ibexes, finally getting behind rocks where he could observe them. He fitted an arrow to his bow, moving slowly. With steady hand he pulled until his thumb rested tightly against his cheek.

TWANG! Before his arrow landed he sent a second one after it. He stood, another arrow notched and ready. Two ibexes had escaped over the hill. He was sure he had hit the other two.

Nephi made his way over the shale hillside to where the animals had been standing. Blood was spattered over the rocks. The tracks and blood-sign of two animals headed down the ravine. He sat on the hillside, waiting for the wounded animals to lie down and stiffen. After half-an-hour he started downward. A hundred steps below, the first ibex was wedged between two rocks. His arrow had traveled true, piercing the ribs just behind the front shoulder—a clean kill. He stripped to his loincloth, and gutted the animal. After wrapping heart, liver, and kidneys in his cloak, Nephi threw the ibex over his shoulder and continued down the ravine. The second ibex, not hit so hard, traveled for some time. Nephi finally found it under a bush almost on the desert floor. It was still alive but an arrow to the heart killed it quickly. Nephi gutted it, hefted an animal to each shoulder, and headed for camp.

As he struggled across the sandy plain, the weight of the two ibexes became a burden he could scarcely bear. His shoulders were pinched and his arms tingled from lack of blood. He glanced over his shoulder in the direction he had come and was surprised to see the dust of riders. He walked faster. It could be dangerous for him to be caught out in this treeless plain. In his effort to get to the oasis, he forgot his pains. The riders were quickly overtaking him, so he put the game down and turned to wait.

There were six riders dressed in plain robes. They were Bedouin, strong and competent. Three of them bore bows across their broad backs, but they didn't seem intent on using them. The one in the lead, a little taller than the others, was armed only with a sword. He sat proudly on his mount, his youthful face blackened by much exposure to the desert sun. As he drew up before Nephi, he smiled openly, his straight white teeth glistening in contrast to his darkened skin.

"Ho, Jew!" he called. "You have been successful with your hunt."

Nephi nodded warily, unsure of their intent.

The young Bedouin dismounted. He strode forward, his arm extended in friendship. Nephi clasped forearms with him. The Bedouin raised an ibex head with his toe. "You are lucky." He regarded Nephi wistfully. "We have hunted for several days but we are unsuccessful." He motioned to a rider. "We will help you get these to your camp."

Nephi started to protest, but thought better of it. He was a poor match for six of them. The Bedouin threw the animals behind the saddles of two men then mounted himself. "I am Artifak." He extended a hand to Nephi. "Come. You are tired from your hunt. We will take you to your camp."

Nephi jumped on behind Artifak. As they rode into camp, Lehi and his remaining men stood ready to meet them. The women were nowhere in sight.

Nephi piled off the horse, followed by Artifak. Another Bedouin unloaded the game and put them at Lehi's feet.

"*Ahlan wa-Sahlan wa Marhaban.*" Lehi said in Arabic, "Welcome to our tent. Our place is now your place." With Artifak by his side, and followed by the others, Lehi entered his tent.

Nephi hung the ibexes on a thorn tree for the womenfolk to skin and cut up, then he joined the men in the tent. Lehi, as host, sat nodding as Artifak talked animatedly about their desert life. Soon everyone was conversing.

Artifak stood and bid goodbye to Lehi, inviting him and his men to join them at their tent at a later time. He nodded to Nephi and the others, then left.

"Whew," Nephi said. "I thought I was in real trouble back there."

They were interrupted by the return of Laman and the other hunters. They had stumbled upon a colony of coneys, and had killed three of them. Laman was hot and tired and cross, and grumbled under his breath when he saw the ibexes.

During the next few days the men shot ducks near the shores of the Red Sea, trapped quail and pigeons in the oasis, and soon had meat enough to continue their journey. They bid the Bedouins goodbye and were on their way, again following the trail to the south-southeast where the ball pointed. They traveled for many days, camping each night near one of the many wells along the trail which earlier travelers had dug and lined with stone. Grooves from the ropes of many years, pulling up skin buckets filled with life-saving water, pitted the limestone well-curbs.

Feeding so many people was a continuing problem. It was necessary to hunt often. The goat herd was now down to one billy and five nannys. These were saved for milk, butter, and cheese. In camp it was necessary to keep a guard on the animals as herds of golden jackals now followed the caravan.

One night they camped at a small oasis where Lehi said the hunting should be good. Nephi, his brothers, and his two brothers-in-law, left the main camp circling toward the nearby hills. As they approached the foothills, they saw a herd of hartebeestes. The meat from these large antelope would greatly benefit the camp. It was decided that, since Nephi had the only bow which could shoot any distance, the others would circle the animals in an attempt to drive them back past him.

Nephi waited on the hillside until almost dark. Tired, he started on the trail of the herd. When it was too dark to see, he settled down in a small depression for the night.

He was awakened by rumblings of thunder. The night sky which had been filled with countless stars was now black. To the west, jagged lightning danced against the clouds. A monstrous bolt of lightning clove the sky splitting into a dozen streaks in the sky around him. A roar of enormous thunder erupted almost over his head. He scrambled out of the ravine, only to meet a great wind howling in the underbrush and whipping against his face. A sudden torrent began to fall and within minutes he was soaked. Sheets of blinding raindrops battered him, driving him backward into the ravine.

The dried-out water course he was in—bone-hard for months—was suddenly fed with water from surrounding hills. Until the last moment, noise of the approaching torrent was muted by thunder. Only as a solid wall of mud-brown water rounded the bend above him like a raging water buffalo did Nephi realize his danger. He scrambled for the bank of the ravine. His foot slipped on wet clay and he fell painfully on his back. Once again he clawed up the bank, pulling himself up by roots and branches of scrub brush which lined the ravine. He was just in time. The debris-laden water roared past. He climbed on out of the wash, then hung to his perch until the flood had passed. He was soaked, muddy, cold and sore, with no place to go for shelter. He suffered through the night, his teeth chattering as he exercised in an attempt to stay warm. The rays of morning sun were welcomed with a thanksgiving he had never before felt.

All day he looked for game as he climbed higher and higher. Toward evening, across a deep, rocky ravine he saw several Barbary sheep high above a cliff. They looked magnificent with their massive spiral, double-twisted horns. He knelt, observing them. Nephi knew he would have to do some fast climbing to get above them before dark. He began his climb, avoiding loose rock, always keeping a ridge between himself and the sheep. Sweating from his exertion, he took off his tunic, climbing in his loincloth.

At last he was above the sheep. Moving cautiously, he raised himself into a position to shoot. Picking out a fat yearling, he let an arrow fly. The other sheep were so fast that before he could loose a second arrow they were gone. The yearling stumbled, sat down on its haunches, then tumbled over the cliff, landing on a narrow, sandy ledge. It kicked sporadically, then was still.

Nephi surveyed the cliffside trying to pick out the best route to get to the dead animal. He decided he would have to circle above the cliff, then climb down to where the sheep lay. The false light of late evening made his footing precarious. Cautiously, he picked his way down the cliff face, sweating with fear at the drop that yawned below him. Finally reaching the narrow strip of sand where the dead sheep lay, he checked himself, half-panting as he teetered on the slippery surface of limestone rock. The difficult descent completed, he carefully gutted the sheep then looked at the magnificent head. He would like to show it in camp, but it would be difficult to carry. He shrugged and cut off the head, twisting the neck until bones crunched and broke apart.

Now to get down. He leaned over the edge trying to pick a path. In the half-light he couldn't see a feasible way. He shrugged. As unpleasant as it might be, he would have to spend the night on the ledge. Making himself as comfortable as possible, he ate a few dried figs, offered a long prayer to his Heavenly Father and tried to sleep. It was a restless night, interrupted with dreams of falling over the ledge. Once again, morning light was a blessed relief.

* * *

In the clear light of a new day he looked over his situation. He could attempt to climb back up the way he had come, or he could descend. Which way? After considering possibilities, Nephi decided to go down. He prayed to learn whether his decision was right. He felt a peace in his mind. That must be the way. Crossing his bow over his back he hoisted the sheep onto his shoulder. One precarious foothold and handhold after another, he descended. Within moments his tunic was soaked with perspiration. He looked down. Only fifteen more feet to a good ledge which would give him a traverse to the side of the canyon.

He slipped. Desperately he jabbed at the rock with his feet, trying to find a crack. There was nothing to hold to and his grip was slipping! Finally he could hold on no longer. He slid down the cliff face, gathering momentum as he fell. The sheep fell from his shoulder, hit the ledge, and tumbled far below into the canyon. He landed hard on the ledge, but as he landed he grasped for anything to hold onto. His momentum carried him over to his back and he heard a crack as something gave way—but he had stopped! He sighed with relief. If he had gone over the cliff . . .? Then he shook his head. No, the Lord had told him he had a mission to fulfill and that he would be protected. "I just need to have more faith," Nephi said aloud.

He lay on his back almost afraid to move, staring into the brassy sky. A trio of vultures circled overhead, close enough that he could see their naked heads and feathers which hung from their beaks like old mens' beards. With his heart finally slowing and his breathing eased, he assessed his situation. He wasn't in pain except for bloody scrapes on his hands and arms. Holding to a rock, he pulled himself into a sitting position. It was his bow! It hung in two pieces from the bowstring around his neck. He held the bow in his hands, looking at it. His fine steel bow that he had prized from youth—broken now, and useless. What would he hunt with? How would they obtain food? His family depended upon him. His brothers were able to get some game, but he was the main provider—and now . . .?

"Well, there's nothing I can do about it," he mused aloud. "My main concern is to get off this cliff." Gingerly he stood, leaning against the coolness of the wall. Facing the cliff, he sidestepped across the ledge until he reached the canyon's edge. It felt so good to stand and walk without fear. He tried to find the dead sheep, searching until the sun was almost overhead, then decided he'd better return to camp. He hated to lose the meat, but it couldn't be helped.

When he arrived at the hunting camp the other men seemed glad to see him until they saw the broken bow on his shoulder.

"You've broken your bow," Nahom said.

Nephi raised his shoulders in mute agreement.

"How did you break it?" Laman asked testily.

"How will we get meat?" Lemuel whined.

Nephi tried to answer their questions but everyone was talking at once. Laman angrily stepped in front of him. "You fool! Didn't you realize that the entire camp is depending upon you for our food? Our bows have lost their spring and are worthless for shooting anything but coneys. Why did you take such a chance?"

Nephi's sun-darkened skin could not hide the sudden flush of his cheeks. Other voices, raised in anger, condemned Nephi. He stood dejectedly, accepting what they were saying as true. Without his bow and hunting skills, their families could starve. The hunters wearily left their camp and returned, empty-handed, to the caravan.

Miriam, sensing that something was wrong, ran forward to greet them. She put her arm around Nephi's waist, escorting him back to the camp, noting the glum expressions of the other men. Nephi smiled tenderly at Miriam and walked with her, arm in arm. Lehi and Ishmael were standing by Lehi's tent. Laman strode up to them.

"Your foolish youngest son, the one you dote on, has broken his bow!" he shouted derisively, gesturing toward Nephi.

Lehi opened the flap of his tent, motioning for the men to come inside. When all were seated, he asked, "What happened?"

Nephi recounted again his story, ending lamely with, "Father, I am sorry. I shouldn't have been so careless."

Lehi said, "We must have meat to live. We have our seeds, but the Lord has told me we will need them to plant in the promised land." He lowered his head into his hands. When he sat back up his tanned cheeks were tear-stained. "Oh, why has the Lord deserted us now? Why would he let this happen?"

A general murmuring of assent hummed in the tent. Nephi ducked his head and offered a silent prayer. Father, I'm sorry that I have brought this sorrow upon our camp. Please forgive my father and brethren for their murmurings against Thee. They are just concerned about our families and how to provide food for them. Please bless us that we may find a way to obtain food so that we may continue our journey.

He stood up. "My brethren. This is a hard time for all of us. I am sorry about my bow. But I know that the Lord will provide." Murmurings of dissent came from Laman and Lemuel and the sons of Ishmael.

Lehi spoke. "My sons, Nephi is right. Please excuse my lack of faith." He paused, then lamely added, "Part of my anxiety is that Sariah is now expecting another child." The men looked up in surprise.

"So is Cleopha," Laman added bluntly.

"And Marni."

"And Esther."

Nephi looked at those who had spoken. It sounded as if every woman in camp, with the exception of Elizabeth and the maids, was pregnant. He didn't mention that Miriam, too, was with child. He waited for the talk to subside. "It is important that we not blame the Lord for what has happened." He then recited once more to them how the Lord had blessed them by bringing them from Jerusalem, helping them to get the plates, bringing Ishmael's family, and guiding them with the director.

"We must keep our confidence in the Lord, but even as important, we must keep faith in ourselves. There will be times when we will stumble and fall, but we must get right back up and go on. We are not defeated unless we just lie there. None of the great heroes, Moses, Joshua, David, had it easy. They were fighters who just kept fighting. From the very beginning the pattern followed by the Lord in granting blessings has been to allow the person seeking the blessing to be tested and tried. Righteous desires are granted only when he has humbled himself and proven his faith."

He paused to look at his father, then he continued.

"I know that if we stay close to His Spirit we won't be overwhelmed by these trials of our faith. Besides, the Lord has promised us that with the Spirit as our companion we can handle any difficulties or trials."

He turned and left the tent, letting them have time to reflect on the things he had said. In his own tent, he fell to his knees. "Father, please give us strength. Help us to find a way to overcome the obstacles which face us."

Chapter 10

Desert Crossing

They were camped in a long wadi, cruelly bare, scarred by a shallow, twisting, dry stream bed braided with heaps of stones. The area was hot and humid. Even at night there was no relief from oppressive heat. Between their camp and the Red Sea was an endless string of cracked and lined mud-flats. It was a desolate place, but here it was that Lehi had chosen to rest for a season. They had planted their grain crops. They hoped to have enough meat to sustain them until the harvest, but now, with Nephi's bow broken . . .?

An old well near their camp provided ample water, but there was little food available. Milk from their camels and the few remaining nannies was saved for the pregnant women. Laman and his supporters demanded that Lehi open the sacks of seeds so they could use them for food but he refused. He had promised the Lord that he would save the seeds for planting in the promised land.

Eastward, at the head of the wadi, were steep, forbidding mountains. The Bedouins in the nearby village called them Mount Jasum and Mount Azd. As Nephi looked at them, their very ruggedness suggested that there must be game. He sat outside the tent, on its shady side. Sweat glistened on his face and body. He was making a sling. He braided long strands of goats' hair into two long, finger-width straps. These were connected in the center with a woven pouch about as wide as his hand. Nephi pulled it taut to test its strength.

For hours he practiced, placing a pebble in the center pouch, holding it with his left hand, then with his right arm whirling the sling around his head several times and then releasing one end. He had used a sling as a child but then it was just for play as he tried to hit a target or knock a bird out of a tree. Now it was a matter of survival. Finally he felt that he was ready. He was still not as accurate as he would like to be, but it would do. He went to Lehi's tent.

"Father," he said as he knelt before Lehi, "please give me a blessing that I may find food for the camp."

Lehi laid his hands on his son's head. "My son, Nephi, I bless you through the power of the Lord Jehovah, that you may be the means of bringing sustenance to this camp. May the Lord bless you that your eye may be quick to see and that your arm may be accurate that we may eat meat once again. . . ."

Nephi returned to his tent, picked up some dried figs and his water gourd, and said a tender goodbye to his now obviously pregnant Miriam. As he made his way through the camp, he stopped and kissed his mother. Sariah was bent over a pot of broth of dried lentils she had salvaged. On the outskirts of the camp he met Ishmar and his sister, Vivian, who were hunkered over an ant hill. With a stick they had dug into the hill until they found the ants' granary from which they had gathered a small pile of seeds.

Ishmar stood as Nephi approached. "May I go with you?"

Nephi put his hand on his friend's elbow as they walked to the edge of camp. "My friend. I would enjoy your company, but you can do more good here than with me. This is something I must do by myself."

Ishmar, disappointed, looked up at his large cousin, then went back to where his sister was still squatting beside the ant hill.

Several hours from camp, Nephi found what he was looking for. In a large clump of rocks at the base of a hill, he saw a quick movement, followed by several shrill warning whistles. It was a colony of rock coneys. They looked like plump rabbits—without the long ears—and lived in holes among rocks. He marked the spot in his mind. Early in the evening the coneys would be out feeding and away from the safety of their rocky homes.

He continued climbing steadily up the steep mountain, not knowing what he was looking for, but the voice within him had said, "Go to the tops of the mountains." He climbed easily, his body in tune with the mountainside. Perspiration ran down his face and back, but he kept his steady pace. He was disappointed that there were no fresh game tracks but he kept hiking. Topping a saddle, right beneath overhanging crags, he found himself in a copse of large, willowy trees. Now he knew why the Lord had led him here. These were *nab* trees—the only good bow wood within hundreds of miles. From these he could make a new bow!

He carefully selected several lengths of the strong sapling wood. Then he cut a handful of young willows—branches that were straight and without knots. He smiled and said out loud, "I can do it! . . . I have never made one, but I can make a wooden bow." Satisfied that he had enough of the springy wood, he started quickly back down the mountain.

The sun was sinking over the sea when he again approached the coney colony. He dropped to the ground and stalked forward. Stopping, he picked out several smooth pebbles from his pouch and patiently waited. Several coneys moved out to browse. He whirled the sling, WHACK. A stone flew straight to the mark, leaving a coney shuddering on its side. All around him now he heard the warning whistles of the colony. He stood, fitted another stone in his sling, SWISH, SWISH, WHACK. A miss. Another stone, WHACK! Another dead coney. One more try. SWISH, SWISH, WHACK. The last one he struck as it was entering its rock burrow. It remained attached to the rock with the suction of its feet, just hanging there.

He picked up the three animals. Carrying his precious bow wood in one hand and the coneys in the other, he headed back to camp. Three coneys would not provide much food, but at least it was meat. A whisper of excitement preceded him through the camp. He strode to Lehi's tent, dropped the coneys on the floor and said, "Father, here is meat for stew."

Sariah slipped up and stood under his arm. She stooped and picked up the coneys. Nodding at Lehi, she turned and left to have the coneys cleaned.

Lehi looked thoughtfully at his son. "What else is it that you have found?" he asked.

Nephi held up the *nab* wood. "I know very little about making a bow," he said, "but I have wood to work with. The Lord has promised us that we would survive to see the promised land. He has now led me to wood from which I can make a new bow."

"My son," Lehi said, "only through your faithfulness has the Lord continued to work with us. You have persisted when the rest of us were ready to give up and quit. You haven't allowed discouragement to get you down."

"Thank you, Father," he responded. "A man needs to feel that he is making a contribution to life."

Lehi paused. "You are right. For the first time in my life I am feeling old—feeling as if something had gone out of me. A man needs to give of himself, knowing that he will always get back much more than he ever gives. I violated that principle and the trust of my people after you broke your bow. I haven't had anything to give since then and that has given me problems."

Taking his father's two big hands in his own, Nephi said, "Father, you are the leader of this family as we journey to the promised land. You have continually shown your leadership and your faithfulness in guiding this caravan." They continued their conversation, with Nephi attempting to help Lehi forgive himself for his complaining and to have him again take the reins of leadership of the caravan.

Supper that night was a real treat with Sariah's coney stew, hot and spicy. After supper, Nephi washed out Sariah's stew pot, filled it with water, and stuck it on the fire. He then cut an old camel hide into small pieces which he put into the boiling water.

"Whew!" Laman said. He and Lemuel had come to see what was stinking so badly. They left quickly, holding their noses and making jokes about "little brother." Nephi paid no attention but continued working on his bow. He first scraped all the bark off the wood, then carefully split it down the middle. He cut and peeled, cut and peeled, far into the night. Before he went to bed he once again stirred the gummy mess in the stew pot.

Nephi awakened before it was light, anxious to begin. He slipped on his tunic, laced up his sandals, and stepped outside. Mountains to the east stood in stark relief, outlined by the pink light of the coming sun. It was a glorious time of day. He faced the sunrise and knelt in prayer—asking that he might accomplish the major task that faced him.

After his prayer he went back to the cooking fire. His pot of goo was still on the fire and warm to his touch. Moving the pot, he stirred dead embers with a stick. A few coals still glowed. Nephi chuffed some bark from the nearby thorn trees, covered it with kindling, and then kneeling beside the embers, blew until a spark flamed up and caught. Bigger sticks were added until he had a small but roaring fire. Nephi waited until the fire burned down leaving hot, glowing coals. Then he carefully took each split piece of *nabwood* and held it over the coals until it was slightly charred. The short, straight willows received even more heat-treatment.

Nephi carried the sticks back to his tent and sat beside the pallet, watching his sleeping wife. She lay on her side, her distended belly resting on the padded blanket. Even though Nephi knew she had been uncomfortable Miriam had not complained. Soon it would be over. Other than rubbing goat's butter on her skin, Nephi felt he had been no help at all during her pregnancy.

Treading softly so as not to disturb her, Nephi slipped back out of the tent. He sat on a stool, scraping his sticks with the flat blade of his bronze knife. Every once in a while, as he scraped, he would match up the sticks. As he worked he whistled a tuneless song. At last he was ready. The wood matched perfectly. He went to get the stew pot. Selecting a short piece of thornwood, he dipped it in the pot and smeared the goo up and down the length of a stick. The pieces were carefully laminated together. He now had a rough bow, curved on both ends. Taking a thin piece of thong, he tightly and carefully wrapped the bow's entire length. One more piece of thong to tie the curved ends together, and it was done. Now all he had to do was let it dry.

Others were stirring around the camp. He checked once more on the sleeping Miriam, then while the bow was drying he scraped his arrows, sighting down each one until it was straight and true. Now he needed help. He walked to the camel drivers' tent and roused Shemin. He had no forge, but soon, with Shemin's help, the coals were glowing white-hot. Taking one of Sariah's old bronze knives, Nephi heated it in the coals, then began hammering it into thin points for his arrows.

"What's all the noise?" a gruff voice shouted behind him. He turned to see Laman striding toward him. "Cleopha is pregnant and needs her sleep, and here you are banging . . ." He quit talking in mid-sentence as he saw the arrows and the bow leaning against the tent. "Ho, what have we here?" He laughed contemptuously. "So little brother is trying to make a bow!" He walked back toward his tent, laughing.

Nephi nodded, his mind already on the excitement of the morrow. The laughing and scorn of others were not going to keep him from his task.

With Shemin's help, he finally had all of the arrows fletched and with sharp, bronze points. Now it was just a matter of waiting.

All day he endured taunts and jibes from his brothers and the sons of Ishmael. He asked Miriam, "Why is it that those you love can hurt you the most? Why do those who aren't doing what they are supposed to try to keep you from succeeding in whatever it is you try to do? Why is it that people have to tear down other people?"

Miriam, in her womanly wisdom, replied, "People have to justify their own weaknesses. It is easier to tear others down than it is to build themselves up."

Nephi nodded. That explained much of his brothers' behavior.

While he waited for the laminated bow to dry, he sat in the tent with Miriam, weaving a fish net from lengths of twisted goats' hair. It was finished before dusk, and he and Miriam left the camp and hiked down to the beach. The Bedouin village was next to the shore. Nephi stopped to watch some villagers building a small boat. He carefully observed their tools and techniques. When it was too dark to watch, he waded out into the water with his net and soon had several small fish to take back to camp.

By morning the glue was dry. Nephi carefully unwound the strips of sinew. Taking a piece of sandstone, he smoothed down the bow and made a notch for the arrows. With the bow against his foot, he stretched the recurve carefully back until he could string it with the new string Miriam had made. He tested the bow, drawing it slowly back to a full draw. It held! It didn't break!

Again he went to his father's tent. Lehi motioned for him to come in. He laid the bow in his father's hands. Lehi held it up, admiring the workmanship, hefting it and drawing it. He looked up at Nephi, his eyes brimming with tears. "Well done, my son. With this bow you will again provide meat for this people."

Nephi quietly accepted his father's praise. "Father, we still need the Lord's help. Where shall I go to obtain food?" he asked.

"Join me in prayer," Lehi said. Together they knelt in the tent's seclusion. Nephi's prayer was interrupted by the agonized moans of his father. Nephi stood and stepped toward him, then realized that his father's agony was not physical, but the agony of the spirit. After several minutes, Lehi dropped his head. "Thank you, Lord," he said. He opened red-rimmed eyes to look upon Nephi. "The Lord chastened me severely," he said, "but He has forgiven me now for my murmuring against Him." He paused, "I will never doubt Him again."

He stood and walked over to a box at the side of the tent, returning with the brass ball. "Go and get your brethren," he said. "The Lord has told me that I must speak to the whole family."

Nephi went through the camp, informing the people of his father's desire. In a few moments everyone was standing before Lehi's tent. It was a hot, uncomfortable day and soon many were complaining about having to stand in the sun. Lehi stepped forth from his tent. Never had Nephi seen him look so stern.

"My sons and family," he said, his gesture including everyone. "The Lord has said for all of us to 'Look upon the ball, and behold the things which are written.' "

He held the ball before him and people crowded around. Those who could read stepped back, astonished looks on their faces. There was a hum as people commented on what they had read. Nephi stepped forward and read aloud so all could hear: *I am the Lord thy God. There are those among you who have sinned exceedingly. Verily I say unto you, beware from henceforth, and refrain from sin, lest sore judgments fall upon your heads.* As Nephi read, he was astonished to see the words fade from view and new words appear. He read on. *Ye call upon my name for directions, and I give them unto you. But when you do not keep my sayings, ye become transgressors, and justice and judgment are the penalty which is affixed unto my law.*

Nephi looked at the men and women who stood around the tent. They appeared to be intent on what he was reading. *Now I give unto you directions of how you may act before me, that it may work for your salvation. I, the Lord, am bound when ye do what I say; but when ye do not what I say, ye have no promise. Follow this ball, but understand that its pointers will work only according to your faith and diligence.* The Lord's words then directed Nephi to go to the top of the mountain to get meat for the camp.

The family members wandered back to their tents, discussing the import of the Lord's message to them. As soon as the evening cooled, Nephi and Ishmar headed for the mountains. The Lord fulfilled his promise: the next evening they were back with two large gazelles. Everyone in camp, even Laman and Lemuel, was ecstatic. Meat was plentiful once again. Lehi called his people around him, this time to offer thanksgiving to the Lord for their deliverance.

Within a few weeks crops were ready to harvest and the caravan to move on. The Lord guided them along the shores of the Red Sea, keeping them to fertile areas where there was grazing for their camels and goats.

They traveled a day at a time, stopping each night to set up their tents. There was no hurry so sometimes they stayed in a camp until the grass was gone. When food was scarce, Nephi would take his bow and head for the mountains. After many days of travel, they entered a dry valley dotted with pistachio trees along a dry, meandering, stream bed. Lehi halted the caravan.

"We will call this the Valley of Nahom," Lehi said. "Here we will rest and plant our crops."

They found a hand-dug well nearer the seashore, and there Lehi directed the women to put up the tents. They would stay in this valley for at
least a season—long enough to harvest a full crop. Nephi could sense that
Lehi was very reluctant to start across the desert with his unskilled group.
Game was plentiful in the mountains south of Nahom, so Nephi spent much
of his time hunting.

While in Nahom, Ishmael's health continued to deteriorate. He hadn't
been well for months and Nephi knew how concerned Miriam was. Coming
in from one hunting trip, Nephi could hear from far up the mountain the
keening wails of mourners. *Ishmael!* He quickened his pace, but with an
antelope on his shoulder he couldn't move very fast. The loud wails of
mourning met him as he arrived in camp, breathless and sweaty. He rushed
to his tent, but Miriam wasn't there. She met him near Ishmael's tent, her
black veil drawn over her comely face. She was sobbing as Nephi enclosed
her in his arms.

As he rocked her gently from side to side, she murmured between sobs,
"It's Father . . . he's dead."

"I'm sorry, my dear."

"Oh, Nephi, now mother will be all alone."

"No, my love. She will never be alone as long as we live."

She hugged him tighter, her sobs becoming muffled. They walked together to Ishmael's tent. His body was laid out on the floor, his head on a
camel saddle. Elizabeth, her daughters, Sariah and all of the maids sat
cross-legged before the body, keening their high-pitched wail, drumming
their fingers on their lips. It was the *saghreed* of the desert people. Miriam
rejoined her sisters on the floor while Nephi looked for his father.

He found Lehi talking animatedly with a Bedouin from a nearby fishing village. As he got closer, he realized that Lehi was negotiating for a
burial spot for Ishmael. Lehi handed the Bedouin a handful of coins signi-
fying the bargaining was over. Nephi stepped up and took his father's arm,
walking with him back to Ishmael's tent. Not only had Ishmael been Lehi's
brother-in-law, but he was also a quiet and faithful friend. Nephi knew his
father would sorely miss him.

That evening Lehi led the funeral procession to a small burial ground
on barren hills near Nahom. Ishmael's clay sarcophagus was carried by his
two sons and the four sons of Lehi. After the burial, the mourners returned
to the camp, quiet in their grief.

Nephi sat in his tent, stroking Miriam's hair, her head on his lap. They
were interrupted by an abrupt commotion outside the tent. Miriam rolled
over and laboriously got to her feet. She and Nephi stepped to the door.
Cleopha, red-faced and angry, stood there with her sisters and brothers.
Laman and Lemuel stood behind them. When she saw Nephi, Cleopha
screamed, "You are the cause of this! If it weren't for you and your dreamer

of a father, our father would still be alive and we would be living comfortably in our own home in the land of Jerusalem." Marni, Leah, and Esther nodded their approval. Laman and Lemuel stood with gloating smiles on their faces.

Lehi emerged from his tent. Cleopha stalked to him and shook her finger in his face. "Because of you our father is dead. Yes, and because of you we have wandered for years in this wilderness, suffering from hunger, thirst and fatigue. We have endured the heat and the goading stings of mosquitoes and flies. If you have your way we will all perish in the wilderness. I want to return to the land of Jerusalem where our babies can be born in a real home, and where they won't have to worry if they're going to live."

The group murmured its assent. Nephi felt very uncomfortable, sorry that his father had to take such verbal abuse. But Lehi appeared unruffled. He stood quietly, his arms folded high on his chest, until Cleopha finished.

Then he said, "My children, I know you are upset. I am upset, too. Ishmael was my dear friend. My wife also mourns her brother's death. But know that if you had stayed in Jerusalem you would have perished. The Lord's vengeance will be unleashed upon that city and it will be destroyed." He softened his tone. "You have suffered much, and you will probably suffer more afflictions, but know this—the Lord has promised us that we will reach the promised land, and the Lord always fulfills his promises!" The last was said with rising inflection. Then Lehi turned and entered his tent.

Sam put his arm around Leah and guided her to where Nephi and Miriam were standing. Grumbling and murmuring, the rest of the group walked away together. They were obviously still displeased with Lehi's leadership and they seemed to be discussing what they could do. In a few minutes Eva and Zoram, a shocked look on their faces, hurried back to where Nephi, Sam, and their wives were standing.

"What happened?" Nephi asked.

Eva seemed reluctant to say anything, but Zoram spoke. "Your brother Laman is trying to stir everyone up." He shook his head, apparently bothered by what Laman had said.

"What has he said now?" Nephi asked.

Zoram told of how Laman, who had been content to let his wife speak before, had stood up and spoken to the dissenters.

* * *

"I am convinced that there is only one thing we can do," Laman said. "We must kill our father and Nephi. It angers me that Nephi continues to try to be our leader and teacher."

Esther and Annah looked shocked. Esther asked Laman, "Are you mad? Kill our own father and brother?"

Laman answered her, "I am angry at both of them. Especially Nephi. He says that the Lord has talked with him, and also that angels have ministered unto him. But behold, we know that he lies . . . he tells us these things, and he worketh many things by his cunning arts, that he may deceive our eyes, thinking, perhaps, that he may lead us away into some strange wilderness; and after he has led us away, he has thought to make himself a king and a ruler over us, that he may do with us according to his will and pleasure." [14]

It had been a long speech, even for the wily Laman. He looked around the group, but most kept their eyes downcast. Though he had tried to stir them up to anger he now knew that he had gone too far. Even Lemuel didn't support him.

* * *

After Zoram told them what had happened, Nephi and Sam, with the others trailing, started toward the dissenters. As they arrived at Laman's tent, a loud clap of thunder boomed from the cloudless sky. A piercing voice surrounded them. *Oh wo, wo, upon you. Unless you repent of your iniquities your houses shall be left unto you desolate and you will perish in the desert.*

Nephi whispered to Miriam, "It is the voice of the Lord!"

The voice said many other things to Laman and his group as they cowered there, causing them to fall upon their knees and ask forgiveness.

Nephi shook his head in sorrow. As he walked back to the tent with Miriam he asked aloud, "Will it never end? Will Laman and Lemuel ever set a steady course of righteousness? They are like streams of the desert, running for a little while with humility and righteousness, then dry and barren of anything." Then he became silent remembering his vision, and knew that it would never end.

* * *

Nephi looked down at the tiny wrinkled face, red and sour, a small fist jammed against its open mouth. "He is very beautiful," he said softly. The baby had been bathed and rubbed with salt as was the tradition. Now he lay wrapped from head to foot in bands of cloth to keep him erect and straight.

Miriam turned on her side, cuddling the baby to her. "What shall we name him?"

He reached down, picked up the tiny baby and lifted him high into the air. "His name shall be Jeremiah. Perhaps he also will become a great prophet."

Miriam responded, a teasing note in her voice, "Jeremiah was a great prophet, but my husband is a greater one."

"No, my father, Lehi, is the prophet. The Lord has just chosen to reveal himself sometimes to me."

He smiled at her. "By the way. You are lovely. You were beautiful when you were pregnant, but now . . ." He left the thought unsaid, throwing out his arms in an eloquent gesture.

She reached up and stroked his cheek. "It is nice of you to say so." A note of concern entered her voice. "Nephi, have you heard how your mother is, and little Jacob?"

His broad smile showed his straight white teeth. "Mother and Jacob are doing fine. He is a beautiful child, with golden eyes." He sat beside her on the mat. "Cleopha, too, has had her baby. They have named it Enoch."

She smiled. "it is appropriate that in this valley where my father died, two of his grandchildren were born."

"Perhaps even more," Nephi chuckled. "We will probably stay here for another season to store supplies. By then Elizabeth should have six grandchildren!"

The thought seemed to comfort Miriam. She closed her eyes and dozed.

Lehi had shared with Nephi the fears he had of the next part of their journey. Just south of their present camp at Nahom, the mountains rose from one high range to another, stair-stepping right down to the sea. When they traveled again, they would have to turn inland, and inland was nothing but a great desert waste. South, beyond the mountains, was the land of the warlike Sabaeans. The Lord would probably lead them away from such a people. Wherever they went, they would have to have plenty of supplies. So, as soon as Miriam had regained her strength, Nephi resumed his hunting. Much of the meat that he now killed was dried and stored. A local Bedouin had shown him how to season it lightly with garlic and salt, and how to dry the meat in the sun until it was dark brown on the outside but still pinkish-red inside. It was sweet to the taste, stored easily, and they could eat it raw.

Lehi and his family had now lived in the wilderness for five years. Still they stayed at Nahom. Each morning Lehi would study the director, which he now called the *Liahona*, looking for directions from the Lord. A voice finally came to him in the night: *Lehi.* It came again. *Lehi.*

He awakened. *Lehi, look on the ball.* He picked up the ball which glowed with a hidden intensity. Written on it were the words *It is time to leave Nahom. Follow the pointers. On your journey do not make fires. I will make thy food become sweet, that ye cook it not. And I will also be your light in the wilderness; and I will prepare the way before you, if it so be that ye shall keep my commandments; wherefore, inasmuch as ye shall keep my commandments ye shall be led towards the promised land; and ye shall know that it is by me that ye are led."* The writing continued. *"After ye have arrived in the promised land, ye shall know that I, the Lord, am God;*

*and that I, the Lord, did deliver you from destruction; yea, that I did bring
you out of the land of Jerusalem.''* [15]

Once again they loaded their camels and started out. Nephi said goodbye to friends he had made in the Bedouin village, then saw that Miriam
and Jeremiah were safely loaded. The caravan trail they followed left the
seacoast and then split as it followed several wadis up through the hills.
Following directions on the *Liahona*, they headed up a winding wadi to
the east.

Their next stopping place was a small village on a mountain plateau
where the trails seemed to come together. It was a peaceful village with
eagles and buzzards turning and soaring overhead in gusty winds that blew
over the plateau. The hills were wooded with small scrub cedar trees. Above
the village the hills were striped with horizontal terraces to catch the sparse
rainwater. With so many babies in the caravan, it was necessary to rest more
often. Another season was spent near the Bedouin village.

Early mornings seemed to be the best times for Nephi to hunt. Sunrise
was a glorious time of day. He watched the sun, half-curtained in fleecy
mist, rise above the desert which lay before him. It was not the desert of
drifting sands which lay beyond, but a rocky desert with dwarfed herbage,
where the surface was strewn with boulders of granite—large gray and
brown stones—interspersed with languishing acacias and tufts of camel-
grass. Birds were plentiful in the area and, as Nephi hunted, lark and chat
and rock-swallow leaped to wing, and desert partridges ran whistling and
clucking out of the way. Occasionally he saw a fox or hyena studying him
from a distance. Over the peaks to the west the vultures sailed on broad
wings in ever-widening circles, black, and silent, and sharp as ink. Each day
he returned to the camp with meat.

When they started again on their journey, fertile land around the village
quickly disappeared and soon they were surrounded by endless desolation—
hills, mountains, plains, and valleys of rock, and shale, and sand. There
were few beasts or birds, almost no growing things. The desert was a picture
of bare landscapes, bold colors, and fiercely bright light—a place of strength
and simplicity. The hills they crossed were gaunt with massive depressions
below almost sheer cliffs. Wide stretches of the *hamada* were covered with
flint and slate and sandstone pebbles as if some distant star had rained
rocks on the earth.

The desert was overpowering to the caravan. The saffron-colored
ground was thick with dust and boulders, and totally flat. The sky was
cloudless, a stark and staring blue—too intense for more than a glance,
glaring with blinding light. Here and there across the plain little spring rills
had run, leaving rope-like straggles of dry amber crawling over the stricken
earth.

It was a land of sharp contrasts. The blazing, desolate heat of midday, without shade or shelter to give relief, was intensified by the silent fury of the breathless *hamsin* wind. Then, at night, they shivered under penetrating cold which came with quick darkness. Occasionally they found hillside caves, their openings like great dry, gaping mouths. The caves, used by countless travelers, gave cooler shelter to the weary pilgrims.

Sandstorms were a continuous and major nuisance. The hot *khamsin* would pick up tiny particles of sand, blowing until a gray film obscured even the sun. The travelers learned quickly to have the camels kneel, providing them some shelter. When storms hit at night, those inside knocked down the center poles of their tents, making the tents fall on themselves and their families so that the storm could blow overhead without ripping the tents from their moorings.

For the most part it was a monotonous life. Their travel was not measured in miles or other distance measures, but by the *saat* or hour, and the *manzil* or halt. The pace of the patient camels dictated the time. Waterholes were further apart across the desert, and even though they were well-marked, thirst was a constant problem. Each member of the caravan became acquainted with the thickness of tongue, the salty crust of drying spittle, the flaking and cracking of swollen lips and the leaden faltering of limbs that were signs of prolonged thirst. Tempers became frayed. Several stopped talking to each other.

Game was sparse and hunting poor. Lehi rationed meat out to members of the party, and murmurings became even more intense. Because of danger of attack by roving Arab bands, they set up camp about an hour before sunset. Following the Lord's counsel, they prepared meals without fire. Often they saw flashes of light from the hilltops—brass mirrors signaling their passage. The desert crossing was a time of great affliction, but they knew that the Lord watched over them as He had promised he would.

Nephi knew that the *Liahona* was their guide. It saddened him to see the miracle of God's guidance become so commonplace that many in the party took it for granted. They became slothful. Often they wandered from the correct trail, suffering even more hunger and thirst. Lehi and Nephi, knowing that the Lord permitted their wanderings because of lack of faith and diligence, pleaded with the people to be prayerful and to have faith, but their words only caused more resentment in the hearts of the faithless ones. Lehi was experienced in the desert but he depended entirely upon the *Liahona*, reverently following its directions.

The desert trek was especially hard on the women and children. Children were born even as they struggled across the desert. Lehi and Sariah had a second son whom they named Joseph. Nephi and Miriam had a daughter whom they named Ruth. Other women also had children, suckling them throughout the desert crossing.

Their affliction extended beyond the oppressive heat and cold and the shifting, gritty sands. It included large scorpions which came into their tents at night. There was also an ever-present danger from snakes like the sand-colored horned viper which would bury itself and then appear when least expected. After over a year of wandering through the trackless wastes, many felt they were about to perish, that their endurance had been stretched too far.

When they thought they could go no further, they noticed a change in the terrain. Once again they were surrounded by scrubby bushes and shrubs, and Nephi again found game. The desert ended against a range of mountains. The weary travelers topped out in a mountain pass which was cool and pleasant after their desert ordeal.

They crowded around Lehi and looked. Before them stretched a velvety jungle leading down to a tropical ocean. Yellow meadows lay along the mountainsides and to the north was a large red sandstone steppe. A shout of joyful relief rose from the caravan. This must be the promised land!

Lehi looked over the land with tears in his eyes. The Lord had led them to a bountiful land, a land of milk and honey. Before descending down the wadi into the beautiful, crescent-shaped coastal plain, he told his people, "We will call this land Bountiful. It is the land to which the Lord has directed us."

The caravan, filled with happy and excited people, descended the mountain slopes into the Land Bountiful. A thick forest slowed their progress, but when they emerged from the trees, they were met by a sight that left Nephi astounded. There, spread out before them, were cultivated fields where peasants tilled the earth or watched over small flocks of livestock. Beyond the fields were several villages, and beyond those was the blue expanse of endless ocean. He had thought that the land of promise would be uninhabited.

That night they pitched their tents by the seashore. Lehi purchased a lamb from a villager, built an altar of stones, and with his whole family gathered around him, offered sacrifice in thanksgiving for the Lord's guidance in bringing them to this lovely place. Standing there, looking out over the great expanse of the ocean, he said, "We will call this ocean *Irreantum*, or 'many waters.' Here we will find a resting place for our families."

Nephi and Miriam sat in front of their tent, watching Jeremiah play in the sand. Ruth slept in her cradle which hung between the tent poles. Miriam had decorated the tent with fresh greenery and sweet-smelling herbs. Everything seemed so peaceful. It was pleasant camping near the great sea; listening to the waves rolling into the beach. Nephi wondered, Now what will the Lord want us to do?

Chapter 11

And They Built a Ship

Lehi and his clan were camped by a beautiful spring surrounded by date palms. The water, during the daytime, was clear to the sand-covered bottom; its taste was fresh and clean. Now moonlight made a golden path across it. Standing beside the pond, Miriam tossed a small pebble into the water. Moonlight glinted in her hair as she idly stretched a bare toe and stirred the cool water at the bank's edge. They had lived in Bountiful for several months. It had been a happy and wonderful time for her. She now had three children. Jeremiah was four, Ruth two, and Nephihah just a baby.

Nephi found her there. He walked up behind her and reached his large arms around her waist. "I love you," he whispered as he kissed her on the neck and buried his face in her fragrant hair.

She turned into him and they embraced. After standing there a moment, she asked him, "Nephi, I have passed through much tribulation. It is so good to be here in the promised land."

Nephi sighed. "My dear, Bountiful is a wonderful place, but I have to tell you I don't think this is the promised land."

Putting her hand to her mouth, Miriam stifled a groan. Not more travel! She waited until she once again regained her composure. Then she asked, "Nephi, how is it that you have such great faith when all that your brothers do is doubt?"

Nephi pondered the question. "I am not sure, my dear. But I feel that faith is merely doing the Lord's will first, hoping that at some time he would explain the reasons why." He paused, then continued. "Faith, my dear, is a statement of belief of future events as if they had already happened. It is acting as if we already had the knowledge."

He smiled as he held Miriam close. "I have found that our success is in direct proportion to our faith and our efforts. It has nothing to do with our circumstances. It seems to me that Laman and Lemuel say, 'I will believe it when I see it.' The concept of faith is 'I will see it only when I believe it.' "

He squeezed her again. "Am I boring you, my love?"

She shook her head.

"I believe the Lord is anxious to assist us. But we have to have faith first. It is a principle of power." He stopped, realizing that he was preaching a sermon to his audience of one. He shrugged his shoulders. "Regarding

Laman and Lemuel . . ." a note of sadness was in his voice ". . . they have had all the blessings of my father's faith, and yet they have not partaken of it. They have seen angels and heard the voice of the Lord, and yet they don't seem to listen or comprehend. It is a mystery to me."

They stood together for a long time, enjoying their oneness and the peace of the night. Miriam again broke the silence. "Nephi."

"Yes, my dear?"

"If this isn't the promised land, why are Laman and Lemuel building rock houses?"

"I don't know. Perhaps it is the promised land. It is just that the Lord has not told us yet. My father still awaits His word."

They made their way slowly back to their tent which had been their only home since their marriage. They prayed, as they had prayed every night, that the Lord would continue to bless them, and that they might know His will. In their bed, Miriam's breathing soon indicated that she slept soundly. Nephi lay awake thinking about their discussion. *Was* this the promised land? Were they to spend the rest of their lives in the land of Bountiful? He dozed, only to be awakened by someone calling his name.

"Nephi." He sat up and looked around in the dark tent. No one was stirring. *"Nephi."* The voice came again. This time he realized that the voice was inside him.

"Yes, Lord," he answered.

"Nephi, arise and get thee into the mountain."

Carefully, so as not to awaken Miriam, Nephi got out of bed and put on his clothes. When he was dressed, he gently touched her cheek and quietly spoke her name. "Miriam." Her eyes came open. "My dear, the Lord has called to me to go into the mountains."

"But why? Are you sure?"

"Yes, my love. He has spoken to me. Will you be all right?"

She was awake now. He sat on the pallet beside her. "Tell Lehi that I will return as soon as I learn what the Lord desires." He kissed her tenderly, then he was gone into the night.

Miriam lay looking at the dark tent, fear churning inside her. Nephi had been gone much of the time hunting for food but never had he been called out in the middle of the night. And so mysteriously. She uttered a short prayer for his safety.

* * *

Nephi was glad for the full moon that shone on the path and guided his feet toward the mountain which loomed above him. He was not sure where he was going, but he trusted the Lord totally. The eastern sky was rose-colored over the shimmering waters of Irreantum by the time he reached a saddle high on the mountain.

He stopped and turned to watch the sunrise. The glory and wonder of the sun coming up each day never ceased to thrill him. The sun, red and round, slowly came over the horizon. Rain clouds, black and threatening, lay over the waters and the sun peered through the slit between the clouds and the sea, shedding a glow that, for a brief moment, washed with glory the rock and wooded hills of Bountiful. A little stream gushed forth cold and fresh from the living rock and Nephi knelt to drink. He remained on his knees and turned his face to the heavens.

"What is it, Lord? What would you have me do?"

He knelt there for some time praying. When no answer came he was about to rise and go further into the mountains, when an audible voice surrounded him as if with thunder. *Nephi*, it boomed, *Thou shalt construct a ship, after the manner which I shall show thee, that I may carry thy people across these waters.* [16]

Nephi was startled. A ship! He had never built anything larger than a wooden bow and arrows—and they had no tools! Yet, when he thought of it, he remembered the many times he had been impressed to watch the ship-builders. He had no doubts that he could do the will of the Lord. The words he had spoken to Miriam the night before passed through his mind. Humbly, he asked, "Lord, where shall I go to find ore so that I can make tools?"

The Lord gave him directions and soon Nephi was on his way. He found an outcropping of copper right where the Lord had told him it would be. He picked up several large chunks from the ground, marked the location so he could find it again, and started down the mountain. By the time he arrived at his tent he was weary—both from loss of sleep and the rugged hike, but he was too excited to rest. He dropped the chunks of ore and went straight to Lehi's tent.

"Father," he shouted. Lehi stepped from the tent. "The Lord has spoken once more to me. He has commanded me to build a ship."

Lehi stepped close to his son. "I am not surprised. I have prayed fervently that we might know if this is the Land of Promise. Now we know it is not. What must we do next?"

"We need to make tools with which to build a ship."

"Good. I have not refined metals, but I am sure the Lord will give us guidance."

Nephi nodded, not trying to hide his excitement. "Yes. He has already shown me where to find ore. We will need to take all the men and carry it to a place of smelting."

He left to tell Miriam the exciting but challenging news, then headed for the tents of Laman and Lemuel.

"Ho, little brother," Laman called derisively as he approached. "What is this we hear about you building a ship?"

"It is true," Nephi answered. "The Lord has directed that we build a ship to cross Irreantum."

Laman sneered. "What makes you think you have the knowledge to build a ship? You are a fool to even consider it. If you think I would trust my family to any flimsy craft you build, you are a greater idiot than I think you are."

Lemuel nodded in agreement. "And if you think we will help you, you're mistaken!"

When Nephi shook his head sadly, Laman laughed. "How can you build a ship? You are immature and lacking in judgment. Besides, we like it here. We have decided to build our homes and settle here with our families. If there ever was a promised land, this is it."

The next day Nephi set up a camp at the base of the mountain for smelting the ore. Without Laman and Lemuel and the sons of Ishmael, he had only half a crew. He was glad that Ishmar had decided to help him, even though Nephi knew that taking a stand against his father had not been easy. Nephi made up his mind to build the ship without his brothers' help.

For three days they worked, chipping off chunks of ore and hauling it to camp. By evening of the third day they were exhausted, but they had enough copper to make the necessary tools. Now all Nephi needed was tin to mix with it to make the bronze.

The mountain was dark now. The last glow in the western sky had faded. A chill was in the air. Tired and silent, he and Ishmar walked side-by-side back to their tent camp.

Nephi walked to the beach, disrobed, and dashed into the surf. With clean sand he scrubbed his body until it was red and tingly. Stepping out of the water, he reached for the clean loincloth Miriam brought him. Holding hands, they walked back to the tent. Miriam had fixed Nephi's favorite meal—honey cakes and curds. The honey cakes were rolled in sesame seeds, shaped and baked like leavened bread but with oil and honey added. Curds were made from thickened, sour milk. For dessert there were fresh grapes, figs, and dates.

Nephi enjoyed his meal. He was glad that he had taken time to build Miriam a clay oven. It was shaped like a beehive with a door on one side and he had built it in a shaded spot. Every day Miriam baked bread for him and he loved it.

During the next days, with the Lord's guidance, Nephi located tin ore. While the men broke the ore into small pieces, he built a clay crucible to hold the ore while it was heated. Then from a goatskin he made a bellows like those he had seen shipbuilders near Shazer use. The neck of the tanned goatskin was fitted around a piece of clay pipe which would be placed under the fire. The four legs of the skin had been folded back and tied off carefully. The back was open, stitched around two parallel sticks. The opened bag was lifted up to draw in air, then pushed down when closed to force air through the tube into the fire.

Now he was ready for the fire. Chuffing bark until it was tinder, he cracked two pieces of flint together. Time after time he struck them. Finally a spark landed in the tinder. He bent down and quickly blew on it until it caught the tinder and leapt into flames. He had fire. Now they needed charcoal. Shemin and the camel drivers had constructed an oven out of sun-dried bricks. Pieces of hardwood were put in and fire built around them. The fires were stoked twenty-four hours a day, and soon there was enough charcoal to process the ore.

Nephi filled the crucible with small chunks of ore, then piled charcoal all around it—even on top. He built a roaring fire to get the charcoal burning, then kept it red-hot with the bellows. It was a laborious process. Heat the ore. Pour off the slag. Cast the ore into ingots for transporting to the seashore, and while that was happening have another batch of ore in the crucible so the process could be repeated. When he felt they had smelted enough ore to make the necessary tools, they hauled their copper and tin ingots to their camp by the sea. Nephi was tired but joyous. They could now make the tools.

He hoped to avoid confrontation with Laman and his supporters, but as he walked through camp the next day, Laman and Lemuel accosted him.

"How is the mighty ship builder?" Laman sarcastically asked.

Nephi tried to walk by but Laman grabbed his arm and spun him around. "What makes you so high and mighty?" he growled. "If it weren't for you and our father we wouldn't be marooned so far from the land of our birth."

"You are just like our father," Lemuel added. "Led away by foolish imaginations."

A small crowd had gathered.

Shazer spoke. "You and your father led us out of the land of Jerusalem, forced us to wander for years. Our women have toiled while big with child; have borne children in the wilderness and suffered all things, save it were death." Then he added, "It would have been better that they had died before they came out of Jerusalem than to have suffered these afflictions."

Cleopha, pregnant with another child, shouted, "Through these many years that we have suffered in the wilderness, we could have been enjoying our possessions in the land of our inheritance. If we had remained there we would have been happy, but this . . .!"

"The people in Jerusalem were a righteous people," Laman called out. "They kept the statutes and judgments of the Lord, and all his commandments, according to the Law of Moses. Yet our father has judged them and has led us away because we listened to him . . . and you are just like him! We refuse to be led further." A hum of agreement came from those around him.

Nephi finally got his chance to speak. "Do you believe that our fathers, who were the Children of Israel, would have been led away out of the hands of the Egyptians if they had not hearkened unto the words of the Lord?" Before they could answer that question, he asked another. "And do you suppose that they would have been led out of bondage if the Lord had not commanded Moses that he should lead them out of bondage? You know that the Children of Israel were led forth by the Lord's matchless power into the land of promise. You also know that they have become wicked and are not following the Lord's commandments. The Lord has told us that the day must surely come that they must be destroyed, save a few only, who shall be led away into captivity."

The hostile audience was silent now, listening to his words. He continued, "The Lord then commanded our father that he should depart into the wilderness because the Jews sought to kill him. But the saddest thing of all is that *you* have also tried to kill him." He heard angry murmurs from the crowd but he continued, his voice rising in anger. "Wherefore, you are murderers in your hearts and you are just like the Jews. You are swift to do iniquity but slow to remember the Lord your God."

He turned back to Laman. "You have seen an angel and he spoke to you. Yes, you have even heard his voice from time to time; and he has spoken to you in a still small voice, but you were past feeling. So, he spoke to you in a voice of thunder which caused the earth to shake as if it were to divide asunder."

Stretching his arms to the heavens, he added, "You know that by the power of His almighty word He can cause the earth to pass away, the rough places to be made smooth, and smooth places to be broken up. You know all of this, so why is it that you can be so hard in your hearts and not understand that He is leading us?"

Shaking his head in sorrow, he sunk to the ground. "My heart is pained because of you. I am afraid that all of you shall be cast off forever." He looked up, a fiery look in his eye. "Behold, I am full of the Spirit of God, insomuch that my frame has no strength." [17]

Laman's face glowed red with anger. He motioned to Lemuel and the other men. "Come. We've had enough of his lying talk. Let's throw this blowhard off the cliff and let him drown in the sea."

"Aye," came a chorus from the others as they moved to grab Nephi.

Sam stepped forward to protect Nephi, but Nephi did not need his help. He stood up, back straight, arms pointing toward the defectors, an unearthly glow in his eyes. "Stop! In the name of the Almighty God I command you to touch me not! I am filled with His power! Whoever shall lay his hands upon me shall wither even as a dried reed, and he shall be as nothing before the power of God, for God shall smite him." [18]

The unruly group stopped, unsure, with Laman in the lead. Nephi continued, "The Lord has commanded us to build a ship, so we are going to build a ship. Stop your complaining and help us."

The men were silent as Nephi went on. "If God had commanded me to do all things I could do them. If he should command me that I should say unto this water, be thou earth, it should be earth. And now, if the Lord has such great power, and has wrought so many miracles among the children of men, how is it that he cannot instruct me that I should build a ship?" [19]

As he continued to talk to them they shrank back from him as though they feared that he was speaking the truth. Still refusing to work on the ship, they slunk away. Yet, with or without them, Nephi was committed to continue the work.

* * *

Nephi put the copper ingots they had brought from the mountain into the crucible, and once again covered it with charcoal. With Ishmar directing the air of the bellows through the long clay pipe, Nephi brought the crucible to a temperature high enough to refine out impurities and consolidate the copper.

While it was heating, he formed molds in the wet sand, carefully designing drills, adzes, axes and other tools he would need. When the ore was molten, he added tin to harden it, then poured the alloy into the molds. When the metal had hardened, and finished tools were pounded into shape, they were smoothed and polished. Now they had shipbuilding tools.

Because he was still frustrated with his brothers, as he talked with Miriam that evening, he drew for her an analogy. "A worker of metals," he said, "will never pound on a cold piece of brass. It has to be hot before it can be formed. The same applies to our lives. We must get excited about something—get hot—then those around us will get excited, too."

Miriam nodded and Nephi continued. "For the next phase of construction we will need the help of every man. I am excited about what we are doing. How can I get Laman, Lemuel and the others to work?"

In his prayers that night, he again approached the Lord. The answer came. *Stretch forth thy hand again to thy brethren, and they shall not wither before thee, but I will shock them. And this I will do that they may know that I am the Lord their God.* [20]

Early the next morning he walked to where Laman had started to build his house. Calling loudly, he said, "My brethren. I have something to say to you." All four men came forward, looking suspiciously at Nephi. "Brethren, I have made the tools. Now I need your help to get logs to build the ship. Please give me your help."

"Never!" shouted Laman, moving no closer. The others nodded their assent.

"Then I am forced to show you the power of God." Nephi stretched forth his hands. At once the four men before him began to quake and shake as though some giant hand grabbed and rattled them. Their screams of terror brought their wives running to see what was happening. Nephi let the shaking continue for several moments, then he dropped his hands. The men sank weakly to the ground, not even left with the power to speak.

Laman finally got up on his hands and knees and looked up at Nephi. "Now we know that the Lord is with you. It must be His power that has shaken us."

The men, filled with superstitious anxiety, attempted to worship Nephi, but he said, "Stop. I am your brother, even your younger brother. Don't attempt to worship me, but worship only the Lord." Then he added, a glint in his eye, "But do honor your father and mother."

As they still lay there, he said, "Now get up and come help so we can build a ship." The men meekly got up and joined the shipbuilding crew.

Nephi soon realized that the Lord had led them to the perfect place to construct a ship. Behind the beach lay a dense forest of almug trees—the best possible wood with which to build a ship. Many of the trees had trunks up to four feet in circumference. The timber was very heavy and fine-grained, black outside and a rich, ruby-red inside. The natives told Nephi that it was "red sandalwood" and that it could be worked beautifully. Also in abundance were *jumaise*, or sycamore-fig trees, some growing as high as fifty feet. Nephi found that wood from these trees was strong, resistant to sea water, and almost free from knots.

Nephi put Laman in charge of cutting and dragging the trees. After they were cut down with crude axes, Laman hooked up teams of camels to pull them down to the beach. He worked hard, and under his direction tons of logs were dragged out of the forests.

Trees with a natural bend were used for the huge ribs. The keel and bow were shaped with drills and planes. Axes were used to rough out the basic shapes of needed timbers, then the adz was used to shape those timbers into keels and ribs. Hand-operated drills, fitted inside a hardwood spindle and rotated by a long rawhide thong in a bow, were used for drilling holes. Wooden planes were made of a block of hardwood with a hand-forged bronze blade wedged tightly in place.

Nephi went often to the mountain where the Lord gave him detailed instructions for the ship's construction. Although Nephi also used what practical knowledge he had gained while watching ship builders in ports they had passed through, this was a ship designed by God and constructed under His guidance.

Logs were split into planks, and the planks tied to the ship's skeleton with coconut-fiber cord the women had made by soaking coconut husks in sea water to soften, then pounding them with wooden mallets. The fibers were then twisted by hand. The hardest task was drilling almost twenty thousand holes through which the fiber would go to be tied around the giant ribs. It was backbreaking toil, and tempers often flared.

The men cut and planed the planks while the women made the cord. Women also sheared the goats and camels and, using the same techniques used in making tents, weaved the hair into long strips. These were then sewn together for sails.

Building the ship became a cooperative effort. Even the children helped. They gathered pitch from the forest and covered the entire outside of the ship to waterproof it. Finally the hull was done.

Nephi went into the forest himself to select a tall, straight-grained tree for the mast. It took all the men, using guy ropes, to insert the mast in the hull. Decks were then built around it, and soon bunks, rooms, and storage areas took shape. Rudder and tiller were fitted last.

After two years of building, the ship was done. It was a day of celebration. Lehi invited natives from the nearby villages to participate. The ship was well-built and solid. Even Laman and Lemuel, as they admired their work, humbly acknowledged the hand of the Lord. Lehi prepared a sacrifice and the women prepared a feast. They enjoyed wild greens and herbs from the hills, wild honey from hives they found in the rocks, freshly baked bread from the ovens, all kinds of fruit—grapes, figs, dates, raisins, pomegranates, bananas, coconuts. A huge tray of freshly cooked meat was served to the men in front of Lehi's tent. It was accompanied by hot bread covered with honey and butter. The men ate with their fingers, stuffing themselves until they could hold no more. They laughed and talked, leaning against their camel saddles in the light from the lamps. They had accomplished a great task. A sense of excitement gripped everyone. The ship was their means to get to the Land of Promise.

* * *

Nephi licked his fingers, then wiped them on linen a maidservant gave him. He was content. The Lord had really blessed them. For almost two years he and his brothers had worked together. It had truly been a lesson on what could be accomplished if only people would cooperate with one another—instead of working against each other. Oh, Nephi thought, if only it could continue.

Chapter 12

Irreantum

Stripped to the waist and glistening with sweat, Nephi stood on shore supervising the loading. Getting provisions together for a long voyage had been a formidable task. He was glad it was almost done. He looked now at the ship. It was big—ninety feet long from stem to stern with a wide, heavy hull. The beam, at its widest point, was twenty-four feet. Nephi was still amazed that they had been able to complete such a huge undertaking. Certainly it could never have been done without the Lord's help.

"Load those citrons carefully," he called to Sam, who, with Zoram, was carrying a wooden box filled with green citrus fruit. He watched as dried meat, fruit, boxes of raisins, goatskins of honey and wine, and boxes and boxes of coconuts were loaded on board. He shook his head, wondering where they would put everything. The ship was large, but he was still concerned as to how they could store all the provisions they might need on board and still be able to house all the people. He was glad that Lehi was on board to supervise the stowing of supplies.

Shouldering a skin of water, he walked up the ramp to see for himself what was happening. He stopped beside his father and silently watched the loading.

Although there were three levels in the ship, Nephi knew how cramped the people would be for a long voyage. The second deck was the primary living quarters for the people. Most of the supplies were being stored in the hold. In addition to work space for sailing the ship, the top deck had two small cabins; one for Lehi and Sariah, the other for Elizabeth and her maid.

Nephi was concerned. Confining people in a small space could mean trouble. His greatest fear was that a rebellion would break out and they would lose all the time and effort they had already put into this journey to the promised land. Since Laman and Lemuel had been humbled, there had been peace during the shipbuilding and gathering of supplies. In his heart, though, Nephi knew the peace was temporary. He had already gone through too many emotional upheavals with his brothers. He sighed thinking, The Lord will provide. He has brought us this far and will not let us down. Knowing Laman and Lemuel as he did, though, Nephi knew he would have to be very careful, that he would have to be sure people had time to exercise off their frustrations.

He watched as Laman, his black hair and beard shining in the sun, carried a box of coconuts on board. His muscles rippled as he walked up the gangplank. Nephi said to his father, "Oh, if only Laman were as strong spiritually as he is physically."

Lemuel trotted up the plank behind Laman carrying a small goatskin of wine. Nephi grinned. What a contrast between the brothers. Laman was physically strong and domineering. Lemuel was slight of build and easily led. His entire life had been spent following Laman. There were few times when they were not together. It seemed to Nephi that Laman enjoyed being the leader even if it were only Lemuel he was leading. Lemuel seemed content to be in Laman's shadow.

Sam led two goats up the ramp. These would be the only animals on board and would supply milk for the children. If necessary, they could also be killed for their meat. Miriam started up the ramp with some wild honey, smiling at him as she walked, almost missing her step on the plank. Nephi winked and smiled back at her. She dimpled and continued on. Oh, what a joy she is, he thought. So comely and pleasant to be with. Never a cross word. He knew the trials she had gone through in the wilderness and yet she never complained.

For hours people toiled up the plank, their arms filled, the hot sun beating down upon them, sweat soaking their shirts and tunics. Finally, the last skin of water was carried on board. Lehi appeared on the deck, and looked inquisitively at Nephi.

"Is that everything?" he shouted. Nephi nodded. "Good. I don't think I could have squeezed in another skin of wine or jar of honey."

Nephi shouted back good-naturedly, "I believe the boat is so heavy we won't even get it to float!"

Lehi flashed his teeth in a smile that was almost hidden in his gray beard. He stood on the edge of the deck, looking over this land they would soon be leaving. The years they had spent here had been fruitful. Mostly they had been a time of peace and cooperation. He cupped his hands to his mouth.

"Prepare to board the ship," he shouted. "We will load by age."

Nephi marked down the names as the people came on board. Lehi assigned spaces to each family. First came Elizabeth and her maid, leaning on each other for support. Sariah came next, holding onto Jacob and Joseph. Sam ran forward and helped his mother up the plank. Then all of the married children came forward:

Shazer, Esther, and their children, Ishmar, Vivian, Zippah, Ursula and Daniel.

Nahom, Annah, and their children, Tamna, Rebecca, Elizabeth and Seth.

Laman, Cleopha, and their children, Enoch, Delila, Noah, Saul and Lazor.

Lemuel, Marni, and their children, Josiah, Seth, Winona and Ukiah. Zoram, Eva, and their children, Bildah, Beth, Adamihah and Simon. Sam, Leah, and their children, David, Daniel, Joshua and Joel.

Miriam joined Nephi, and together they walked to the ship followed by their children, Jeremiah, Ruth, Nephihah and Naomi. Counting his family there were fifty people! How their small family had grown in the ten years since they had left Jerusalem!

The camel drivers and maids stood on the beach watching the proceedings. Lehi and Nephi walked back off the ship. Lehi strode up to the camel drivers, clasping forearms with each of them. From his robe he pulled out a piece of parchment. "I have written out a bill of sale," he began, "which gives you possession of our camels. There are twenty-two camels. Shemin will see that they are divided fairly among you." He paused, his emotions high. "You have all been very faithful, suffering with us as we crossed the great desert, living with us and actually being a part of our family. It is hard to say goodbye, but so it must be. May the Lord bless you."

Nephi pulled Shemin forward with him. "My friend, will you remove the block when we are ready to leave?" Shemin nodded, too choked up to speak. Nephi swallowed, holding back his own tears, and whispered huskily, "Thank you for being such a loyal friend." Arm in arm they walked to the ship.

By Nephi's calculations, it was the second week of November. He looked up and studied the rigging. The ship almost cast a spell over him. With God's help they had put together a craft of wood and bronze and rope which would be propelled by wings of goats' hair fabric. It was poised on the beach ready to surge forth. "What adventures await us?" he mused aloud.

He called to the men to hoist the sails. The inexperienced men ran forward to carry out his commands. The raised sails caught the wind. Nephi signaled Shemin, who took his large wooden mallet and knocked out the block that held the ship. With a lurch the ship surged forward almost throwing Nephi to the deck. The goats' hair topsails filled and the mainsail billowed in the breeze. The sun sparkled on the gentle waves of Irreantum, the wind shifted to the eastward, and they were on their way.

Lehi had named the ship "Miriam," over the protests of Laman and Lemuel. It was named after Miriam, the sister of Moses who had been such a help and support to Moses during the Exodus. Lehi said, "We are on our own exodus and this ship will support us on our journey." He recalled the song of Miriam, "I will sing to the Lord, for He has triumphed gloriously; . . ." She had sung her song after their safe crossing of the Red Sea. "We will sing the same song when we have safely crossed Irreantum."

The first part of the voyage went smoothly as the *Miriam* ran across the fairly calm water. Nights were pleasant for Nephi, and often, after getting the children to sleep, he and Miriam stood silently at the rail in the warm darkness, watching the mastheads circling the stars above them. It was a peaceful and wonderful time in their lives.

The *Miriam* ran steadily southeast, picking up the monsoon winds, logging about eighty miles a day. Life aboard ship settled into a daily routine. Morning prayer was led by Lehi, followed by breakfast of bread and dates. The *Liahona* guided them and they trusted completely in the Lord. The ship handled well, seeming to sense her way through the sea. The people chatted, tended children, sang, dozed on deck, and rigged fishing lines in the wake. Twin balconies hung over the sides of the ship for lavatories. On hot nights people took showers on the balconies, dipping up water from the sea.

After a month at sea an island loomed ahead of them. It looked like paradise with its dazzling white beaches and dark green forests. They beached the Miriam and went ashore, glorying in the feel of land under their feet. It was a good time to replenish their fresh water supplies. Nephi and Ishmar went into the forest, returning in several hours with two freshly killed boar. More fruit was gathered, and they were ready to resume their journey.

As they headed south through the Strait of Malacca, the evenings grew longer and the mornings misty. The sky was still blue and the sun hot, but the sea now was gray and running high. Then the blue sky turned to gray and the first rain they had known for weeks wetted the decks. The flurry of rain increased on the decks. The wind began rising and swooping more violently than usual and the ship heeled sharply. She started laboring under her sails. Nephi called for the men to slack off the mainsail. The squall struck like a slap, staggering the ship and swinging her broadside to the wind. She plunged heavily into a trough between giant waves. There was a crash below as women and children were thrown from their bunks. She rose again, still laboring, the water creaming under her bows. As she plunged into the waves, water poured over the deck, the wind whipped spray around them. On deck, Nephi and Sam braced themselves against the ship's heart-stopping angle. Sam leaned on the tiller, pulling it hard over.

The bow swung slowly back into the wind, the ship straightened, and once more surged forward. The storm ended as quickly as it had begun. An hour later the ship was back on course with the rigging again tracing an elegant pattern against the sky.

Several months went by. They sailed past several islands, but only stopped when low on water or fresh food. Two days out from their last stop, the *Miriam* reached the limit of the southeast trade winds. The sails draped limply from the rigging. They were becalmed.

For a week they sweltered in the middle of nowhere, ocean on every side as far as sight could reach. The men finally rigged fishing lines and dropped them overboard. Soon half-a-dozen fat fish flopped in a basket on the deck. As soon as people started hooking fish, a score of sharks gathered around the boat, their fins cleanly cutting the water as they circled the ship. Laman cut a fish, baited a large hook and threw it over the side. He stepped to the rail with a heavy line coiled in his hand. A small striped fish flashed this way and that about the bait, followed by a huge fish—just an ugly, yellowish blotch in the blue water. It rose under the bait, turned over on its side, and gulped it down.

Laman had hooked a shark! The rope sailed from his hand. Lemuel and Shazer jumped forward to help hold it. They were wringing with sweat when they were finally able to bring the huge, thrashing fish on board. It flailed around on the deck like a demented monster, snapping at anything within reach of its jaws. Nephi stepped forward with an adz to kill it, but Laman grabbed the tool from his hand.

He growled, "This is my fish. Keep away from it." He stepped forward, waiting for just the right moment, then struck with the adz. The shark was dead.

All afternoon they worked on it, cutting it in narrow strips, then salting the strips and laying them out to dry in the sun. Laman, who had never been the hunter that Nephi was, gloated. He had brought in the most meat of the entire voyage.

That night Laman and his group celebrated. They brought skins of now very potent wine from the hold. They drank and danced and sang. Nephi and Lehi were worried. Hoping to keep peace on board ship, they had been careful not to upset Laman or his supporters. They stood back now, watching warily. Soon the drunken voices of the men boomed out, shouting rude sayings and obscenities, cursing God and taking credit for being where they were.

Nephi could take it no longer. Drunkenness was bad enough, but blasphemy was not acceptable. He stepped up on the cabin and shouted to the ribald mob.

"Stop it. Do you realize what you are doing? The Lord has brought us here by His power. If you continue He will be angry with us and smite us. I for one do not desire to be swallowed up in the depths of the sea." An angry murmur rose from Laman's group. Nephi ignored it. "Why do you tempt the Lord? He has guided us and protected us for over ten years. Would you destroy all of that in a moment of indulgence?"

Laman swaggered forward. "You have attempted to be a ruler over us for the last time. From now on I am commanding this ship." A roar of support went up from his followers. "Seize him," Laman yelled. Before Nephi could move, he was pinned against the cabin. Lehi stepped forward to intercede but was rudely shoved backward. Nephi's hands were cruelly yanked behind him and rough ropes were wrapped tightly around his arms and wrists. Over the shouted protests of Lehi and the sobs of Miriam, he was dragged to the mast and trussed up against it. Lehi pleaded with the miscreants to let Nephi go, but to no avail. Miriam, holding little Naomi in her arms, stepped up to Laman, her eyes flashing fire. The blood had left her face but she bravely told Laman, "You let my husband loose. You cannot treat him like this."

Laman laughed and pushed her back toward the hold. "I'll treat him any way I please," he said, "and what do you think you can do about it?"

Nephi strained at the ropes, but they would not budge. Even his prayers weren't answered this time. He was helpless.

The party on deck continued most of the night. When morning came, the face of the sea sparkled in bright sunshine. Laman and his followers were sprawled all over the deck. Sam, knife in hand, tried to get to Nephi to cut his ropes. Laman rose behind him, spun him around, and knocked the knife from his hand.

"You touch those ropes and I'll throw you overboard, stupid little brother." The look in his eye was a dare to Sam to attempt anything.

Nephi called, "Be careful, Sam. He means it. Stay with Mother and Father. They will need your help."

Laman stepped in front of Nephi and slapped him hard across the face, bringing blood to his lips. "You talk only when I tell you you can talk," he said gruffly.

As he said this, a noisy flapping came from above. The sails were filling with wind. The doldrums were over. Laman hustled aft. He assigned Lemuel to handle the tiller and soon the ship was once again cutting cleanly through the water.

Laman sent Shazer for Lehi. Lehi came forward, bent and stooped with age, sick at heart over what his older sons were doing. He kept his eyes on the deck, refusing to look at his wayward son. "Father," Laman said gruffly, knowing that he was in disfavor. "I can't get this stupid compass to work. The needles just keep spinning around in circles. What do I do now?"

Lehi, his eyes filled with anguish, looked at Laman. "My son," he whispered, "the compass only works when we are keeping the Lord's commandments. You have broken the commandments, tied up your brother, dishonored your father, and yet you expect it to work?" Shaking his head sorrowfully, he turned and shuffled off.

Laman belligerently said, to no one in particular, "It doesn't matter. We'll sail this ship without a compass." Then he scratched his head in puzzlement. He wished that he felt that confident. There was no sign of anything but ocean in any direction, horizon to horizon. He looked at the sun. He wasn't sure what time of day it was, but felt it must be nearly noon. He shrugged his shoulders and shouted at Lemuel, "Steer that way," and he pointed off to the right. Lemuel obediently turned the tiller and the ship started circling to the new course.

Nephi's legs burned. The cords that bound him cut so deeply that little blood reached his arms or legs. For two days he had been tied to the ship's mast, unable even to move his feet. His arms were wrapped behind the rough-hewn pole and he was trussed from head to toe. His legs concerned him most. They had been numb for the past day. He had no feeling at all in them. Even though he was exhausted, he had been unable to sleep. He couldn't remember ever being so weary. He sagged against the ropes, not having strength to hold himself erect. As he drooped there, his mind wandered. He thought of all the events which had taken place since they had left Jerusalem.

He was brought back to the present by the touch of soft, cool hands on his fevered forehead. Opening his eyes, he saw his beloved wife before him. His dry lips formed her name, "Miriam," but no sound came. She embraced him, wetting his face with her tears as she leaned close against him. She placed a gourd of water to his lips. When his thirst was eased he murmured, "Thanks, my dear. I love you."

"Oh, Nephi," she sobbed, "what can we do? Your parents and my mother are sick in their beds because of their grief over the wickedness of Laman and Lemuel. I'm afraid they are going to die. Jacob and Joseph are also sick, sorrowing over their mother." She looked pleadingly at him. "Can't you call down fire from heaven, or something?"

He smiled through his cracked lips. "My dear, I appreciate your faith in my powers, but I really have none. It is only the Lord who can do such things."

"But why is He allowing this to happen?" she asked.

"He is letting this happen so He might show His power unto the fulfilling of His word which He has spoken concerning the wicked." He saw her puzzled look. "It is necessary that people have freedom to act for themselves, to condemn themselves or raise themselves up. It is Laman's and Lemuel's decision to choose wickedness over righteousness."

He so wished that he could just put his arms around his wife and comfort her. "Dear Miriam, do not grieve. I am constantly praising the Lord for His goodness. It is necessary for us to have our faith tried. Please have faith and expect a miracle. He will take care of us as He has done in the past."

He could tell that she wasn't convinced. He thought to himself, That's probably the hardest principle of faith for people to live. It is difficult for us to have the faith to see the future as we desire it, when we are so concerned about what is happening in the present. Aloud he said to Miriam, "My darling, in all of our history I have never seen a great person who quit when he was beaten. We cannot get discouraged. The Lord will take care of us in his own time." He paused in thought, searching for an example. "Remember Bountiful?"

She nodded.

"Picture yourself as being in such a lovely place again. See our family as if we had already arrived in the Land of Promise. Keep that picture in your mind and don't think about the present. If you can see that it will make it easier." Then he added, "That's really what faith is—just seeing yourself as having already arrived at your destination."

Miriam tried to be cheerful. She chatted briefly about the children and what they were doing. She told how Jeremiah had gone to Laman and pleaded for Nephi's release, and how Laman had just laughed at him. Nephi's eyes misted as he thought of his brave little son. Miriam fed him honey-water and cheese, and then left.

Just before dawn of the third day of Nephi's bondage, there was a groaning in the rigging. Nephi felt the uneasiness of the ship. He waited, feeling as though stricken by a blind man's helplessness—not able to act. Lightning quivered faintly as if flashed in a dark cave. The sea, which had been calm and mysterious in the half-light of morning, suddenly changed, becoming black with foaming crests. The ship began to rear and plunge through the growing swells. From behind the ship an awesome array of storm clouds rolled and churned like smoke from a great fire. Nahom and Shazer, on watch, were taken aback by the suddenness of the storm. They rushed around the deck working to secure all openings.

The storm exploded around the ship like the sudden smashing of a pot of wrath. It was if they were caught by a flash flood in a wadi. There was an overpowering concussion and a rush of great waters. As the mast swayed, Nephi swayed with it, feeling it strain in the gale. He hoped that Miriam and the children were all right. The door to below decks was closed, and no sound could be heard.

* * *

Laman must have been asleep. What was that loud noise? Wind? A whistling could be heard from outside. Straddling his legs to keep his balance, but still staggering, he forced his way to the door. He attempted to open it and the wind caught it. Clinging to the handle, he was dragged out over the doorstep, and at once seemed engaged in a struggle with the wind to see who had control of the door. A current of air scurried in and licked out the flame of the lamp. A confused clamor filled his ears. It was tumultous and loud— made up of the rush of wind, the crashing of the sea, the prolonged deep vibration of the air like the roll of an immense and remote drum.

Ahead of the ship was darkness, punctuated by white flashes. Suddenly he was afraid. Should he untie Nephi? He strained his eyes to see the mast with Nephi still tied to it. *No!* He would not release him. He, Laman, was the leader now. A plunge of the sea ended in shock as if the ship had hit something solid and a lofty flight of spray drove hard into his face. With all his strength he pulled the door shut. He stood there panting. Lemuel came up behind him and his frightened voice came out of the darkness, "Are we going to sink? Should we release Nephi?"

"No to both of your questions," he gruffly replied, hoping he sounded sure of himself.

He carefully moved back to his bunk, falling heavily in the dark. Cleopha whispered, "Laman, I'm afraid. What will happen to us?"

Another voice came out of the darkness, "Oh, if only we had light. I am going mad."

Marni added, "I can't even see my own baby. It's terrible lying here just waiting for the ship to sink."

The quiet voice of Miriam penetrated the din. "Why didn't you think ahead of the consequences when you tied up my husband? At least you are safe and dry down here while he has probably drowned."

"Enough of that!" Laman shouted crossly. "Nephi deserves to be tied up and if he has been swept off, so much the better."

His tirade was greeted by silence. As the ship pitched and tossed, the people held onto whatever they could to prepare themselves for the worst. Several expressed concern about how their aged parents were doing up in the main deck cabins.

* * *

The storm raged all day and into the night without letup. The sails had been blown to shreds and the ship floundered through the sea. Nephi was alone on the deck, caught in the middle of the maelstrom. He had never seen such violence or such fury. The elements seemed determined to destroy everything. The sea foamed and broke around him, but he had a feeling of peace. He knew the Lord would protect him. He squeezed his eyes tightly against the saltwater. When he ventured to open them, it was as if they were still shut—it was so black—except for the intensity of the lightning. In one of those flashes he had seen Laman poke his head up. Nephi hoped Laman would keep everyone below decks until the storm was over. It was too dangerous on deck. An alarming tearing sound ran the full length of the ship. With a thunderous crack the mast broke away just above his head and fell into the sea.

In the crackling flash of lightning, Nephi saw the black figures of Laman and Lemuel, faces framed as if petrified. Darkness again settled over the ship. In another flash he saw the head of a huge wave rearing over the ship. The wave toppled over, adding the might of its crash to the already tremendous uproar raging around him. He had lost sight of his brothers.

* * *

Laman had heard the mast go and knew that he had to do something. The weight of leadership was heavy on his shoulders. He hesitated, unsure of himself. Finally he called, "Lemuel."

A timid voice came out of the darkness behind him. "What?"

Feigning bravery, Laman called over his shoulder, "We need to check out the ship."

He barely managed to close the door before the gigantic wave hit them. It tore away his grip and after a crushing thump on his back he found himself struggling for breath and borne upward in the water. He knew he must have been swept overboard. As he was being tossed, flung, and rolled in great volumes of water, he kept praying. "Oh, God of my fathers, save me, save me. God of my fathers, save me. I will turn Nephi loose. Have mercy on me. . . ." He threshed around with his arms and legs, finally encountering something solid. He clawed ferociously at it, lost it, found it again, lost it once more and finally was himself caught in the clasp of a pair of arms. He returned the embrace and found his arms around a lean body . . . it was Lemuel.

He held tightly to Lemuel as the water let them down with a brutal bang against the upper cabin, bruised and with the breath knocked out of them. Very frightened, he held on while waves poured over him as if trying to pull him from his hold. He breathed in gasps, choking on the salt water he swallowed.

The ship's motion was savage. Her lurches had an appalling helplessness. She pitched into the void, seeming to find a wall to hit every time. When she rolled she was brought back upright by such a demolishing blow that Laman felt the ship reeling. Then she would tumble again as if dropped back into a boiling caldron. The sea, flattened in the heavier gusts, would rise and engulf both ends of the ship in snowy rushes of foam, rising and sinking, rolling continuously.

Laman felt helpless. "She's done for," he shouted to Lemuel. Nothing could stop its destruction now. The ship could not last. To have suffered and almost die on the desert, and now to die in the middle of the ocean . . .!

* * *

Inside the ship it was cold, black and dismal. Men, women and children hung on to each other and to anything solid, attempting to keep from flying across the hold. Almost everyone was seasick and the sour stench was overpowering. Every roll and toss of the ship brought more groaning and screams from the people trapped inside, adding even more to Nephi's misery and frustration. He strained against the ropes, but the water had stiffened them around him. He was helpless to act. The only thing he could do was continue to pray. In his misery he had lost track of time. How many days had he been tied to the mast?

* * *

Laman and Lemuel clung tightly together, hoping to wait out the storm. Laman's arms were weary from clinging to the stanchion and Lemuel. But, instead of letting up, the storm seemed to be increasing in intensity. The wind had thrown its weight on the ship, trying to pin her down among the seas. Breakers flung themselves onto the ship and when a grey dawn finally came there was no relief—only a ghostly light as the sea continued to crest over the ship which could not shake itself clear of the water, but began to jerk and plunge as if berserk.

Lemuel knew the ship was floundering. He whined, "Laman, let's let Nephi go. The judgment of God is upon us."

A mighty column of water rose above them, then fell with a mighty crash, burying them, filling their ears, mouths, and nostrils, suffocating them in its rush. After wrenching their arms, it seethed away swiftly. All that was left were piled-up masses of foam dashing against what looked like the fragments of the ship.

The great physical tumult beating about their bodies finally broke even Laman's determination, bringing a profound trouble to his soul. Above the steady roar of the hurricane, he shouted to Lemuel, "You are right. The Lord is punishing us for our iniquities. Let us release Nephi."

When a lull came they lurched to the mast where Nephi had been captive for so long. Laman sawed through the ropes and Nephi fell flat to the deck. He moaned in anguish as the blood rushed back to his swollen limbs. He felt himself slowly sinking into the relief of unconsciousness. His clothes, full of water, were heavy on him, cold and dripping like a slow spring from a rock. Shivering, he shook himself back to wakefulness. He dragged himself back to the mast and held on, massaging his feet with his free hand, attempting to get some feeling back into his tingling and useless limbs. The howls and shrieks of the gale seemed to take on something of human rage and pain.

He could not use his legs, but struggled on his stomach toward where the tiller had been. It had been swept away. Twice he banged his head, but even though dazed he continued. His mind concentrated on one task. He must get to the *Liahona*. Through the *Liahona* the Lord would work His miracles and stop the storm. Slowly he inched himself along until he was at the box. He was glad that they had been given the vision to enclose the compass so it would be protected against such a storm as this.

He opened the box and pulled forth the compass. In his hands it was working! He lay there by the box, one arm around the rail, and prayed a prayer of thanksgiving to his Father. Fervently he prayed for the storm to cease. Even as he prayed, the winds began to abate. As the winds slowed, the waves gradually shrank back to their normal size. Within a short time the storm was over.

Laman and Lemuel, open-mouthed at such a miracle, could only gape at their brother.

Still weak and sore, Nephi crawled to the door and threw it open. A gasp came from inside as he was recognized in the light. He wearily motioned with his hand, then pulled himself out of the way as the families trooped onto the deck. Everyone was miserably wet, but now Nephi was at least able to walk. After a quick embrace of Miriam and his children, he stumbled over to the deck cabins. He was distraught at the condition of his parents—lying on their sodden and stinking pallets, soaked with sea water, hugging each other for what warmth they could get. He carried his frail mother out onto the deck while Sam helped Lehi to a spot next to her. There were no dry blankets or clothing on the entire ship. They would just have to sit in the sun until they dried off and warmed. Annah and Esther dutifully sat beside their parents, massaging their cold bodies.

Leah and Miriam had hurried to their mother's cabin. The maid, sitting in one corner of the cabin—wet, wide-eyed and silent—was in shock. Miriam knelt beside her mother. She looked up in panic at Leah, then put her ear to Elizabeth's chest. She raised up, dry-eyed. "She's dead."

A howl of anguish rose from Leah's lips. Shazer and Nahom came running. "What is it?"

Miriam looked at them accusingly. "Our mother is dead." The other sisters pushed into the tiny, crowded cabin. Miriam brushed past them without speaking, walked over to Nephi, and resignedly sat beside him. He looked at her, a question in his eyes.

It was moments before she could speak. Then looking at her hands in her lap, she said, "Mother is dead."

Nephi reached over and pulled Miriam's head onto his shoulder, clasping her tightly to him. He knew how she had loved her mother. He hoped that she would cry and let the hurt out of her system, but she didn't. Her feelings of hurt and resentment were too intermingled with her grief.

* * *

Elizabeth's body was sewn into shreds of what was left of the sail. Lehi was still too weak and too sick to conduct the short funeral so Nephi took charge. He praised Elizabeth for her faithfulness to God; for her courage in standing up for what she thought was right; for her uncomplaining attitude during their afflictions in the desert. He told the group, "The Lord expects us to be patient in affliction, not complaining about our problems or discomforts." After the funeral, they laid her body to rest in the vast ocean.

The sun was glorious in the sky, shedding warmth and light upon the bedraggled and hapless assemblage. Everyone was quiet, thinking their own thoughts. Laman and Lemuel had not uttered a word since the calming of the storm. Now they sat isolated from the group. It was not a happy time for anyone. But there were still things that needed to be done.

Nephi stood and motioned for the men to join him on the aft deck. When everyone was there, he spoke. "I am holding no grudges for what has happened. What was done was done. I forgive you, but it is up to you to put yourself in tune with the Lord so He can forgive you.

"Right now it is important that we assess our situation. We are drifting in the middle of Irreantum. We don't know where we are, we have no sails, no tiller, and no mast. We can be thankful that with the exception of our parents, no one is seriously injured, although I've noticed that several are badly bruised."

Ishmar spoke up. "There's more," he said. "I was just down in the hold to get some supplies. We are leaking badly. The seams were tight when we left Bountiful, but not now."

Nephi grimly acknowledged Ishmar's report. "Then it is even more imperative that we find land soon." He looked around at the group. "We have several choices. We can just drift and hope that we find land before our supplies run out or we sink, or we can put our total faith in the Lord and ask him to help us." He looked around at the group of men. He knew he could count on Sam and Zoram. Ishmar would probably be cooperative. The only unknowns were Laman, Lemuel, Shazer and Nahom. He looked at them pointedly, awaiting their reaction. Laman was the leader of that faction. Even though he had made some mistakes, Nephi was sure that there was much good in him. As he fixed a steady gaze upon him, Laman uncomfortably shifted from one foot to another.

Finally Laman cleared his throat. In a gruff but contrite voice he said, "It's my fault that we are in the predicament we are in." He swallowed self-consciously. "I say we follow Nephi and the Lord." The other men nodded their agreement. Nephi's heart sang at Laman's repentance. If only that repentance would last!

They rejoined the women and children. After carefully explaining their predicament, Nephi commented, "The trial of faith we have just gone through should convince us all that we cannot succeed by relying on the arm of flesh. The Lord has said that 'After much tribulation come the blessings.' My dear family, the time has come when we have to be united in our prayers. The Lord wants to bless us, but we must ask for those blessings. The Lord is much more anxious to help us than we are to be helped."

"But why doesn't the Lord just bless us with what we need, without us having to ask?" Nahom asked.

Nephi patiently explained. "The Lord wants us to have the blessings. We are His children and He loves us, but our asking for the blessings is a manifestation of our faith in Him."

Lemuel, in a teachable mood, asked, "How do we go about asking? What do we do now?"

"First, we have to go to the Lord in earnest prayer," Nephi responded. "We also have to be conscientious in following his commandments. It is important that we make commitments to Him as to what we are willing to do." He turned to the group. "Are all of you ready to unite in prayer?"

Everyone nodded in agreement. Nephi turned to Lehi. "Father," he said, "are you well enough to lead us?"

Lehi nodded. When everyone was kneeling on the deck, he began. "God of our fathers, . . ." Nephi listened carefully as the great patriarch petitioned the Lord. Lehi's faith was complete. He asked the Lord for a current to carry them to where they could repair the ship; he asked that their lives be preserved; and then he asked that they be carried safely to the promised land. When he had finished the prayer, everyone remained kneeling for a few moments, adding their personal and private prayers of faith.

Knowing that faith must be accompanied by action, Nephi organized people. Some he sent to the hold with buckets to bail out the water; some took rags and rope to calk the leaky seams; others were assigned to clean up the mess from the storm. Aware of Laman's desire for leadership, Nephi asked him if he would form a crew to tear down the deck cabins and use the materials from them to build a new tiller. By day's end things were again starting to look shipshape on board the *Miriam*. She was still without mast or sails, but at least they could steer her.

Nephi continued his prayer that the Lord would guide them to the nearest land. As he looked at the sea streaming past, he knew they were now moving faster. They had caught an ocean current. The *Liahona* continued to point in the direction they were drifting. The Lord was answering their prayers. All day and all night they drifted, but there was no longer a feeling of hopelessness among the people.

Before it was light, Nephi relieved Sam at the tiller. The stars paled in preparation for the dawn and the rosy light grew stronger in the east. The velvet of the heavens faded and turned blue, then the sun, still below the horizon, began to tint the little scattered clouds with changing shades of pink and violet. It was as if the Lord were responding to their prayers by saying, "All is right, Nephi. This is a new day."

Miriam had quietly come up beside him. "What a glorious sunrise," she whispered.

Nephi turned to her. "Yes. To me every sunrise is a promise that the Lord still loves us."

She bent her head. "Do you hear that sound?"

Nephi listened. He had not heard it before, but now he could hear a pounding. "It sounds like breakers." He strained to see, and there it was. Over to their right, but still at some distance, he saw a volcanic island, its mountains clothed in tropical foliage. The noise they heard was the sea breaking on a coral reef which was much closer to them. Behind the reef was a calm lagoon. Nephi could now make out the belt of flat beach, glistening white in the early light.

"Could this be the promised land?" Miriam asked.

As Nephi looked at the vivid emerald of tropical vegetation covering the mountains, the rich foliage, steep green cliffs rising above the white line of breakers, he hoped that perhaps it was. But the spirit whispered to him, "No, my son."

Holding Miriam close, he said, "No. It is not the promised land, but it is a place where we can fix the ship." He stepped to the door and called below. "We see land! Come help!"

Excited and anxious people piled through the door and lined the rail to look at the beautiful island. Now the only problem was how to get the ship through the breakers. Laman stood beside him on the deck. He pointed, "There's an opening in the reef to the left."

As every one watched, the *Miriam* drifted helplessly toward the reef.

"It'll be close," Nephi said. "Laman, keep the tiller all the way to the left." Closer and closer the ship approached the reef, but the gentle current it rode seemed to carry it right through the opening. Calmness of water inside the reef came as a real relief for the passengers, but it spelled trouble for the ship. A faint breeze ruffled Nephi's hair, then stronger gusts brushed his cheeks. They were moving again. Small waves raised by wind carried them toward the beach. Laman, followed by men whose names he called, jumped onto the beach. With ropes they pulled the ship until it rested solidly on sand.

The island provided the voyagers a pleasant respite from the sea. With their tents erected on the beach, they set about replenishing their supplies and repairing the ship. The lagoon was a veritable marketplace. The women were able to gather shellfish and crabs. Near the beach they found a hollow tree filled with honey. Myriads of sea birds nesting on rocks were easy to catch. Albatross were so tame that the men were able to walk among their nests to gather eggs while the big birds responded with grave bows. Breezes blowing faintly from the highlands brought a heavenly scent of strange flowers; even the ground smelled good to the sea-weary travelers.

While men chopped down a tree for the mast, the women were busy stitching together the torn sails, patching them with clothing and blankets. When they were done, the sails looked like patchwork quilts—but they would hold the wind.

After a month on the island, they were finished. The new mast, its yellow wood contrasting with the old timbers, stood straight and tall above the ship. Repaired sails were laid out ready to raise.

Several were so content with the island that they had no desire to get back aboard ship. However, Nephi received word through the spirit: *"Nephi, I am ready to lead you to the Land of Promise."*

Amid grumbling of several couples, the *Miriam* was once more loaded and prepared for the sea. Even Nephi had regrets about leaving the island. It had been a refuge of peace and safety for them.

Two days were required to shovel sand away from the hull and push the ship into the lagoon where it once again floated free. With careful maneuvering they got the ship through the breakers. Sails billowed and filled and they were on their way. The compass pointed due east and the wind blew them forward on a straight course.

Breeze in the rigging ropes played a harmony of a thousand high-pitched tones and overtones, heard in every part of othe ship. That, with a slow creaking of the ship's timbers, created a joyous serenade—a song of happiness and peace. The wind had not failed when Ishmar, standing on the masthead, caught sight of a mountaintop as light faded in the western sky.

He cried, "Land!"

Everyone rushed to the decks. Straight ahead outlines of a mighty mountain rose from the sea, pale blue and ghostly in the evening light. The people gazed with awe and wonder. As they approached more closely they saw a whole range of mountains, rising majestically with wooded peaks and spires. As they drew nearer they could see waterfalls, looking like threads of burnished silver, plummeting down mountainsides.

An enormous bay lay before them, and that night the *Miriam* dropped anchor a hundred feet offshore of the promised land. This was the last night the travelers would spend aboard ship, and many, unable to sleep, stood on deck and chatted through the night.

In morning light they again observed the mountains. They saw a long mountain range—a chain of old volcanoes truncated and weathered down by the passage of time. The upper part of the mountains was a warm gray. A solid belt of green clothed their base, unbroken save where lesser volcanoes jutted out. With the gentle breeze still pushing, the boat ran softly aground on a beach of golden sand.

Chapter 13

The Land of Promise

Shaking his head in his anguish, Lehi turned from his tent and strode to a nearby mahogany tree. He leaned against the rough bole, his shoulders rising and falling with his breathing as he worked to control his emotion. It was hard for him to accept the fact that his wife of thirty-seven years was dead even though, for months, he had watched Sariah's health deteriorate. She had never recovered from her illness brought on by the great storm on the ship when Nephi had been lashed to the mast and Elizabeth had died. Since that time Elizabeth's maid, Ephreda, had taken care of Sariah in her illness and had been a good companion for her.

Nephi walked up and placed his hands on his father's shoulders. Lehi, dry-eyed, turned to him. "She's gone," he whispered hoarsely.

Nephi had no words of comfort to give. His mother's death was a great blow to him, too. He merely squeezed his father's shoulders, then pulled him close. Nephi thought it was natural for Lehi to seek comfort from the tree. Nephi remembered that Lehi had told him "a tree has its roots in the ground while it has its head in the sky." Lehi had added, "When you're lonely and sad, put your back against a tree. It can give you amazing strength."

"She was a good woman," Lehi commented lamely, his eyes focused on some distant object over Nephi's shoulder.

"Yes, Father. We will miss her greatly."

Lehi sighed. After a few moments he said, "I'm worried about Sam. He and his mother were so close." He closed his eyes and shook his head sadly.

Nephi thought to himself, "That's just like Father. Even in a time of great personal sadness he is concerned about others." Many other thoughts flew through his mind as he stood there by his mourning father.

A year had gone by since they had arrived in the Land of Promise. Most of the people were still living in tents, but several families had built makeshift homes of willows and mud. The settlement was beginning to look like a regular village. The ground was very fertile, and during the rainy season there had been plenty of water. The first crops, planted soon after landing, had been harvested. New green shoots from the second crop were peeking out of the rich brown earth with promise of another bountiful harvest. Crops seemed to grow without much effort, but it was now the dry season and men, women and children carried water to irrigate the young plants.

Nephi, Ishmar, and Sam had gone often into the forest to hunt. They had been surprised at the abundance and diversity of wildlife. Birds filled the forests. Robins, grackles, wrens and crows resembled those in the land of Jerusalem but here also were birds—red, orange, flashing blue—birds with such brilliant plumage they scarcely seemed real.

Wild pigs and deer were plentiful. Several animals they saw resembled domesticated animals of the old world so closely that the new colonists caught and tamed them. A few, like the tapir and wild cats—the jaguar, ocelot, and puma—were unlike any animals in their old homeland. Swamps were infested with alligators and caymans.

The land itself was a land of great contrasts. They had built their village on a flat, grassy plain not far from the beach where they had landed. Lowlands were predominantly grasslands. Bordering the grassland was a thick, dense forest. Beyond the forest, jagged mountains rose into the sky like giant canine teeth forming a natural barrier to the east. There were no harbors, and behind the beaches were wet lagoons choked with mangrove trees. The coastal plain was wide here. Volcanic alluvial soil was fertile and easy to cultivate even with their primitive tools.

For the first time since leaving their homes in Jerusalem, obtaining food wasn't a problem. Daily tides brought in a plentiful harvest of lobsters, sea urchins and barnacles. There was a profusion of easy-to-dig clams along the beaches. Other shellfish and fish were abundant. Rookeries along the coast provided fresh birds' eggs and fresh meat.

Now Laman and Lemuel and the sons of Ishmael and their families no longer had to depend on Nephi for their food. Daily they became more distant to him and the rest of the family. It was almost as if there were two settlements instead of just one. Nephi was grateful for the continued friendship of his cousin, Ishmar. Soon after their arrival in the promised land, Ishmar had married Tamna, daughter of Annah and Nahom. Since there were no more tents, Nephi helped him to build a willow and mud home for his new family. They had woven the eelgrass, which washed up on the beaches in great masses, through the willows to make a solid wall. For bedding they used dry seaweed.

Nephi really enjoyed his own family. He adored Miriam, and now she was expecting their fifth child. Jeremiah, who was almost seven, was old enough to accompany his father on hunting trips into the jungle. Nephi had been teaching him how to shoot a bow. Often they would go to the beach together to spear fish in the shallow water. Ruth, though still quite young, helped her mother with cooking and tending the younger children. Little Nephihah and Naomi just seemed to be into everything.

Theirs had been a pleasant life so far in the promised land, except for Sariah's illness and the bad attitudes of Laman and Lemuel.

Now Sariah was gone. Nephi's thoughts returned abruptly to the present. His hand was still on Lehi's shoulder, and he gently patted his back. He wished he could express more eloquently how much he loved his father.

He knew how lonely his father would now be. Lehi's life had revolved around his wife and family. For as long as Nephi could remember, Lehi had turned to him to discuss important matters. He was now twenty-six, born when Lehi was thirty. That would mean Lehi was fifty-six. His mother was six years younger so she was fifty at the time of her death.

He closed his eyes, picturing the many wonderful experiences he had enjoyed with his mother. They had been very close. He was glad that his children also had the opportunity to be close to their grandparents. That was very important to Nephi. People needed the foundation a family heritage could give them. Without such a heritage, life lacked permanence and became shallow.

"Father," he said.

Lehi looked up.

"With mother gone, Miriam and I want you to move into our tent. Jacob is Jeremiah's age and he can hunt and fish with us. Joseph can help Ruth and Nephihah with the household chores."

Lehi looked at him for a moment then he shook his head. "No. We will continue to live in our own tent. Ephreda can cook my meals and take care of Jacob and Joseph." He paused, then shook his head again as if to clear it. "No. It would not work out." He gently shook off Nephi's hand, and returned to his tent to supervise funeral and burial arrangements for his mate.

After Sariah's funeral, Lehi retreated more and more from active participation in leadership of the community. He spent his time working on his writings, which left the responsibility of leading the settlement almost entirely on Nephi's shoulders. Relationships continued to deteriorate and sometimes Nephi felt as if he were walking on eggs, trying to lead the people without upsetting his older brothers. He prayed for guidance, prayed that things would work out between him and his brothers.

Soon after they landed, a violent storm had dashed their ship against the shore, pounding it until it fell apart. Nephi had wanted to use it to explore up and down the coast but since he could not he spent more and more time in the forest, using the excuse that fresh meat was needed to feed the growing settlement. It was really his escape from tension that seemed always present in the village. Besides, there was much to explore in this new land. Jeremiah went hunting with him in the region close to the village. They also enjoyed walking the beaches, seeing what had washed up during the night. During shrimp spawning season they built a willow fence across an estuary and trapped hundreds of shrimp on the outgoing tide.

Often they would find tell-tale tracks of a huge turtle returning to the sea, and by backtracking they would find where she had laid her eggs. Turtle eggs were a real delicacy. They also hunted turtles which fed in shallow waters of the lagoons. Turtle meat was delicious, the bones were used for tools, and the large shells made excellent storage vessels for seeds and corn.

When he hunted alone, Nephi would sometimes be gone for a week at a time as he explored further and further into the mountains. Miriam had been very tolerant of his need to get away, but as the time drew closer for her delivery, she took a firmer stand, pleading with him to spend more time at home.

One day he had come home without meat, but very pleased with himself. In the mountains where he had been exploring he had found marvelous deposits of ore—gold, silver, and copper. Now they could make new tools and weapons. He went to Lehi's tent to share the good news.

Lehi continued carving on a turtle flipper he was making into a sandal. He sat in thought, pushing his lips in and out through his beard as he worked. Finally, he spoke. "My son, I feel that it is best at this time that you not tell anyone of your discovery. Such ore could be turned into tools to make our lives easier, but . . ." his voice broke and he continued in a whisper ". . . but the same ore can be made into weapons with which to kill."

Nephi returned to his own tent, very sobered. So Lehi was aware of the developing contention in the village. Twice before his brothers had attempted to kill him. Was his father hinting that such a thing might happen again?

In his tent that night, Nephi prayed for guidance. Exhausted, he finally crawled onto the pallet by Miriam's side. The night was stifling. Miriam was so large and so uncomfortable. He lay there listening to her troubled breathing, his own thoughts fluttering through his mind like the ragged sails of their ship. At last he fell into a restless sleep. He was awakened by a voice ringing in his mind. *Nephi. Nephi. Take the ore you have found and make plates of gold on which to engraven a record of your people. Transcribe your writings from the parchment onto the plates to be a permanent record— a record that will not decay nor be destroyed.*

Nephi rose before dawn and awakened Miriam. "The Lord has spoken to me once more. He has commanded me to return to the mountains. I desire to take Jeremiah with me."

"How long will you be gone?" she asked anxiously.

He knelt and put his arms around her. In a comforting voice he said, "We shall only be gone a week."

She frowned. "Nephi, I almost think you enjoy being away from me, as much as you are gone," she said petulantly.

Shaking his head, he said, "My dear Miriam, you know better than that. I'll return very soon and be here for the birth of our child."

Her voice softened and she raised her lips for a kiss. "I'm sorry. It is just that I get so lonely when you are gone. And Jeremiah . . .?" Her eyes widened as she thought of what he had asked her. "Is it safe for him to go that far with you? What about the wild cats you told me about? Why can't Sam or Zoram go with you?"

He smiled, amused at her fears. "I will take good care of Jeremiah. He has hunted with me before, and besides, he needs to learn how to take care of himself in the forest. And Sam will be going." He patted her arm and stood.

After waking an excited Jeremiah, he filled a pack with their supplies, waited for Sam, and they were on their way.

Following the Lord's instructions, they dug the ore and smelted it on the spot. Nephi used the brass plates as a pattern and hammered the gold into sheets almost as thin as his parchment. Then he made a thin stylus from one of his knives. He was ready now to transcribe. They carried the materials back to his tent. Miriam greeted them with a voice filled with relief.

For the next few months he spent all his free time inscribing on the plates. From his parchment he copied off the record of their wanderings in the wilderness and the prophecies and visions which the Lord had shown him. He also transcribed all of Lehi's journals which included his prophecies and his history. He was commanded by the Lord to call the plates *The Plates of Nephi* but he named the first segment of the plates *The Book of Lehi.* From the brass plates he copied the family genealogy from Joseph to Lehi. Then he wrote about their journey to the promised land.

During the time he was so busily engaged in the copying project Miriam delivered their fifth child, a beautiful dark-haired, brown-eyed girl. They named her Helen and Nephi built for her a cradle out of a large turtle shell.

With the plates and his family taking all of his time, Nephi had ignored the leadership of the village. Miriam, a worried look on her face, told Nephi about the increased grumblings in camp. He shrugged helplessly. "What can I do that hasn't already been done?"

A pleading look was in Miriam's eyes and Nephi nodded resignedly, "All right, I will see what can be done."

The next morning, after a breakfast of fruit, he went to his father's tent. He was surprised to see Ephreda sitting beside his father on the rug. A curious expression passed over Lehi's face—it was almost as if he were blushing. He slowly stroked his beard, his eyes contemplating the floor.

Clearing his throat, Lehi said, "Ephreda and I have decided to be married. Since Sariah died it has been a lonely time for both of us."

Nephi smiled broadly. "That is wonderful!" he exclaimed. "When will the wedding take place?"

Lehi looked a little embarrassed, but he seemed pleased that Nephi had understood. "Soon. We will announce it at the family gathering tonight."

"Father, the meeting tonight is why I came here. Miriam has told me of the people's grumblings. I wanted to speak to them tonight, but what can I tell them that we haven't already told them? They know the Lord's commandments and desires. Yet they still grumble. It is difficult for me to understand how to work with them or what to say to them. What do you suggest?"

Lehi pressed his lips together in exasperation, then sighed. "For some it is easier to complain than to work. It has been too easy for our people. They are getting soft and lazy. As long as they have things given to them they are satisfied, but if they think someone else has a little more than they have, they become dissatisfied and begin to murmur." He stared at the tent top for a moment. "It is a sad thing that when some people have a choice between working and complaining, they choose complaining." He shrugged eloquently, "It is also human nature that when things go wrong people always try to find someone else to blame."

Nephi waited for his father to continue.

Lehi lifted his bent shoulders, then let them fall, spreading his hands in a helpless gesture. "I am not sure what is best, my son." Then he squared his shoulders, a fiery look in his eyes. "Yes, I am sure. It is important that we get our records in order before I die. You work on the records. I will take care of the murmurers."

Nephi continued to transcribe the records from his and Lehi's parchment to the gold plates. The time came when he ran out of plates and needed more ore. Nephi's brother, Jacob, asked if he could accompany him and Jeremiah. With Lehi's blessings, and with Jeremiah and Jacob gamboling at his heels, he again left the village. After struggling through the green, leafy forest of cedar and mahogany trees, they climbed a tortuous, twisting trail up the mountain slopes. The trail led along breath-taking gorges that plunged hundreds of feet below. As they climbed higher, they entered forests of pine and giant oak. In the mountain valley where Nephi had smelted his gold, the climate was sunny and mild. In contrast to the fierce humid heat of the coastal plain below, this was a land of eternal spring. The hillsides were ablaze with bright flowers. As Nephi trudged along he thought of his mother, Sariah, and how much she had always enjoyed beautiful flowers. He knew she would be pleased that Lehi would have companionship in his declining years.

When enough gold was smelted, they returned to the village. On the way home Nephi killed a large tapir. His family would enjoy some red meat after living on fish and shellfish for so long.

Copying Lehi's journal onto the plates was time-consuming. One day, as he sat in contemplation, he noticed how much little Nephihah had grown. As he looked at his second son, he suddenly realized that Nephihah was growing up and now needed to be trained in hunting and fishing. His brother

Joseph also needed attention, and Lehi was too old to teach him. Both Jacob and Joseph seemed to look up to him. He needed to spend more time with them. He made new bows and arrows for Nephihah and Joseph, then took the four boys with him hunting in the forest. It was good for him, too, giving him a break from the tedium of inscribing on the plates. He was thrilled when Jeremiah shot his first wild pig. His children were growing up. He resolved that, as important as the plates were, his family would be his first priority.

Often he sat on the floor of the tent playing bone games with his children. To Jeremiah and Nephihah, their father was their idol. Miriam, a perfect helpmeet, tried to keep the children outside playing while he wrote, but he enjoyed having them come in and watch. Jacob, who revered Nephi, was especially interested in the plates. Nephi took time to teach the boys how to read and write Hebrew and also the Egyptian hieroglyphics. Jacob was quick to understand and soon could read everything Nephi had written. Remembering his own schooling, Nephi found some clay and soon had each boy writing with his stylus on a clay tablet. Soon the girls came in to watch and learn. Miriam knew reformed Egyptian and she was able to read the plates. Often, in the evening, she would stand behind Nephi, her hands on his shoulders, reading as he wrote. Nephi had quoted extensively from Zenock and Zenos, and it almost frightened her when she read:

"Thus spake the prophet: The Lord God surely shall visit all the house of Israel at that day, some with his voice, because of their righteousness, unto their great joy and salvation, and others with the thunderings and the lightnings of his power. And the rocks of the earth must rend; and because of the groanings of the earth, many of the kings of the isles of the sea shall be wrought upon by the Spirit of God, to exclaim: The God of nature suffers." [21]

"When will all of this take place?" Miriam asked.

Nephi stopped writing to answer. "The prophets have said that the destruction will take place at the time of the death of the Lord, who will be crucified by his own people in Jerusalem."

"How awful. His own people? What will happen to them?"

Nephi read from the book of Zenos: "And those at Jerusalem shall be scourged by all people, because they crucify the God of Israel, and turn their hearts aside, rejecting signs and wonders, and the power and glory of the God of Israel."

He continued, writing the words as he told them to Miriam: "And because they turn their hearts aside, saith the prophet, and have despised the Holy One of Israel, they shall wander in the flesh, and perish, and become a hiss and a byword, and be hated among all nations." [22]

"Will the people be condemned forever?"

"No," Nephi answered. "The prophet has said that when they no more turn their hearts against the Holy One of Israel, then He will remember the covenants which he made to their fathers. Then he will gather in His people from the four corners of the earth. At that time He will bless all people."

"What a glorious day that will be," Miriam murmured.

Miriam spent many days with her sisters gathering food. While standing knee-deep in mud in the estuary feeling for mollusks, or scrounging for croakers or anchovies in the lagoons and sandy beaches, she listened to the women. She kept Nephi up-to-date on the news and gossip of the village, mostly the same old things: who had complained or grumbled, who was pregnant, what someone had said. One piece of news really excited him, however. Ephreda was pregnant! Lehi, even in his old age, would once again be a father!

Each Sabbath day Nephi taught the people in the synagogue they had built. He read them what he and Lehi had written; he quoted to them from the writings of Zenos and Zenock; he taught of the coming to earth of the God of Israel. He also spent much time reading from the brass plates so the people would know how the Lord had worked with their forefathers.

He especially liked to read from the books of Moses and Isaiah. He said to the congregation, "Hear ye the words of the prophet, ye who are a remnant of the house of Israel, a branch who have been broken off; hear ye the words of the prophet, which were written unto all the house of Israel, and liken them unto yourselves, that ye may have hope as well as your brethren from whom ye have been broken off." [23]

Nephi felt that the words of Isaiah had been written directly to this people: "Hearken, O ye house of Israel, all ye that are broken off and are driven out, because of the wickedness of the pastors of my people; yea, all ye that are broken off, that are scattered abroad, who are of my people, O house of Israel. Listen, O isles, unto me, . . ." [24]

Jacob, now a spiritual youth of twelve, asked, "What do these things mean? How can we understand them?"

"They were given to the prophet by the voice of the Spirit," Nephi responded. "By the Spirit all things are made known. So, my brothers, to understand them we must pray for the spirit. From this prophecy it appears that the house of Israel will be scattered over all the earth, and among all nations."

There was silence for a moment, then Laman asked suspiciously, "Do you mean we aren't the only ones who have left Jerusalem?"

"The Lord has said that many are lost from the knowledge of those who are at Jerusalem. Most of the people have been led away and are scattered throughout the earth, even upon the isles of the sea. Since they have been led away, the things I have read have been prophesied concerning them, and also concerning all those who shall be scattered and be confounded from this time forth.''

Laman persisted. ''Do you mean the people will remain scattered forever?''

''No,'' Nephi responded. ''The exciting thing is that the time will come, after all the House of Israel has been scattered and confounded, that the Lord will raise up a mighty nation among the Gentiles upon this very land. They will scatter our descendants, and then the Lord will do a marvelous work among the Gentiles which will be of great benefit to our descendants. Isaiah, speaking of that time, said it is likened unto their being nourished by the Gentiles and being carried in their arms and upon their shoulders. Not only will it benefit our posterity, but that great work shall benefit all of the House of Israel by making known to them the covenant which Heavenly Father made with Abraham: 'In thy seed shall all the kindreds of the earth be blessed.' I want you to know that the Lord God will proceed to bring his covenants and his gospel unto all those who are of the House of Israel.''

Lemuel whined, ''I'm still not sure what that means.''

''What it means,'' Nephi patiently explained, ''is that the Lord will then gather together the House of Israel in the lands of their inheritance. At that time they will know that the Lord is their Savior and their Redeemer.''

Nephi continued teaching the people about the last days of which Isaiah had spoken. He taught them concerning those who would fight against Zion; of how they would be destroyed. He taught them of the time when Satan would have no more power over the hearts of men; of the time when the proud and wicked would be burned as stubble.

''The Lord will not let the wicked destroy the righteous. He will preserve the righteous by his power, even to the destruction of their enemies by fire. The righteous need not fear, for the prophets have all said that they shall be saved. . . . 'but all they who fight against Zion shall be cut off.' ''[25]

Another time Nephi spoke to them concerning the coming of the Savior. He quoted from Moses. ''A prophet shall the lord your God raise up unto you, like unto me; him shall ye hear in all things whatsoever he shall say unto you. And it shall come to pass that all those who will not hear that prophet shall be cut off from among the people.'' Then he declared to them the prophet of whom Moses spake was the Holy One of Israel who would execute judgment against the wicked.

He ended his sermon with, ''And now I, Nephi, make an end; for I durst not speak further as yet concerning these things. Wherefore, my brethren, I would that ye should consider that the things which have been written upon the plates of brass are true; and they testify that a man must be obedient to the commandments of God. Wherefore, ye need not suppose that I and my father are the only ones that have testified, and also taught them. Wherefore, if ye shall be obedient to the commandments, and endure to the end, ye shall be saved at the last day. And thus it is. Amen.'' [26]

In his tent that night, he inscribed what had been said onto the plates. Then he noted in his journal: "It has been fifteen years since we left Jerusalem. A daughter was born yesterday to my father and Ephreda;" and, "During the past month I have traveled clear across this island, finding the ocean on the other side. The side we landed on is hot and dry. There is a magnificent ridge of mountains running down the middle of the island, and the other side is a jungle—hot and humid." He noted, "If we ever have to leave this place it would be pleasant to live in a valley of the mountains where the temperature is more like Jerusalem."

Chapter 14

Death of Lehi

Gray hair and his wrinkled face told the story of Lehi's age. But his eyes continued to hold the light of youth. Though he smiled cheerfully, he realized he had little time left. He asked Nephi to call his family together. Nephi had made a trumpet from the shell of a large gastropod. Now he used it to call the people to assemble. Then he and Sam helped their father walk the short distance to the synagogue.

When all were crowded into the open meeting place, Lehi began. He reminisced about their trials in the wilderness. He chastized those who had taken part in the previous rebellions, especially while on the waters of Irreantum when the mercies of God spared them from being swallowed up in the depths of the sea.

He taught of how blessed they were that the Lord had brought them out of Jerusalem to this land of promise. He reminded them about prophecies concerning the destruction of Jerusalem.

"I was shown in vision," he said, "that Jerusalem has been destroyed. Had we remained there we would also have perished. But in spite of our afflictions," he continued, "we have obtained a land of promise, a land which is choice above all other lands. The Lord has covenanted this land unto me, and to my children forever, and also to all those who should be led out of other countries by the hand of the Lord."

Lehi was radiant. His gray hair and beard became a halo around his face. He continued in a softer voice. "I, Lehi, prophecy according to the workings of the Spirit which is in me, that none shall come into this land unless they be brought by the hand of the Lord. This land is a consecrated land. If those who come here will serve the Lord and keep His command- ments, it shall be a land of liberty to them. They shall never be brought into captivity. However, if iniquity ever abounds in this land, the land shall be cursed. But to the righteous, this land will be blessed forever."

Nephi wrote quickly, transcribing his father's words. Lehi continued, "I have obtained a promise that those who keep the Lord's commandments shall prosper upon the face of this land, and they shall be kept from all other nations, that they may possess this land unto themselves. No other people will molest them or take away the land of their inheritance. They shall dwell here in safety forever."

A shadow passed over his face as he added, "But if the time comes that the people dwindle in unbelief, after they have received so many great blessings from the hand of the Lord—having been brought by his goodness into this precious land of promise—behold, I say, if the day shall come that they reject their God, behold, His judgments shall rest upon them." He paused and looked sadly around at his family. "He will bring other nations here and will give them power, and He will take away from our people the lands of their possessions and will cause them to be scattered and smitten."

A fit of coughing hit Lehi. He clutched his chest and Nephi eased him to a seat. "No, let me continue," he gasped. "As one generation passes to another there shall be bloodshed. Oh, my sons, please hearken unto my words."

He shut his eyes and breathed deeply. Leaning heavily on Nephi and Sam, he pled, "My children, hear the words of a trembling parent whose body you must soon lay down in the cold and silent grave from whence no traveler can return."

He slumped once again. "A few more days and I go the way of all the earth. But behold, the Lord has redeemed my soul from hell. I have beheld His glory, and I am encircled about eternally in the arms of His love."

He paused and smiled tenderly at Ephreda who sat before him with his two daughters on her ample lap. "But my heart has been weighed down with sorrow, for I have feared that the Lord would come out in the fulness of his wrath upon you. In vision I have seen that some of you will be cut off and destroyed forever. A cursing will come upon you for the space of many generations. You will be visited with the sword, and with famine, and will be hated and led according to the will and captivity of the devil."

He faced Laman and Lemuel who squirmed uncomfortably under his gaze. "O my sons, that these things might not come upon you, but that you might be a choice and a favored people of the Lord. But behold, His will be done for His ways are righteousness forever." He paused, coughed again, then spread his arms wide. "The Lord has promised us that 'Inasmuch as ye shall keep my commandments ye shall prosper in the land; but inasmuch as ye will not keep my commandments ye shall be cut off from my presence.' And now that my soul might have joy in you, and that my heart might leave this world with gladness because of you, rise up my sons, and be men. Be determined, with one mind and in one heart, united in all things, that you may not come down into captivity and be cursed."

Once more his piercing eyes sought out his two oldest sons. His voice hoarse he said, "My sons, put on the armor of righteousness. Shake off the chains which bind you. Rebel no more against your brother, Nephi, whose views have been glorious. He has kept the commandments from the time that we left Jerusalem. The Lord has used him as an instrument in bringing us forth into the land of promise. Were it not for him, we would have long ago perished with hunger in the wilderness." He shook his head. "Nevertheless, you tried to kill him. He has already suffered much because of you."

Laman's face was bloodless and a rage burned within his eyes.

Lehi was very tired but he continued. "I fear because of you, knowing that he shall suffer again. You have accused him of seeking power and authority over you. I know that he has not sought for power nor authority over you, but he has sought the glory of God and your own eternal welfare."

Lehi continued. "And now my son, Laman, and also Lemuel and Sam, and also my sons who are the sons of Ishmael, behold, if you will hearken unto the voice of Nephi you will not perish. And if you will hearken unto him I leave unto you a blessing, yea, even my first blessing."

New strength came to him as he looked directly at Laman and Lemuel. "But if you will not listen to Nephi, I take away my first blessing from you and give it to Nephi."

Laman looked at Nephi, his eyes filled with hatred as Lehi turned to Zoram.

"And now, Zoram, I speak unto you. You were Laban's servant but came to dwell with us. I know that you are a true friend to my son, Nephi. Because you have been faithful your seed shall be blessed with his seed. They shall dwell in prosperity long upon the face of this land. Wherefore, if ye shall keep the commandments of the Lord, the Lord hath consecrated this land for the security of thy seed with the seed of my son." [27]

Once more he was seized by a fit of coughing. Recovering, he looked sadly around the group, knowing prophetically what would happen to his descendants. He hoarsely whispered to Nephi, "Take me to my tent."

Nephi helped his aging father to his feet, and with Sam's help, half-carried him to his own tent. Jacob, Joseph, Ephreda and her two small daughters followed behind.

After they were gone, Laman whispered in Lemuel's ear. "When Father dies, we'll put an end to Nephi and our younger brothers who have tried to rule over us all of these years."

In the tent, Lehi rested on his pallet. Ephreda cooked him some bird soup. Holding his bowl in both hands, he sipped the steaming broth. He asked that Jacob be brought to him. He leaned against a tent pole, hands resting heavily on Jacob's head, as he gave him a father's blessing. Nephi wrote the blessing on parchment.

"And now, Jacob, I speak unto you. You were my firstborn in the wilderness. You have learned the greatness of God and he shall consecrate your afflictions for your gain. You shall be blessed, and shall dwell safely with thy brother, Nephi. Your days shall be spent in the service of the Lord."

He continued Jacob's blessing, telling him of the redemption which would come through the Messiah, of the necessity of opposition in all things, for without opposition, he said, "righteousness could not be brought to pass." He told Jacob of the necessity for laws and then rehearsed to him the concept of the creation and the fall of Adam—how Adam's fall was an important part of the Lord's plan.

"And now," he said, "behold, if Adam had not transgressed he would not have fallen, but he would have remained in the garden of Eden. And all things which were created must have remained in the same state in which they were after they were created; . . . and they would have had no children. You see," he added, "all of these things were done through the wisdom of God. Adam fell that men might be; and men are, that they might have joy." [28]

After reviewing again the coming of the Messiah in the last days, he closed Jacob's blessing, and leaned back, wan and tired. Nephi thought to himself that this had been one of Lehi's greatest sermons.

Lehi hardly had strength enough to sit up, but weakly motioned that Joseph come sit before him.

Nephi stepped to him. "Father, isn't that enough for today? You need your rest. You can bless Joseph tomorrow."

Lehi shook his head. "No, it has to be now." He motioned to Joseph, who knelt before him. Placing his hands on his youngest son's head, he blessed him. "And now I speak unto you, Joseph, my last born." Lehi spoke to him of his lineage from Joseph who was sold into Egypt. He told of the promises that came from Joseph, and that "Joseph truly saw our day. And he obtained a promise of the Lord, that out of the fruit of his loins the Lord God would rise up a righteous branch unto the house of Israel; not the Messiah, but a branch which was to be broken off," and Lehi quoted from Joseph's prophecies: "Out of that branch a seer shall the Lord my God raise up, who shall be a choice seer unto the fruit of my loins." Then Lehi told of that latter-day seer who would be raised up like another Moses, with power to bring forth new revelations from the Lord to the people.

After much prophesying concerning this latter-day prophet, Lehi concluded, "And now, behold, my son Joseph, after this manner did my father of old prophesy. Wherefore, because of this covenant you are blessed. Thy seed shall not be destroyed, for they shall hearken unto the words of the book. . . . And now, blessed are you, Joseph. You are still young so listen unto the words of your brother, Nephi. Remember the words of your dying father. Amen." [29]

He motioned with his arm and Nephi hurried to his side. "My son," Lehi whispered, "I have yet to give you your blessing."

"Can't it wait until you are rested?"

"No, my son. There is not time." Lehi then gave Nephi the blessing of the firstborn, the blessing which normally would have gone to the eldest son. Nephi, his head bowed, listened as his father recited the marvelous

blessings which the Lord had promised him. When he was finished with the
blessing, Lehi's hands slipped weakly from Nephi's head.

Concerned about their father, Jacob and Joseph stepped beside Nephi.
Jeremiah joined them. Faithful Sam sat at the tent door to insure his father
some rest. Ephreda was at Lehi's feet, watching patiently. Several hours
passed, and then Lehi called again. Nephi quickly went to him.

"Yes, Father?"

Lehi took him by the hand. "My son," he whispered weakly. "Bring
the children of Laman and Lemuel and the sons of Ishmael. I must also
give them a blessing." Nephi eased him back onto a pillow, then hurried to
do his father's bidding. It took some time to gather all the children of his
elder brothers and the children of the sons of Ishmael. Finally he had them
at Lehi's tent. Lehi called first for the sons and daughters of Laman.

With several pillows, Nephi propped his father up so he could look at
the children. "Behold my sons and my daughters, who are the sons and
daughters of my firstborn, I would that you would listen carefully to my
words." He looked around proudly at his grandchildren. "The Lord God
has said, 'Inasmuch as ye shall keep my commandments ye shall prosper in
the land; and inasmuch as ye will not keep my commandments ye shall be
cut off from my presence.' "

Once more he looked at the faces before him. "Behold, my sons and
my daughters, I cannot go down to my grave unless I should leave a blessing
upon you. I know that if you are brought up in the way you should go you
will not depart from it. So, if you are ever cursed, I leave my blessing upon
you that the cursing may be taken from you and be answered upon the
heads of your parents. Because of my blessing the Lord God will not suffer
that you shall perish, but He will be merciful unto you and your seed forever."

After he had completed his blessing upon the children of Laman, he
called for Lemuel's children. He gave them a blessing similar to that given
Laman's children, noting that the Lord would not let them be utterly destroyed.

Following the children of Lemuel, Lehi blessed Ishmael's sons and their
children who were also his grandchildren.

Then he called for Sam and his children. Tears stood in his eyes, giving
them a radiance as he looked over the children of his special, voiceless Sam.
He laid his hands on Sam's head and blessed him. "My dear son, Sam.
Blessed are you and your seed. You shall inherit the land with your brother,
Nephi. Your seed shall be numbered with his seed. You shall be even like
your brother, and your seed like his seed, and you shall be blessed in all
your days." [30]

When his blessing was finished, Sam stood, tears coursing down his
bronzed cheeks. He bent to kiss his father then turned and embraced Nephi.

After Sam's blessing, Nephi again hustled the people out of Lehi's tent.
Ephreda sat by the great patriarch's side, stroking his arm and comforting him.

"Do not mourn," he said in a hoarse whisper. "I look forward to being released from this old tired body and to see my Sariah once again." He smiled, apparently in anticipation. "She will be in the bloom of her youth." He closed his eyes, and his breathing slowed.

Nephi knelt and touched his father's face. "Father. Father. I love you. Don't forget that I love you."

Sam picked up one of his father's limp hands, then fell to his knees, burying his head in his father's breast and sobbing. He raised his head and Nephi could see him mouthing the words, "I love you."

Nephi squeezed Sam's shoulder. His vision was blurred by tears. "All the pain is over for you now, Father," he whispered. "Goodbye."

He reached over and helped Sam to his feet. They walked out of the tent. Their father was dead.

Chapter 15

A Divided Family

"The time has come," Laman bellowed, slamming his fist into his palm. "I will not be lorded over by my younger brother one more minute!"

"But Laman, we have a good life here," Cleopha tried to calm him. "Everything we need is available. Why fight with your brothers?"

Not even Cleopha could calm Laman's anger. He stood there red-faced and fuming, jaw clenched, veins standing out on his forehead. "Lemuel," he yelled.

Lemuel ran into the hut, big-eyed and breathless. "What is it?"

"Summon Shazar and Nahom," he commanded. "We need to have a conference of war."

Cleopha looked up from the oysters she was prying open. "Isn't that a little strong? To be talking of war?"

Turning to her angrily, Laman retorted, "No, it isn't too strong. What we are going to have is war. It is time that we destroyed Nephi and all those who support him."

Cleopha shrugged helplessly and went back to preparing dinner. She was about to remind him of what happened the last time he had threatened to kill Nephi, but . . . what was the use when he was in this kind of mood?

Shazer and Nahom, led by an excited Lemuel, crowded into the hut. "What's this about war?" Shazer asked.

Laman licked his lips, looking at the others in turn. Then he said, "It is time for war. Our younger brother thinks to rule over us. I say we've had enough of him." Heads nodded. Laman looked around cunningly. "The only way we are going to be free of him is to kill him! Then we who are the lawful rulers will lead this people."

The others nodded again, then Lemuel spoke. "Just this week he called us into the synagogue and told us we all needed to repent."

Shazer agreed. "Since your father died he has truly been trying to set himself up as the ruler over us. Now he wants to instruct our children and grandchildren in his so-called religion."

The four men plotted long into the night, planning how to kill Nephi and any others who opposed them.

* * *

Nephi, unaware of his brother's scheming, was also up late. He felt an urgency to complete the transcription from his journal to the plates. By flickering candlelight he wrote some of the admonitions which he had spoken to his brothers since Lehi's death. No matter what he said to them, all he got was angry and bitter words from Laman and Lemuel. He had prayed repeatedly to the Lord, asking how he might help them, but no response had come.

He was almost through writing when a scratching on the tent distracted him. He stepped out of the tent into the quiet of the moonless night, but saw nothing. He turned when he heard a "Pssst." In a dark area behind the tent, Nephi saw a dim outline. As he approached, he could see it was Ishmar.

Pulling Nephi with him, Ishmar dropped into the tall grass.

"Why so secretive?" Nephi asked.

"Shhh!" Ishmar said. He looked around as if the very grass had ears. "I need to talk with you. Can we go away from the camp so we won't be seen?"

They went into the darkness behind the village, then Ishmar stopped and turned to Nephi. He put his hand on Nephi's shoulder. "My friend and uncle," he began. "We have played together, worked together, and hunted together since we were children."

Nephi nodded in agreement, curious as to what Ishmar was trying to say.

Ishmar blurted out, "Your older brothers and my father and uncle are planning to kill you and anyone else that opposes them."

Nephi was not surprised, though it saddened him to think once again that his brothers would want to kill him. He had felt the undercurrents of rebellion for several weeks. "They have tried that before," he said.

"I know that," Ishmar pleaded. "This time they're serious. They're still in Laman's hut, planning. I eavesdropped outside, then came quickly to tell you."

Nephi cupped his hand behind Ishmar's neck, pulling him close. "Thank you very much, my friend. You are truly my brother. It is important that you not be seen talking to me. I will seek counsel from the Lord as to what we should do. Again, thank you."

Ishmar squeezed Nephi's shoulder and hurried back to his own hut.

Kneeling where he was, Nephi prayed. "Dear Father. Thou has blessed me since I was a youth. Whenever I have needed Thy help, You were there. Now I need Thee again. If what Ishmar tells me is true, I must make plans to save my family from the wrath of Laman and his supporters. What should I do?"

He prayed for a long time before the Spirit whispered to him. *Nephi, what Ishmar has said is true. Your elder brothers seek your life. The time has come to depart from them and flee into the wilderness. There you will become a separate but a mighty people.*

Nephi asked, "But what of those who remain?"

The voice whispered, *Inasmuch as they will not hearken unto thy words they shall be cut off from My presence. I will cause a cursing to come upon them, yea, even a sore cursing, because of their iniquity. For behold, they have hardened their hearts like flint against Me. Therefore, I will cause a skin of blackness to come upon them so they will appear loathsome and not enticing to your people. And cursed shall be the seed of him that mixeth with their seed; for they shall be cursed even with the same cursing.* [31]

"But they are my family. Can't the curse be removed?"

"Only if they repent of their iniquities," responded the Lord.

Nephi hurried back to his tent. He carried a candle in and sat beside the sleeping Miriam. Gently, he shook her. She looked up at him. "My dear," he whispered, "the Lord has told me that we are to leave the village. We must do so tonight. We will need to be packed and leave while it is still dark."

"What has happened?" Miriam asked.

Nephi told her of Ishmar's visit and of what the Lord had said. Then he added, "We won't have very much time to pack. I'll put Jeremiah and Nephihah in charge so you won't have to do any heavy work."

"It won't take long," she said. "I've had a feeling that this would be coming, so I've put things aside." She reached up and put her arms around his neck. "But thanks for being concerned about me."

"I am always concerned about you," he smiled. "You are in my thoughts all of the time."

Nephi woke Jeremiah and his wife, Beth, and put him in charge of the packing, then slipped out to warn the others. He went to Sam's tent first, telling him what had happened; then to Zoram's, and finally to his father's tent. Jacob, the same age as Jeremiah, immediately took charge, making sure that Ephreda and the little girls were taken care of.

The last stop Nephi made was at Ishmar's hut. Careful not to awaken Tamna, he quickly told his friend of their plans to create a separate colony in the wilderness, then he invited him and his family to join them.

Nephi could see that Ishmar was torn. If he went, he knew he would be the only one from that side of the family. He said, "Give me a few minutes. I will have to talk with Tamna."

Nephi whispered, "I'll be back as soon as I see how the loading is coming." He squeezed Ishmar's hand and vanished into the blackness of night.

When he returned, Ishmar and Tamna were already packing. Several of their children were young, and it would be a hardship on them, but Nephi remembered their journey across the desert and he knew that the Lord would protect them—small children and all.

They worked through the middle of the night, loading household goods, packing tents, loading seeds and tools. Nephihah and Adamihah had the responsibility for gathering a small herd of sheep and goats. These were moved out early so that the cries of the animals would not alert the rest of the village.

They were nomads once again.

* * *

Nephi was thankful for exploring done on his hunting and ore-gathering trips. By the time it was light enough to see where they were going, they were almost to the foothills. Because Jeremiah had hunted with him so often, and knew the forest and the mountains, Nephi sent him ahead to scout out the best trail. He assigned Jacob to bring up the rear and to watch for pursuit by Laman or his people. Jeremiah had been given instructions to turn north at the foothills and travel through the forest. The next day they would tackle the mountains.

Most of the tents had been left standing in the village, in order to deceive Laman and Lemuel as long as possible. The smaller tents had been packed on the camel-like llamas. Nephi was very thankful for the foresight to have tamed them though at the time he had assumed all he would use them for would be to haul ore from the mountains from which to make more plates. Now the llamas were really useful although men, women, and children each carried a pack as they followed Nephi single file through the forest.

The last thing Nephi had done before leaving the village by the sea was to get the brass plates and the *Liahona* from his father's tent. He didn't trust anyone else to carry them, but had them in his own pack. Joseph and Nephihah carried the gold plates he had been working on. Everyone else carried personal and family items they would need in the wilderness. Most of their possessions, however, had been left behind.

As the sun came above the horizon, Nephi stopped and observed the people as they gathered around him. These were his people—the people who believed in the warnings and revelations of God and who had listened to him as their leader.

Just as he had done when they boarded the ship to cross Irreantum so many years before, Nephi counted those who were accompanying him into the wilderness:

His father's family consisted of his widow, Ephreda and her young daughters Phyllis and Oletha.

Jacob had married Zoram's daughter, Bildah, and they had a small child.

Joseph had married Nephi's daughter, Ruth, and she was large with child.

Sam and Leah, with their six children, David, Daniel, Joshua, Joel, Mary, and Sam.

Nephi and Miriam still had five children under their care: Nephihah, Naomi, Helen, Omni, and Francis.

Jeremiah had married Zoram's second daughter, Beth, and they had two children, Lehi and Sariah.

Zoram and Eva only had two children still with them, Adamihah and Simon.

Ishmar and Tamna had six children, three girls and three boys.

There were thirty-eight people in the group, none with a spirit of contention. What a pleasant situation, Nephi thought. With no contention, the Lord's Spirit can dwell with us as a people and we will raise up a righteous generation.

He put his arm around his daughter, Ruth. "How are you feeling?"

She smiled tiredly at him. "I'll make it." She patted her big belly. "Our baby is getting close, though. I don't know how long it will be."

Nephi hated to cut their rests short, but he was fearful of pursuit. He wasn't sure what Laman would do when he found them gone. Would he be angry and follow them? Or would they just be glad to be rid of him and his people?

When the sun was halfway down the sky, Jacob caught up with Nephi. He couldn't talk until he caught his breath. "I waited in the forest where we turned north. Laman and his men are about four hours behind us." He paused again, gasping for air.

Nephi patted his brother on the shoulder. "Thank you. When you are rested, Jacob, drop back again and keep an eye on them. Find out if they are armed." He looked at the sky. "About four hours until dark," he mused aloud. He called the men to him and told them what was happening. To Jeremiah he said, "You stay in front with me. We'll lead the women and children. The rest of the men, and any boys who can handle bows and arrows, bring up the rear. We won't take any chance of their surprising us."

After preparing themselves for defense, they continued on through the forest. As Nephi walked, he prayed. Dear God, we need Thy help. You have commanded me to leave the village of my father. Now give us protection so we can become a separate but a mighty people.

By nightfall they had arrived at the trail Nephi had forged up the mountain. Near the base of the hill they found a sheltered cove in which to make camp. They would tackle the mountain in the morning when they were fresh.

Around the small campfire that night, Nephi held a council. He looked around at the men. They were a stalwart crew. Several were mature and well-developed like himself, ranging in age from Zoram, the oldest, down to Ishmar's boy, Ben, who was ten. If forced to, they would put up a valiant fight.

Jacob reported that the fires of Laman's group were several hours down the trail. Laman and his followers, a total of seven men, were lightly armed. Jacob had crept close enough to their camp to hear them talking. Smiling, he reported that several had appeared frightened to be this far away from their village.

Nephi smiled. Perhaps there wouldn't be a fight after all. He assigned lookouts to watch their back trail with Adamihah and Daniel taking the first watch. For another hour he discussed possible strategies with Sam, Ishmar, and Zoram. After his brother and two friends went to bed, he walked back down the trail, checking the guard. As he walked he prayed, and a feeling of peace permeated his whole body. An assurance came to him that the Lord would protect him and his band.

By first light they were up and packed. They ate a cold breakfast of dried fish and wheat, and were on their way. All day they toiled up the steep mountain slope, passing through tall mahogany trees and hillsides where only scrub brush grew. They had little time to look at scenery that was exquisitely beautiful. The trail wound up a steep hogsback ridge, with breathtaking gorges on either side. They climbed over beds of loose rock where they slipped and slid, bruising their shins and tearing sandals and clothing. The trail was so steep in places that they held on to brushy limbs to pull themselves along. It was a grueling hike, especially for the women and children. Nephi was most concerned about Ephreda who was heavy and out-of-shape, and his daughter, Ruth, who was close to delivering a child.

As they climbed higher on the mountain they passed small stands of tall pines and fir trees. By noon they had reached the pass and started descending into the first mountain valley. There Nephi called a halt so they could rest. He was very concerned about Ruth. It would not be good if she had her baby along the trail. As he was checking each family, he was interrupted by Jacob's hail.

"Nephi, come quickly." Jacob, several hundred yards back on the trail, was waving urgently to him. Motioning for Sam to join him, he picked up his bow and trotted up the trail.

Jacob was excited. "Laman's party is still in camp at the base of the mountain, but he has sent his son, Enoch, ahead under a flag of truce. He should be here in minutes. What should we do?"

Nephi was puzzled. "Are you sure the rest of them have not broken camp?"

Jacob nodded.

Nephi said, "We'll just have to wait and see what Enoch wants."

They didn't have long to wait. Within the hour Enoch, carrying a piece of white cloth on a stick, came from the trees high on the trail.

Enoch was breathless from running. His legs were scratched and cut from rocks and brush. He seemed very glad to see them. He and Jacob and

Jeremiah were the same age and had been friends in the past. They clasped arms, then he faced Nephi. Between labored breaths he said, "Father said to tell you he won't stop you from leaving. But he says that you have stolen the brass plates which belong to his people. He says that if you return the brass plates he will leave you alone. If you do not . . ." He left the sentence unfinished.

Nephi looked at the young messenger with compassion as he shook his head. "No. The plates belong with us. The Lord has directed that we make a record of this people. The brass plates are part of that record." He sighed. "Return to the camp of your father. Tell him that we desire peace with him and his people, but we will never give up the brass plates."

Enoch looked around at the small group, turned, and slowly headed back up the trail. Nephi was silent as Enoch disappeared into the trees, then he walked back to their camp. Miriam looked at him expectantly.

Nephi's face was grim. "Laman has found the excuse he needs to harass us," he said. "He is accusing us of stealing the brass plates."

"But they don't even follow the teachings of the plates," Miriam remarked.

"That's true, but it makes no difference. Laman needed some reason to convince his people that we were in the wrong. I'm afraid that this thing will be a contention between our peoples from now on."

As they traveled, Nephi used every trick he knew to avoid being followed. He wanted to avoid all trouble with his older brothers. He was thankful for rains that came every afternoon. They soaked the travelers, but they also washed out signs of their passage. The way was not easy. Rushing mountain streams filled with huge white boulders were in every ravine.

Toward evening of the sixth day, tired as he was, Nephi was gripped by excitement. He recognized landmarks. They were close to their destination.

On the morning of the seventh day, they crossed over a pine-covered saddle. Before them lay a beautiful valley isolated by high snow-capped volcanic peaks. The valley floor was a profusion of bright-colored flowers. This was the valley Nephi had discovered on one of his hunting expeditions, the destination to which he had been leading them.

Miriam stood beside her husband, her hand in his. "It is beautiful."

Others crowded around them as they looked down upon the high mountain plateau. Almost below them glittered a deep-blue lake. Far in the north sun glinted on another, larger lake. To the west, a line of cone-shaped mountains rose to the sky. From one of the mountain tops smoke billowed. The whole valley seemed almost a fairyland scene.

Nephi spread his arms wide, encompassing everything before them. "My family and friends," he said, "this valley will be our home."

There was silence in the group as they contemplated the idyllic scene. Finally Bildah, Jacob's wife, spoke. "Let's call it the Land of Nephi."

A murmur of assent rose. Then Jacob added, "Yes, and we will be called the People of Nephi." Again heads nodded in affirmation.

* * *

As twilight drew in, the weary travelers crossed the valley floor. Wind veered until it blew directly from the west. Thunder rumbled and rain fell in a slanted torrent. The sky grew suddenly dark as heavy clouds rolled overhead. Thunder beat across the sky and eerie zig-zags of lightning flashed down. Rain plopped like drumbeats against the mud, then as suddenly as it had come, the rain was gone.

That night, wet and tired, they camped by the small lake. Clouds had vanished from the sky and stars glittered in profusion.

Some of the group wanted to settle by the lake, but when morning came, Nephi led them on. He knew where he was going. About a day's march east of the lake he showed them where he wanted to build the city. A lovely little valley beside a sparkling river, it was curtained with the perpetual green of pine forests on the hillside. It was close to timber for their homes, and the valley floor was sunny and fertile. Springs of fresh water bubbled from the mountainside. It was a perfect spot for their settlement. As soon as they were assured that this was the right location the women began to pitch their tents.

Nephi took the men exploring. He wanted them to see the things he had found in his earlier explorations. The volcanic soil was rich and fertile; the forests had good timber for homes and temples; the river not only had plenty of water for irrigating their crops during the dry season, there was also gold sand in its bottom; the outcropping of copper and tin were within a half-day's journey. If there was a perfect spot to build their city and establish their people, Nephi felt this was it.

Their tents had served them well for many years, but now they were frayed and worn. Nephi wanted this to be a permanent settlement so he taught the men in the use of tools in making lumber. Within a few months each family had a home. Most of them were built with pine logs, chinked with mud. For roofs they used smaller branches with a layer of mud over the top. Nephi was pleased. The people had lived in tents for almost twenty-five years. Now they had homes.

The Lord had promised them many times that if they would keep the commandments he would prosper them in the land. They did prosper. The land produced bounteous crops, their flocks of sheep and goats constantly increased. Bananas, mangoes and papayas grew wild in the surrounding forest. It was a time of peace and plenty for the People of Nephi.

Harvest season came and went, and never had there been such a harvest. They saved seed for the next planting, but there was still plenty of food for the entire village. They found and cultivated edible wild plants. Wild maize became one of their favorite foods. Grain and squash, planted from seeds brought from their old country, were staples in their diet. They learned to cultivate sweet potato, arrowroot, manioc and cassava. Fish were plentiful in the nearby lake and game were plentiful in the hills. Except for occasional mild earth tremors, they dwelt in peace. The Lord's promise was certainly coming true: the Land of Nephi was indeed a land of prosperity.

To have the people build their homes was only one of Nephi's projects. He had seen problems caused by people with not enough to do. The people of Laman and Lemuel, with all the food they needed available without effort, had become an idle people, full of mischief and subtlety. Nephi did not want that to happen with his people, so he taught them to work with their hands and to be industrious. They planted and worked their crops. From the ceiba tree they harvested kapok and made mattresses. Cinchona trees provided them quinine for medicine.

As soon as their homes were built, the people worked together to build a synagogue. With that completed, Nephi began the most ambitious project of all. For almost thirty years, ever since they had left Jerusalem, he had longed for a temple. It had been in many of his dreams. He had taught his people how to make adobes out of mud, and they used the adobes to begin construction of a temple. It was a slow process, but one that accomplished several of Nephi's objectives: it kept the men busy, and they were constructing a house of worship to the Lord.

Daily rain was always a problem. After a few storms roofs would begin to leak and more mud had to be put on the roofs and smoothed down. Many times adobes they were making would melt in the rain and they would have to start all over. In Moses' writings on the brass plates, Nephi had read of putting straw in the bricks, so he had the men gather long grass from the meadows and mix it in with the mud. Adobes were stronger then and held up better. But in spite of rainstorms, the climate was pleasant. It wasn't humid like air along the seacoast. Days were warm and nights were cool. Zoram called it the "land of eternal spring."

Nephi could hardly believe how pleasant his life had become. The close-knit group of people obeyed the laws of Moses and kept the Lord's commandments, a welcome relief after the contention and stress of the seacoast village.

One night he sat on the porch of his house with Miriam as she held one of their grandchildren. He could hear crickets singing and the beat of a nighthawk's wings; even the occasional chirp of a bat darting to and fro. It had been raining and water dripped from the eaves of the house. A few stars shone through clouds, then the moon rose over the eastern hills, large and round and yellow-gold. Sitting under the tattered sky, Nephi had a special feeling—a closeness to nature and a nearness to God. He placed his arm gently around Miriam. They sat there in total contentment, with no words necessary. Miriam snuggled against him.

Finally he broke the silence. "The people have asked me to be their king."

Miriam nodded imperceptibly. "Yes, Ruth told me."

Nephi smiled. Village rumors always beat any news he wanted to share with his wife.

She looked at him closely. "What are you going to do?"

Nephi pursed his lips thoughtfully. "I have not wanted the people to have a king. There are too many kings who rule unjustly." He thought of those he had known in Jerusalem. Most of them had been wicked men. "I feel that having a king is like having fire. It can be a wonderful but dangerous servant. A king can also be a fearful master." Miriam nodded as Nephi continued. "My only concern is to help the people. Perhaps I can help them best as king."

Smiling in the darkness, Miriam said, "Whatever you decide to do, I know you will do it well."

He looked at her to see if she was teasing him, but he knew she was serious. "I will be a good king for the people," he said.

Five years passed from the time they separated from Laman and his people, a time of prosperity and peace. The temple was now almost finished. It was a large building, patterned after the temple of Solomon which Nephi had admired so much as a youth in Jerusalem. It wasn't as ornate nor as richly decorated, but Nephi was proud of what they had done.

With gold and silver plentiful, he had taught the people how to smelt gold and to craft it into ornaments. His brother, Joseph, a natural goldsmith, had made most of the temple decorations and they were beautiful. Soon they would be able to use the temple for the sacred ordinances which the Lord would give them.

Though it was not yet completed, Nephi taught in the temple each week. He wanted the youth to know of their heritage, of their life in Jerusalem before their flight to the promised land. He talked often of their grandparents—Lehi and Sariah—who had been such noble parents to him. As the Lord had given him visions, he taught the people the gospel of Jesus Christ, who would come.

But peace was not to last: Nephi was warned in a dream that he should prepare the people to defend their land against the Lamanites. He was saddened. War—after they had enjoyed such peace! But he didn't want his people to be caught unprepared, so again he led his men into the mountains. They mined iron, copper, and tin to make weapons. Using adobes to make a furnace, Nephi built a forge. Iron, after its first smelting, was spongy and interwoven with impurities. He showed the men how to get the iron red-hot and how to hammer it into its final shape on the anvil.

As a model, he unwrapped and brought out the sword of Laban which he had carried with him all of the years. Zoram's son, Adamihah, was muscular and a natural metal worker. He learned very quickly when the metal was just right to work, and how to hammer the swords until they would hold an edge similar to the edge of Laban's sword. For handles, they smelted copper and tin to make bronze. By adding slightly more tin they could make the metal harder, though it was more brittle.

Adamihah created closed molds out of clay into which he poured molten metal for handles. The molds were in two pieces which could be fitted together leaving a cavity in the center in the shape of the handle. Liquid metal was then poured into the closed mold through filler holes and allowed to harden. Adamihah would then break open the mold and finish off the handle by filing and polishing.

David, Sam's oldest son, had become very proficient in carving stone during the building of the temple. One morning he walked over to the forge and handed Adamihah a perfect two-piece mold carved out of stone. From then on all they had to do was separate the mold and reuse it.

Soon every man in the camp was armed with a sword. In addition, Nephi had trained them in the use of their bows and arrows. Though Nephi had seen in vision the fighting that would take place between his people and the Lamanites, he prayed nightly that they would never have to use their weapons.

Ishmar wanted peace as badly as Nephi did. One morning when the dew was still on the grass, he came to Nephi's door. His face had a look of determination tinged with sadness. "My dear uncle," he said, "we have been together for many years."

Nephi nodded. Yes, they had been together as friends for forty years. With a heavy heart he suspected what Ishmar was going to suggest, but he was silent as Ishmar continued.

Averting his gaze, Ishmar said, "Nephi, I have decided to return to my own people."

Even though he had suspected what Ishmar wanted to say, Nephi was still startled. "But why?"

Ishmar drew a deep breath. "During the past months we have prepared for war against my people. I know it is best to be prepared, and yet my heart is torn. It will be my brothers, my relatives who will be coming against those swords." He stepped forward and grasped both of Nephi's arms. "My friend, you know that my loyalty is to you and to this people. Tamna and I have loved the years we have lived here with you, but I am feeling a necessity to try to teach our people to live in peace. It is good to be prepared for war, but if I can convince my own family to remain at peace? . . ." He left the rest unsaid.

Nephi, eyes filled with tears, pulled Ishmar close, embracing this man who had been a brother to him. He could find no words to say. They stood there for many moments.

Finally Nephi held Ishmar away as he struggled for words. "Ishmar, go with my love. I pray that your mission will be successful . . . but if the time comes when it is not, please know that you and your family are loved and welcome here."

In a few days Ishmar and his family were gone.

* * *

Sitting in his house a year later, Nephi had a sense of impending trouble. In that year he had not heard anything from Ishmar. Was he successful in preaching peace to the Lamanites? Would they ever see each other again?

It was dark outside. Rain had begun, first a fine mist like a spray, then a heavy, steady drizzle which drummed on the roof of their house. Would troubles come to his people like the rain—a little at first and then a flood? What would the future bring?

Chapter 16

Death of Nephi

Nephi, my son. The voice seemed to reverberate and to fill the temple where Nephi prayed.

"Yes, Lord."

My son, I commend you for your faithfulness over the years. For thirty years, ever since you left Jerusalem, you have been faithful.

Nephi, his tawny hair and full beard now streaked with gray, remained on his knees on the hard rock floor, waiting for the Lord to continue.

Nephi, you have also diligently kept the records of this people. Now I give you a new assignment. I want you to make another set of plates. These plates will have a special purpose, known only to me. On these plates you will engrave many things which are good in my sight, for the profit of thy people.[32]

"Lord, I will do whatever thou should ask. What is it that you want me to write upon this new set of plates?"

Write on the plates the most precious parts of your ministry and your prophecies. The things which are written upon them will be kept for the instruction of my people who should possess this land, and also for other wise purposes which are known only to me.[33]

"It shall be done, my Lord." Nephi waited to see if there were further instructions. After a few minutes he rose laboriously. He had knelt for so long that he was stiff and his feet tingled. He walked for a few minutes to get his legs limbered up, then hurried to the annex of the temple where his scribes had smelted gold and hammered it into plates. He noted that there was a plentiful supply of blank plates. He was well prepared to write.

At home, as Nephi thought about the assignment the Lord had given him, he knew that writing a new set of plates would take his full time. Reluctantly he called his brothers, Jacob and Joseph, to him. Putting an arm around each of them, he walked into his garden. "My dear brothers," he said, "the Lord has given me an assignment to write another set of plates— a record of our ministry and prophecies."

"That will be exciting writing for you," Jacob exclaimed.

"Yes, but time-consuming," Nephi responded. "Therefore I have decided the time has come to ordain you to the ministry."

After telling them what would be expected of them, he laid his hands on Jacob's head and ordained him as a priest and a teacher to the people.

Then he did the same for Joseph. After clasping their arms, he said, "Now yours will be the responsibility to teach the people. However, I will still want to teach. It is important that the people hear prophecies the Lord has spoken unto me."

With the responsibilities of the priesthood delegated to Jacob and Joseph, Nephi had time to begin his writing. He titled the plates, "The Plates of Nephi." After summarizing some material from the large plates, Nephi wrote, "I do not write anything upon (these) plates save it be that I think it is sacred."

From then on, as Nephi received visions and revelations, he inscribed them on the plates. The most important visions to him were those that dealt with the coming of the Savior.

He wrote: "And behold he cometh, according to the words of the angel, in six hundred years from the time my father left Jerusalem." He read back through the brass plates, remembering that some of the writers had prophesied about the Savior—especially his death. After again reading these prophecies, he continued writing:

"And the God of our father, . . . yieldeth himself, . . . into the hands of wicked men, to be lifted up, according to the words of Zenock, and to be crucified, according to the words of Neum, and to be buried in a sepulchre, according to the words of Zenos, which he spake concerning the three days of darkness, which should be a sign given of his death unto those who should inhabit the isles of the sea, more especially given unto those who are of the house of Israel." [34]

He told of the great joy of the people when the Lord would visit the house of Israel, and of suffering of Jews at Jerusalem; of how they would be despised and become a hiss and a byword and hated among all nations. He told of the time when they would remember their covenants and return to a belief in the God of Israel. He was excited as he wrote: ". . . then will he remember the earth shall see the salvation of the Lord, saith the prophet; every nation, kindred, tongue and people shall be blessed." [35]

One morning as he was writing on the plates in the temple, he was disturbed by a commotion outside. He stepped to the door and was almost knocked over by Sam and Zoram.

"Come quickly," Zoram said. Sam's brow was wrinkled with worry. He motioned to Nephi to follow.

Nephi hurried after them. They led him to the spring where he was astonished to find Ben, Ishmar's oldest son. He lay by the spring still gasping for breath. His almost-naked body was bruised and scratched from thickets he had forced his way through.

Nephi knelt beside him. "Ben, what has happened?"

Ben's eyes were bloodshot. "I hurried as fast as I could." He gasped for another breath. "The warriors of Laman are coming."

A sickening feeling came over Nephi. "On their way where?" he cried, clenching his strong hands.

"One of Laman's scouts discovered your village. They have organized a war party. They are coming to destroy you. Father sent me to warn you."

Nephi turned to Zoram. "Warn the villagers. Organize the men."

He turned back to Ben and patted his shoulder. "Thank you, my son. You have saved many lives."

Leaving Ben in the care of young Omni, Nephi hurried to his people. He had known this day would come. He hoped his people were ready. Jacob and Joseph, protesting, took the women and small children into the forest where they would be safe. In preparation for just such a day as this, Nephi had organized the men into four groups. He himself, Sam, Zoram and Jeremiah were each in charge of a warrior group. Now he deployed them in the edges of the forest around the village. While they waited for the Lamanites, Nephi put away the plates he had been working on along with the brass plates and the *Liahona*. He would not forgive himself if anything happened to the precious plates.

From their concealed positions they watched the Lamanites come down the other side of the valley. It was raining and the ground was slick. The warriors stumbled and slipped in the mud. They appeared to be loosely organized and when they hit the river they just waded through. By now rain fell heavily and Nephi could see the wet, glistening bodies of the Lamanites.

He shuddered. This was the first time he had seen any of his brothers' families since they had come under the curse. Their skins were bronzed and dark like the sword Nephi held in his hand. Silently he lamented, Oh, my brothers. Why did you have to harden your hearts? Why couldn't you have followed the Lord's commandments and dwelt in peace? But now it was too late. They were in *his* land, bent on bringing war and destruction to his people.

Simon, who was standing beside him, spat between his teeth. "When do we attack?"

Nephi motioned him to silence. The rain was slacking. The Lamanites were in battle lines. Nephi looked across the hollow where the Lamanites waited. He could see the rain-freed sun glinting from their swords. He wondered who had helped make them.

A quiet period of nearly an hour passed while the two small armies looked at each other across the vacant meadow. Finally the Lamanites started forward again. Nephi waited until they were struggling up the slope to the trees, then he had Joel blow the conch horn. At the signal, his men loosed a deadly stream of arrows into the front ranks of the Lamanites. Many warriors fell and there was great confusion in their ranks. As he watched, Nephi was sure this was their first battle. Many dropped their swords and ran. Nephi took advantage of the confusion, leading his men from the trees. They fell upon the Lamanites, their swords rising and falling. The ranks broke. The men staggered backwards pursued by Nephi's young warriors. Nephi moved slowly behind his men, giving encouragement where he could.

"Watch out!"

He heard the cry and whirled just as Sam, grizzled with age, stepped between him and a young, wounded warrior. The Lamanite had been ready to bring his sword down upon Nephi's skull. Sam deflected the sword from Nephi but it cut through his own arm. He stumbled, a surprised look on his face. Nephi didn't have time to stop and help him. The Lamanite youth facing him was about seventeen, just beginning to raise fuzz on his cheeks. His left arm hung useless at his side, with blood running from a deep wound near his shoulder. He started for Nephi once more, stumbled, and fell to the earth.

Nephi turned to Sam who stood with his sword and his severed arm on the ground before him. Blood spurted from his stump. Nephi gathered his brother into his arms and staggered back to the trees where he laid him down. He did what he could to stop the bleeding, but it was no use. A glazed look came into his brother's eyes. He grunted something to his brother and died.

Sam had died defending him! Nephi put his head against the tree and cried. His shoulders shook as he sobbed. Dear Sam. So faithful. Ever wanting to please. Other than Miriam and his own children, Sam had been closer to him than anyone in the world. He would sorely miss him.

The battle was over by the time Nephi stood up. He was weary and sick at heart. As his men regrouped, he counted their dead. Including Sam, they had lost three men. Several others were badly wounded. A score or more Lamanites lay dead. Nephi picked up a discarded Lamanite sword. It was made of wood! The craftsman had carved the blade out of a long, thin piece of wood. A row of sharp pieces of obsidian were wedged into both edges. Though not as sharp as the metal swords of his people, it was a deadly weapon. Nephi was glad he had never taught Laman or Lemuel the art of metalworking.

By the time the sun was down they had buried their dead and also the dead Lamanites. It had been a senseless slaughter. Still grieving Sam's death, Nephi looked into the heavens and offered a prayer. It had started. What he had seen so many times in vision had begun. Sadly, he shook his head. He knew how it would end; with the complete destruction of his own people. The boles of the trees were pale, the evening was gloomy as he made his way home.

Thoughts of that first battle continued to haunt Nephi. Night after night he prayed to the Lord that he might understand what would happen to those who would be led away by the slick tongue of Satan. One night, after praying mightily to the Lord for comfort, he fell into a fitful sleep and dreamed. In his dream, the Lord appeared to him in person, looked upon him with compassion, and spoke to him. *My son, cursed is he that putteth his trust in man. . . . Wo be unto the Gentiles, . . . for notwithstanding I shall lengthen out mine arm unto them from day to day, they will deny me.*

"Will they be lost, then?" Nephi asked.

The Lord answered, *No, I will give unto the children of men line upon line, precept upon precept, here a little and there a little; and blessed are those who hearken unto my precepts, and lend an ear unto my counsel, for they shall learn wisdom; for unto him that receiveth I will give more; and from them that shall say, We have enough, from them shall be taken away even that which they have. I will be merciful unto them if they will repent and come unto me.*[36]

The Lord then pledged to Nephi that he would honor the promise He had made to Lehi and also to him, that He would remember their descendants.

Words of the Savior were still on his mind when Nephi arose the next morning. He inscribed them onto the plates, then wrote his own testimony of the Savior: "I have seen Him. . . . Behold, my soul delighteth in proving unto my people the truth of the coming of Christ; for this end hath the law of Moses been given; and all things which have been given of God from the beginning of the world, unto man, are the typifying of him. . . . my soul delighteth in his grace, and in his justice, and power, and mercy in the great and eternal plan of deliverance from death. And my soul delighteth in proving unto my people that save Christ should come all men must perish."

He rubbed a hand through his beard. Why couldn't all people see the logic? He wrote: "For if there be no Christ, there be no God; and if there be no God, we are not, for there could have been no creation. But there is a God, and he is Christ, and he cometh in the fulness of his own time."[37]

Every afternoon, as if signaled by the position of the sun, the rains came. For some it was dreary, but Nephi enjoyed sitting by the window, watching the clouds weep. As a youth he had enjoyed walking in the rain, laughing as the rain dripped from his nose. Now he was content just to watch it. One day, as he was watching, a magnificent rainbow arched into the heavens with ends dipped to each horizon. It seemed as if the Lord was offering a special blessing upon him. Oh, how much the beauties of the earth had meant to him in his life!

After each rain Nephi went back to his reading. He had read and reread scriptures in the brass plates. He never tired of them. Each time he read he gained new ideas and new insights. Even though his eyes were dim with age, he spent most of his waking moments either reading or writing. Often he would read a passage and would meditate upon it. Then the Lord would open up a vision to him of the meaning. Of late, he had difficulty sleeping.

Sometimes he would awaken in a sweat in the middle of the night, having dreamed he was again tied to the mast of his ship, or looking down, sword in hand, at the drunken Laban, or seeing the fatally wounded Sam standing before him. At such times his anguish was real, and he wrote in poetic form what he was feeling.

As a child his favorite hero had been King David, and now to be able to read David's psalms thrilled him. David had experienced many of the same things that he had. Nephi thought back over his youth. Once again he saw himself and Miriam in their carefree days. He thought of the many experiences of his life. Then he picked up his brush and wrote his own poetry on a piece of parchment. He poured out his heart, his psalms, his "songs of the heart."

He transcribed part of what he had written onto the plates. To preface his psalms, he wrote, ". . . upon these plates I write the things of my soul, . . . for my soul delighteth in the scriptures, and my heart pondereth them, and writeth them for the learning and profit of my children."

FIRST PSALM OF NEPHI

Behold, my soul delighteth in the things of the Lord;
My heart pondereth continually upon the things which I have seen and
heard. . . .
Nevertheless, I know in whom I have trusted.
My God hath been my support;
He hath led me through mine afflictions in the wilderness;
He hath preserved me upon the waters of the great deep.
He hath filled me with his love, even unto the consuming of my flesh.
He hath confounded mine enemies, unto the causing of them to quake
before me.
Behold he hath given me knowledge by visions in the nighttime.
By day have I waxed bold in mighty prayer before him;
Yea, my voice have I sent up on high; And angels came down and ministered
unto me.
Upon the wings of his Spirit hath my body been carried away into exceeding
high mountains.
Mine eyes have beheld great things, yea, even too great for man. . . . O then,
if I have seen so great things,
If the Lord in his condescension unto the children of men hath visited men
in so much mercy,
Why should my heart weep and my soul linger in the valley of sorrow,
And my flesh waste away, and my strength slacken, because of mine
afflictions?
Why should I yield to sin, because of my flesh?
Yea, why should I give way to temptations.

That the evil one have place in my heart to destroy my peace and afflict
    my soul?
Why am I angry because of mine enemy?
Awake my soul! No longer droop in sin.
Rejoice, O my heart, and give place no more for the enemy of my soul. . . .''

Nephi's second psalm was a song of praise.

THE SECOND PSALM OF NEPHI

Rejoice, O my heart, and cry unto the Lord, and say,
O Lord, I will praise thee forever;
Yea, my soul will rejoice in thee, my God and the rock of my salvation.
O Lord, wilt thou redeem my soul?
Wilt thou deliver me out of the hands of mine enemies?
Wilt thou make me that I may shake at the appearance of sin?
May the gates of hell be shut continually before me,
Because that my heart is broken and my spirit is contrite!
O Lord, wilt thou not shut the gates of thy righteousness before me.

. . . O Lord, wilt thou encircle me around in the robe of thy righteousness!
O Lord, wilt thou make a way for mine escape before mine enemies!
Wilt thou make my path straight before me!
Wilt thou not place a stumbling block in my way—
But that thou wouldst clear my way before me,
And hedge not up my way, but the ways of mine enemy.''

From the other psalms that he had written on the parchment, he selected
one more to include on the plates.

THE THIRD PSALM OF NEPHI

"O Lord, I have trusted in thee, and I will trust in thee forever.
I will not put my trust in the arm of flesh;
. . . Cursed is he that putteth his trust in the arm of flesh. Yea,
Cursed is he that putteth his trust in man or maketh flesh his arm.
Yea, I know that God will give liberally to him that asketh.
Yea, my God will give me, if I ask not amiss;
Therefore I will lift up my voice unto thee;
Yea, I will cry unto thee, my God, the rock of my righteousness.
Behold, my voice shall forever ascend up unto thee,
My rock and mine everlasting God. Amen.'' [38]

* * *

Nephi loved to read the words of Isaiah. He longed also for his people
to have an opportunity to read those words. He wrote about Isaiah: "I will

liken his words unto my people, and I will send them forth unto all my children, for he verily saw my Redeemer, even as I have seen him.''

Nephi wrote: ''I will send their words forth unto my children to prove unto them that my words are true. . . . By the words of three, God hath said, I will establish my word . . . And now I write some of the words of Isaiah, that whoso of my people shall see these words may lift up their hearts and rejoice for all men. Now these are the words, and ye may liken them unto you and unto all men.''[39]

* * *

As the years passed, Nephi's people multiplied, built more villages, and started scattering throughout the Land of Nephi. Nephi felt it was important to visit each village and to teach the people so they wouldn't stray from the truth. In vain Jacob urged him not to strive so vigorously. He replied to such urgings with a smile. ''If I am to teach the people about the Savior who will come, then I must press on. When the time comes for me to die, then will I sleep. Till then, my task is not complete.''

He didn't tell Jacob that he still thrilled at just being a part of the beauty that surrounded him. He enjoyed the radiance of the sky, stark beauty of the mountains, the freshness of the open air.

Once more the Savior visited him, and again taught him concerning His gospel which would come to the earth in its fullness. The Lord said, *Behold, I am God; and I am a God of miracles; and I will show unto the world that I am the same yesterday, today, and forever; and I work not among the children of men save it be according to their faith.*

Then for those who did not have the faith, but approached religion from a shallow point of view, the Lord continued, *Therefore, I will proceed to do a marvelous work among this people, yea, a marvelous work and a wonder, for the wisdom of their wise and learned shall perish and the understanding of their prudent shall be hid.*[40]

The next day Nephi taught again in the temple, giving his testimony of the Savior who would come. The thoughts of the Savior permeated his being. He told the people what had happened in Jerusalem, how the city had been destroyed and the Jews who still lived had been carried away captive into Babylon. He prophesied that the Jews would return again to Jerusalem and possess the land as the land of their inheritance.

He told them that . . . ''They shall have wars, and rumors of wars'' until the coming of the Only Begotten of the Father. Then the Jews would reject Him. He said, ''Behold, they will crucify him; and after he has laid in a sepulchre for the space of three days He shall rise from the dead, with healing in His wings; and all those who shall believe on His name shall be saved in the kingdom of God.'' [41]

Nephi then predicted the scattering of the Jews and their eventual return to a belief in Christ. At that time, the Lord would "proceed to do a marvelous work and a wonder among the children of men." In his dream the Lord had manifested to Nephi that the plates upon which he was writing would be an important part of that marvelous work of conversion.

As he taught in the temple, Nephi bore his testimony of Christ as often as he could. It became the most dominant force in his life. "I say unto you, that as these things are true, and as the Lord God liveth, there is none other name given under heaven save it be this Jesus Christ, of which I have spoken, whereby man can be saved. . . . we talk of Christ, we rejoice in Christ, we preach of Christ, we prophesy of Christ . . ."

Jacob noticed that Nephi's face was pallid, and that he was weaving as he stood before the congregation. He stepped forward to help him, but Nephi wasn't through. He added in closing, "I have spoken plainly to you, so you will understand the right way. The right way is to believe in Christ and not deny Him. If you deny Him, you also deny the prophets and the law. Christ is the Holy One of Israel, therefore you must bow down before Him and worship Him with all your might, mind, and strength."

By now, age and his many experiences and trials had turned Nephi's hair and eyebrows pure white. His face was wrinkled but he walked upright and straight. His eyes still commanded attention, and his voice still rang with authority. But he was weary. His magnificent body had carried him well for over sixty-five years.

He missed his friends. Zoram had passed through the veil. Sam had been killed in battle, and Ishmar, hoping to convert his family, had returned to the land of his father. His beloved Miriam was still with him. She was his constant support and companion. Each night Nephi praised the Lord for letting her continue to live. His other happiness came from his children and grandchildren. His joy in his family was boundless.

Recurring visions of the future destruction of his descendants haunted Nephi. He continually taught the people what he had seen, the falling away and the great destruction. Then he told of how the righteous would be spared, and of how the Savior, after he had risen from the dead, would appear to those righteous people in this land. He prophesied of the peace that his people would have for three generations after the coming of the Savior. Then in anguish he predicted the destruction of his descendants. "For the Spirit of the Lord will not always strive with man. When the Spirit stops striving with man then destruction will come, and this grieves my soul."

One night Nephi dreamed he was carried away to the top of a high mountain—a mountain similar to those which surrounded the Land of Nephi. In his dream he saw the people who would live in the promised land in the last days. He saw the book which had been translated from the plates he had so diligently written. Not only did he see it translated, but he saw three witnesses testifying of its truthfulness.

He knew that there would be those who would scoff and not believe. Many would say they had need for the additional witness that this book would give. The Lord had an answer for those who felt they had no need for additional witnesses. *Know ye not that there are more nations than one? Know ye not that I, the Lord your God, have created all men, and that I remember those who are upon the isles of the sea; and that I rule in the heavens above and in the earth beneath; and I bring forth my word unto the children of men, yea, even upon all the nations of the earth? Wherefore murmur ye, because ye shall receive more of my word? Know ye not that the testimony of two nations is a witness unto you that I am God, that I remember one nation like unto another? Wherefore, I speak the same words unto one nation like unto another. And when the two nations shall run together the testimony of the two nations shall run together also.*[42]

From his vision he wrote down the conditions of those who lived in the last days, of the building up of many churches, of the false teachings of those who would be living during that time. He told of how the devil would lull some into carnal security until they were fully ripe in iniquity.

Nephi loved to walk through the village with Miriam. Hand in hand they would stroll, greeting old friends, enjoying the brightness of each day. The warmth of the sun and the friendliness of his people were both soothing to Nephi. He went often to the temple, praying, writing, and teaching. As questions arose among the people, he would petition the Lord in prayer, and answers would come.

One day Jacob asked him concerning the Holy Ghost. Nephi knelt and prayed for knowledge concerning this Personage. The voice of the Lord came to him, telling him that those that are baptized in His name are given the Holy Ghost. After people repent of their sins and demonstrate their willingness to keep the commandments by submitting themselves to be baptized, then through the Holy Ghost he was told that they would also receive the baptism of fire.

The Father's voice came to Nephi, affirming that what had been said was true, that those who endured to the end would be saved.

This knowledge excited Nephi. On the next Sabbath he taught about the Holy Ghost to the priesthood assembled in the temple: "Again I say unto you that if you will enter in by the way and receive the Holy Ghost, it will show unto you all things that you should do."

He prophesied concerning the book which came from the plates he was writing; that it would go to the Gentiles, and how the Gentiles would take it back to the descendants of Laman and Lemuel. Tears came to his eyes as he contemplated the blessings that would come upon the descendants of his brothers. He knew how happy his father, Lehi, was to know that all of his descendants would have the opportunity of having a faith in Christ.

Nephi continued with his prophecy, "And then shall they rejoice; for they shall know that it is a blessing unto them from the hand of God; and their scales of darkness shall begin to fall from their eyes; and many generations shall not pass away among them, save they shall be a pure and delightsome people." [43]

On Nephi's seventieth birthday, Miriam invited their children and his brothers and sisters for dinner. They had barbecued a wild pig and the aroma was delightful. Miriam also had platters of fresh bananas, mangoes, and papayas, and vegetables fresh from her garden. Nephi enjoyed his family so very much. At the dinner, Jacob and Joseph honored him with a new golden amulet, one Joseph had made himself as a tribute to his older brother.

Several weeks later, Nephi requested that Jeremiah help him to the temple one more time. He knew this would be his last sermon. He looked into the eyes of the people—people whom he loved and who loved him.

"My brethren," he began, "Jacob and Joseph have been given the power and the authority to carry on as priests and teachers to you. Give heed to their word. Listen to them and they will teach you the things you should do. Today I shall speak unto you plainly. I admonish you to do the things which I have told you. Remember that the gate through which you enter is repentance and baptism by water. Then comes a remission of your sins by fire and by the Holy Ghost. Then you are in the straight and narrow path which leads to eternal life. My beloved brethren, I ask you that after you have gotten on this straight and narrow path, is all done? No. If you will press forward, feasting upon the word of Christ, and endure to the end, the Father has promised that you shall have eternal life."

He looked around at all of the familiar faces. These were his people. "And now, behold, my beloved brethren, this is the way; and there is none other way nor name given under heaven whereby man can be saved in the Kingdom of God . . ." [44]

Nephi ended his sermon, his last in mortality. With Jeremiah he walked slowly back to his home. Once more he brought out the plates and inscribed on them the important words he had spoken. He sighed. There was so much more he could say, but now that would be Jacob's responsibility. He had decided that Jacob should keep the small plates and that the large plates would be Jeremiah's responsibility.

Before turning over the plates to his brother, he wrote a final comment. "And now I, Nephi, cannot write all the things which were taught among my people; . . . But I, Nephi, have written what I have written, and I esteem it as of great worth, and especially unto my people. For I pray continually for them by day, and mine eyes water my pillow by night, because of them; and I cry unto my God in faith, and I know that he will hear my cry.

"And now, my beloved brethren, . . . hearken unto these words and believe in Christ . . . if ye believe in Christ, ye will believe in these words, for they are the words of Christ, and he hath given them unto me; and they teach all men that they should do good. . . . Christ will show unto you, with power and great glory, that they are his words, at the last day; and you and I shall stand face to face before his bar; and ye shall know that I have been commanded of him to write these things, notwithstanding my weakness. And I pray the Father in the name of Christ that many of us, if not all, may be saved in his kingdom at that great and last day."

He sat there for a few moments, stylus in hand. Miriam came over and stood beside him, her arm around his neck. He smiled up at her and then wrote. "And now, my beloved brethren, . . . I speak unto you as the voice of one crying from the dust; Farewell until that great day shall come. . . . behold, I bid you an everlasting farewell, . . . Amen."[45]

He put down his stylus and sighed. His work was done. He pulled Miriam down beside him. They sat together, their backs against the cool outside wall, united in that bond that required no words. They were together, in their spirits as well as in their bodies. He smiled. He was ready to go to that Paradise that Lehi had so often spoken of, but he didn't want to leave his sweetheart behind.

The next day he sent for Jacob. Greeting him warmly, he said, "My dear brother, you have been faithful to the Lord's commandments all of your life. It has been a joy to share with you His words. I thank you for your loyalty to me and to the Lord. Jacob, I have finished my writing. I am turning the plates over to you. They will now be your responsibility. I have written of the things of God, with the intent of persuading men to come unto Him and be saved. I have not attempted to write the things which are pleasing to the world, but the things which are pleasing unto God."

He looked intently at Jacob. "My brother, do not write trivial things on the plates. Write only those things which you consider to be most precious. The history of the people will be kept on the other plates. If there are sermons, or revelation, or prophesying, write them."

Nephi gently handed over the sacred plates. Jacob took them reverently. "I will treasure these plates, dear brother Nephi. I will write in them those things which the Lord would have me write." He held Nephi's hand for a moment, then turned and walked away.

Only one more task remained. Nephi called for Jeremiah. He was proud of his stalwart son—now middle-aged. Jeremiah sat on the floor before him.

"My son," Nephi said, "the Lord has blessed us greatly. He has brought us to this beautiful land from the land of Jerusalem. Here he has protected us and taught us His ways.''

Jeremiah nodded in agreement.

Nephi continued. ''It is important that we govern the people wisely in order that dissension and discord do not creep in.'' He placed his hand on Jeremiah's shoulder, then smiled. ''My son. Is it too late in life for you to change your name?''

Jeremiah looked surprised, apparently not knowing what his father meant. Nephi smiled again, his eyes crinkling. ''My son, the people have requested that each king carry the name of Nephi. I would like you to be known from this time forth as Second Nephi—I desire to annoint you as the king of this people.''

Jeremiah seemed shaken by what his father had said. His eyes brimmed with tears. He was speechless. He embraced Nephi and buried his head against his father's thin shoulder.

The aging king pushed Jeremiah to arm's length. He said, ''I know you understand what a great responsibility this will be.''

Jeremiah understood. Nephi had been king for over thirty years. He had governed his people with fairness and dignity. The people had loved him. For most of that time there had been peace in the land, with the exception of the few times the Lamanites had raided the villages.

''Thank you, Father. I will not betray your trust in me.''

Remember, my son, that as Jacob will keep the record of the ministry, yours will be the responsibility of inscribing the history of this people on the large plates.''

''Yes, Father. You have taught me well. I will not disappoint you.''

* * *

Nephi lay on the bed, his white hair moist with the mist of sweat that covered his forehead. His skin was clammy and mottled. Miriam, white-haired and weak herself, sat by his bed, holding his limp hand. Jeremiah and Ruth stood near the foot of the bed. Ruth was crying softly. Miriam leaned over, wiping his forehead. His eyes were closed, but his lips moved as if he were trying to say something. Jeremiah put his ear close to his father's lips, but there was no sound. Joseph came into the room and leaned over Ruth's shoulder, touching her, saying nothing.

Suddenly Nephi's eyes opened. He stared at the ceiling of the dim room. A smile appeared on his blue-gray lips. Then he whispered, ''Lord, you have come.'' His eyes closed, but the smile remained on his lips. His gallant heart had beat its last beat. Nephi was dead.

Ruth, overcome with anguish, uttered a cry of grief. Joseph pulled her close. ''He is now where he wants to be,'' he said gently.

Miriam sat quietly by his side, still holding the hand of the man who had been her husband for over fifty years. She would miss him greatly. Tears welled from her eyes and ran softly down her wrinkled cheeks.

Jeremiah's eyes were also filled with tears. Then with the dignity befitting the noble love he had for his father, he eulogized: "My father was a man of vision. He was a man who believed in life. A man who had too much to do to worry about fame. But fame is now his. He will be forever remembered—not only by this people, but by millions who will read his words."

Miriam squeezed Nephi's lifeless hand and rested her head on his breast. "I will come to you soon, my love," she whispered.

Epilogue

The life of Nephi had been a most eventful one. He had passed through many trials and afflictions and although he was often in positions of peril, he never yielded, never faltered, never shrank from any ordeal to which he was exposed.

Understanding as he did the government of the Lord, before whom there are no privileged classes, he respected the rights of the people, and while he knew there must be officers to bear responsibility and a properly organized government, he knew also that it should be based upon the consent of the people. He brought with him to the "promised land" a respect for the principles of human equality and the rights of men. As a statesman, he organized a society upon a firm and permanent basis and laid the foundation for civil and religious liberty.

We here close the life of Nephi. He has shown us how much a mortal man, who devotes himself to God and his work, can accomplish for himself and his fellow mortals, and how near, by the exercise of faith, man can draw to God. He was the revered founder of a nation.

Jacob, who followed Nephi as high priest, said, "The people had loved Nephi exceedingly, he having been a great protector for them, having wielded the sword of Laban in their defense, and having labored in all his days for their welfare. Wherefore, the people were desirous to retain in remembrance his name. And whoso should reign in his stead were called by the people, second Nephi, third Nephi, and so forth, according to the reigns of the kings."[46]

Though Nephi had seen the future, it still had to be lived. The reign of kings continued down through the centuries, and the two sets of the Plates of Nephi continued to be inscribed upon by kings and prophets. The kings were, as a rule, righteous men and wise rulers. The Nephites multiplied and grew exceedingly rich in the wealth of this world. Their artisans and craftsmen became expert builders and creators.

The people spread abroad on the face of the land of Nephi and were scattered throughout the lands both north and south. The Lamanites followed them from the land of their first possession, and continued to harass them through the years which led to numerous and bloody wars which were often disastrous for the Nephites.

Spiritually, the Nephites had many seasons of faithfulness to God when they listened to and obeyed the words of His prophets. Unfortunately, they also had many seasons of apostasy at which times the judgments of God fell upon them. The Lamanites were often used by the Lord as a sharp instrument to bring His people to repentance and reformation.

By the time of the Prophet Jarom, the Nephites had grown from a powerful tribe to a wealthy nation. The people were generally industrious, honest and moral. Their prophets not only instructed them in the Mosaic Law, but also expounded the intent for which it was given, and while so doing, directed their minds to the coming of the Messiah, in whom they taught the people to believe as though he had already come. These pointed and constant teachings preserved the Nephites from destruction by softening their hearts and bringing them to repentance.

Shortly before Jarom died, he delivered the sacred plates to his son Omni. Omni kept them for about forty-four years, then handed them to his son Amaron, who in turn transferred them to his brother Chemish. Chemish, when his end drew hear, placed them in the hands of his son Abinadom, who afterwards gave them to his son Amaleki.

Then three kings, who were also prophets of God, created a new dynasty. When Mosiah became king, in him was again united the kingly and priestly authority. Both sets of the Plates of Nephi were once more in the hands of one person. Kings Mosiah, Benjamin, and the second Mosiah ruled the people in righteousness. It was a new age for the Nephites—a time for new heroes.

Notes

1. Jeremiah 7:8-11
2. Jeremiah 20:6
3. Proverbs 3:5, 6
4. 1 Nephi 1:13-14
5. 1 Nephi 2:1
6. 1 Nephi 2:19-24
7. Reference 4, page 1057
8. Reference 5, page 55
9. 1 Nephi 3:29
10. 1 Nephi 4:3
11. 1 Nephi 4:10-13
12. 1 Nephi 5:2-5
13. 1 Nephi 16:2, 3
14. 1 Nephi 16:37, 38
15. 1 Nephi 17:12-14
16. 1 Nephi 17:8
17. 1 Nephi 17:47
18. 1 Nephi 17:48
19. 1 Nephi 17:50-51
20. 1 Nephi 17:53
21. 1 Nephi 19:11, 12
22. 1 Nephi 19:13, 14
23. 1 Nephi 19:24
24. 1 Nephi 20, 21
25. 1 Nephi 22:16-19
26. 1 Nephi 22:29-31
27. 2 Nephi 1:1-31
28. 2 Nephi 2
29. 2 Nephi 3
30. 2 Nephi 4
31. 2 Nephi 5:21-23
32. 2 Nephi 5:30
33. 1 Nephi 19:3
34. 1 Nephi 19:8-10
35. 1 Nephi 19:16, 17
36. 2 Nephi 28:30-32
37. 2 Nephi 11:3-7
38. 2 Nephi 4:15-35
39. 2 Nephi 11:3, 8
40. 2 Nephi 27:23-26
41. 2 Nephi 25:13
42. 2 Nephi 29:7, 8
43. 2 Nephi 30:1-6
44. 2 Nephi 31:17-21
45. 2 Nephi 33
46. Jacob 1:10-11

References

1. Book of Mormon
2. Holy Bible
3. George Reynolds. "The Story of the Book of Mormon," West Jordan: reprinted in *Early Church Reprints*, 1888.
4. W. Cleon Skousen. *Treasures of the Book of Mormon*, Vol. 1, W. Cleon Skousen. Skousen, 1974.
5. Vernon W. Mattson, Jr. *The Dead Sea Scrolls and Other Important Discoveries*, 1980, Salt Lake City: 1980. Buried Record Publications, 1980.
6. George Reynolds. "A Dictionary of the Book of Mormon," West Jordan: reprinted in *Early Church Reprints*, 1891.
7. George Q. Cannon. "The Life of Nephi," West Jordan: reprinted in *Early Church Reprints*, 1883.
8. George S. Stewart and Gene S. Stuart. *The Mysterious Maya*, National Geographic Society, 1977.
9. Hugh Nibley. *An Approach to the Book of Mormon*, Salt Lake City: Deseret Book Co., 1978.
10. J. I. Packer, et. al. *The Bible Almanac*, Carmel: Guideposts, 1980.
11. Peter Farb. *The Land, Wildlife, and Peoples of the Bible*, New York: Harper and Row, 1967.
12. *The World of the Bible*, New York: Educational Heritage, Inc., 1959.
13. Winifred Walker. *All the Plants of the Bible*, New York: Doubleday, 1979.
14. Olive L. Earle. *Camels and Llamas*, New York: William Morrow and Co., 1961.
15. Merrill T. Gilbertson. *The Way it Was in Bible Times*, Minneapolis: Augsburg Publishing, 1959.
16. Nelson Glueck. *Rivers in the Desert*. New York: Farrar, Strauss and Cudahy, 1959.
17. William E. Berrett. *Discovering the World of the Bible*, Salt Lake City: Deseret Book, - - -.
18. M. Rostovtzeff. *Caravan Cities*, New York: AMS Press, 1971.
19. Gail Hoffman. *The Land and People of Israel*, Philadelphia: J. B. Lippincott, 1972.
20. Howard Fast. *The Jews*, Story of a People, New York: Dell Publishing, 1968.
21. *Great People of the Bible and How They Lived*, New York: Readers Digest Association, 1974.
22. *Atlas of the Bible*, New York: Readers Digest Association, 1981.

23. Lynn and Hope Hilton. *In Search of Lehi's Trail*, Salt Lake City: Deseret Book, 1976.
24. George Reynolds and Janne M. Sjodahl. *Commentary on the Book of Mormon*, Vol 1, Salt Lake City: Deseret Press, 1955.
25. David A. Palmer. *In Search of Cumorah*, Bountiful: Horizon Publishers, 1981.